THE WEEKEND BUCKET LIST

THE WEEKEND BUCKET LIST

a blossoming friendship between unlikely people...

mia kerick

interlude **press** • new york

Published by Duet, an imprint of Interlude Press
www.duetbooks.com
Cover Illustration and Book Design by CB Messer

10 9 8 7 6 5 4 3 2 1

interlude 🧩 press • new york

To cherished friends, far and wide.

Love is not only made for lovers, it is also for friends who love each other better than lovers. A real friend is very hard to find, difficult to leave and impossible to forget.

—Anonymous

THE WEEKEND
BUCKET LIST

1. go skinny-dipping
2. stay out all night
3. face a fear
4. sleep under the stars
5. take a road trip
6. get drunk
7. have a first kiss
8. run naked on a beach
9. sneak into a movie
10. spend twenty-four hours with no electronics
11. get pierced and tattooed
12. say thank you to someone

PART ONE
CHAPTER 1

cadence

SINCE IT'S ONLY FRIDAY, WE decide to start small. We have plenty of time this weekend to screw up our lives in monumental ways.

"You go first," he says. "Ladies before gents."

I'm a consummate eye-roller and I can't hold back. But still I bend over, grab the hem of my denim skirt, yank it to my ankles, and then kick it into a pile of leaves. "And you're *such* a gentleman."

He stares at my bare legs. "Does this one count as facing a fear, too?"

"No—it *only* counts as skinny-dipping. Now take something off."

Cooper whips his Mario Kart 64 T-shirt over his head. If a pale, freckled belly has the capacity to blush, that is what's happening to his. "We been joined at the hip since freshman year, Cady, so how is it we've never caught a glimpse of each other wearing nothing but a smile?" he asks. He's trying to distract me from accomplishing our list's *mutually agreed upon* number one.

"Well, you've seen my boobs before—and don't try to deny it." I unbutton my plain white blouse. I'm not one for flamboyant patterns, lace, or frills. My twin brother Bradley labeled me a tomboy when I refused to put on the dress that Mom picked out for my first day of kindergarten. I won that standoff; the other moms at the bus stop thought Bradley and I were twin brothers until October. "Remember Halloween night of sophomore year, when we went trick-or-treating?" I shimmy my shoulders until the blouse hits the forest floor.

And he has the balls to laugh. "Yeah… your toga slipped." Cooper hesitates, but finally pulls his shorts down without unbuttoning them. "For Sparta!" He tosses them high in the air and they get stuck on a low branch.

We gawk at each other. "Plain white boxers? How dull," I say, although they work for me.

"Your bra doesn't match your panties," he counters.

"My *underwear*. 'Panties' is a porn word." I rip them off quickly, before I have a chance to change my mind.

In a blur of sudden movement, Cooper's boxers take a swift trip down his skinny legs to the forest floor. There follows a frantic scramble and a splash in the marshy part of Tamarack Lake, which is thankfully well beyond the public beach.

"That was graceful, Murphy." *Pale and freckled from head to toe,* I think as I unhook my bra. "Good thing you're gay, 'cause my boobs are going to underwhelm you."

"Who says I'm gay?" Cooper corrects in a defensive tone. He takes me in from head to toe as I march my ninety-two-pound frame in the direction of the water—head held high. Not that he's looking at my head. "And no worries, Cady, I don't have my glasses on."

I refuse to let him in on my intense relief—both at his insistence that he's not *necessarily* gay and his serious nearsightedness—and

2

I go with some distraction of my own. "I hope there aren't any leeches in here."

"Ewww…"

I have a fairly good idea of his mental image.

SETTING UP THE TENT IS a challenge. It's nothing like the play Army tent I had when I was a kid; that tent popped open as soon I pulled it from its camo bag. But with the sense of accomplishment from having successfully gone skinny-dipping under my figurative belt, my confidence is surging. "We can do it, Coop… I think we've actually got this."

"What we've *got* is a freaking extra pole." Cooper uses it to brush the damp red hair off his forehead. His hair is as long and shaggy as I've ever seen it, and he has little time to get it cut before he has to read his speech at graduation on Monday night. The time for a man bun is nearly upon us. "This can't be good."

"For a math geek, you aren't much of a tent-erector."

"*Tent-erector…*" He repeats my words and giggles. High-school-boy humor is so completely caveman.

I grab the extra pole and toss it toward the trees. "But it's standing, so let's get in."

Using my computer clashed directly with the concept of taking in the great outdoors, but after one glance at the nylon sack filled with a bunch of metal poles and what seemed to be *another*, larger, nylon sack, we had no choice but to conduct an online search: how to set up a two-person dome tent. Now, we need to consult the bucket list. Thank God, I've got an excellent wifi service plan. I can get online anywhere, even here at the swampy end of the Wellington Town Beach.

And it's as if Cooper's a mind reader. As we climb into the tent, he tells me, "I've memorized the list, Cady. Number four is sleep under the stars."

We sit next to each other in the two-person green tent that I found at the back of the garage in a box of junk labeled *BRADLEY*. He won't need it while he's in rehab, so I snatched it without a second thought. I choose to ignore my intense guilt that I'm glad he's "locked away" where he can do himself no further harm. Safe and sound.

"Are we technically 'sleeping under the stars' if we crash in a tent?" I ask.

He shakes his head, and I'm surprised. Cooper usually chooses the easy route. "The stars are *out there*." He nods toward the unzipped tent door. "That's why we set up in a clearing, right? We can bring our sleeping bags outside when we're ready to go to sleep."

"I'm coming in if the bugs start to make a meal of me," I say, but he knows that if he wants me to I'll brave the mosquitos all night.

"Sounds like a plan, Cades."

I CLOSE MY LAPTOP TO save the battery; because of number ten we won't need it for the whole weekend. Cooper flops onto his back on the tent's nylon floor and closes his eyes.

"I'm starving," he mumbles.

Lately, I never miss an opportunity to study him. His face draws me in—a pointy chin and nose, smart eyes that hide behind thick-rimmed black glasses, and a perpetual smirk on his lips.

He tries to take cover in his mop of shaggy, dark red hair too, but he can't hide from me.

Ever since we skipped the junior prom together last spring—neither of us is the type to participate in overrated school events, especially ones that involve dancing—and came to this very spot at the end of the Wellington Town Beach, I've felt a flicker of "something more" for my longtime BFF. It wasn't exactly a romantic evening—we listened to eighties music and downed a full bucket of Kentucky Fried Chicken while gazing at Tamarack Lake—but for me, our relationship changed. When Cooper touched my face that night I was overwhelmed by an urge for something completely new and different and dangerous: I wanted to kiss him. The urge has been lurking since that night, but right now, it's stronger than ever. I want so badly to drop down on top of him and plant my lips on his, just to find out how it tastes... *just to find out how it feels.* But I don't because it isn't next on the list.

And because I just don't.

"How does Micky D's sound for dinner?" I ask. Food is always a good distraction for my attraction to my best friend. I have no clue why I'm so determined to distract him tonight.

"Better than good." Cooper opens his hazel eyes and finds me staring down at him. He doesn't seem surprised—like I said, it isn't the first time this has happened. "Well, what are you waiting for, Cady? Let's get this show on the road."

I'm caught in one of the "is this genuine attraction or is it merely the random hormone surge of a classic late bloomer?" quandaries I've been suffering more and more. I gawk at Cooper until he grabs my hand and squeezes it hard enough to make me wince. And *still* I have to shake my head to break the spell.

"I'm pretty hungry, too," I finally admit. "You better keep your slimy fingers out of my french fries." But we both know that I'm the french fry thief in this relationship.

CHAPTER 2

cooper

SHE ACTS AS IF THIS was *my* big idea, but The Weekend Bucket List has got Cady LaBrie's name written all over it. She's persuasive, though—the girl has almost got me believing *I* came up with the idea to do everything we never did that "normal" kids do in high school, all in the forty-eight hours before graduation. We have a lot of lost time to make up for.

"These fries are so good." Cady's eyes are closed like she's in goddamned ecstasy. I'm not sure why, but I look away.

"How can you eat so freaking much and stay so freaking skinny?" I ask, as Cady starts in on her *second* large order of french fries. And these are just appetizers.

"I'm *petite,* Cooper. Not skinny… and you're skinny, too."

I shrug and suck futilely on the straw that stands straight in my vanilla shake.

"Whatever." It doesn't matter how thick the shake is; I'm in no rush to suck it down. Cady's the talker in this relationship, so all I've got to do is sit here and listen.

"I don't see how adults can be so naïve? I mean, they fell for my line," she says, finally opening her gray-blue eyes.

Cady's right. It was almost too easy. My parents had zero problems with me "spending the weekend at Cady's house" either.

mia kerick

"See, it was Tuesday night, I think, and I was scraping the last of the SpaghettiOs from my bread bowl, when—"

"Your mom put SpaghettiOs in a *bread bowl*?" That's just plain wrong—a crime against bread bowls.

"She's trying to be more creative in the kitchen so she doesn't obsess over stuff she can't deal with, like Bradley being in rehab. See what I'm saying?"

I don't see shit, but still *yuck*.

"And we can't all have a gourmet chef in the family. Anyway, when I asked Mom and Dad if I could stay at your house this weekend, Mom said, 'Of course you can, dear, and thank you for *never* giving us *one minute* of trouble during your high school years, *the way your brother did*.'"

"Major guilt-infusion, huh?"

"Um… *yeah.*" Cady stuffs a final stack of fries in her mouth and then unwraps her double cheeseburger. You've got to respect her dedication to junk food consumption. "Mom actually got up from her seat, leaned across the table, and *kissed* me."

I can't help but imagine an orange-sauce lip print on Cady's forehead—it's not *my* fault I giggle.

"So it was as if my burden of guilt was physical as well as emotional." She frowns. "And it's not a laughing matter, Murphy."

"Uh, sorry… that *so* sucks." This about sums it up. I take off my glasses and rub my eyes; I'm determined to keep a straight face when I put them back on.

"Yeah, it does. I was going to call you and cancel the whole dumb bucket-list idea."

Hello! It was your dumb idea! I want to scream this in her face, but I'm so freaking glad she didn't cancel on me that I keep

8

my mouth shut. Cady thinks this weekend is all about checking items off a bucket list, as if this will magically turn us into cool kids. But I know better. What we're doing this weekend means way more than being able to say, "been there, done that" to a gathering of college dudes at a frat party.

At least, it does to me, which is disturbing—and hopefully not soul mate splitting.

I can't deny it any longer, and maybe I don't want to: since prom night last year shit between us stopped being as simple as "we're best pals." I remember the exact moment it happened. The bucket of extra crispy chicken was empty, except for a few crumbs in the bottom, Cady had just finished licking her fingers—which sounds cliché but is true—and the Human League's *Don't You Want Me* was playing on the little iPhone speaker I purchased specifically for that night. And it seemed like Cady was *trying* not to look at me; she stared with round eyes out over the lake, like it could provide her with the answers to the mysteries of the universe. Suddenly, I wanted Cady to look at me. Maybe I *needed* her to. So I did something completely unlike me; I reached out with a shaky hand and touched her cheek so she'd turn her head and look at me. And she did.

What I saw in her expression wasn't simple friendship, although it wasn't burning passion either. If I had to label the look in Cady's eyes, I'd call it "morning has broken"—like something truly amazing was dawning on her. I'd also describe her expression as conflicted. And it scared me… but was still so compelling. I didn't look away for just a second too long. In that split second, everything changed.

I shake my head to clear my mind.

"But I shook off the guilt, so here we are." Her double cheeseburger is already history. She didn't even take the proper time to chew each bite before gulping it down. She goes on to open a ten-piece box of Chicken McNuggets. Cady LaBrie's ability to inhale fast food is legendary, as is her willingness to brag about her 'highly efficient" metabolism. These are only two of the many things I admire about her.

"So here we are," I echo, and finish the last well-chewed bite of my *one* McChicken sandwich. I don't intend to dwell on the possible outcomes of our weekend excursion.

"It's our last weekend together." Cady stares at me with an expression so forlorn I can hardly stand to look. She snatches a few strands of her shoulder-length brown hair and pulls it forward over her eyes. It doesn't reach her turned up nose—a nose that I consider just a tad too big to qualify her as adorable—and she says, "Just shoot me."

Cady's not nearly as good at hiding as me, although she tries like hell. Maybe it'll come with practice, but I hope not. "Nobody's gonna shoot you," I assure her, "and we have all summer to hang together. So chill."

"Well, this is our last weekend before graduation that we're going to be... like... you know, *kids* together."

She's got a point, so I nod reluctantly.

"We have to do everything we never did together. We *have to*, Cooper."

"Who's arguing?"

Cady stands, brushes the salt off her fingers and onto her denim skirt, and heads for the door. "Let's go back to the tent and get started on number two." I pick up her wrappers, put them on the tray next to mine, and toss it all in the trash before I follow her out the door.

I HOPE SHE DOESN'T CRY. I can't cope when she cries. I'd do anything to make her not cry!

We lie shoulder-to-shoulder in the grassy clearing with our sleeping bags pushed together. "I can't see any stars, Cooper."

"It isn't a starry night."

"Does it still count as sleeping under the stars?"

As usual, Cady's over-focused on the wrong details. "Yeah. I'd say so." I inch my sleeping bag closer to hers. When I glance her way, she's staring at the moon, not at me. I'm unreasonably disappointed. "What's on the list for tomorrow?" I ask, as if we haven't been over the plan a thousand times.

"Well, we're going to start the day by taking showers at the Wellington Racquetball Club. Remember I told you we just got a family membership?"

I nod, although she's still not looking at me.

"Tomorrow morning, we face our fear—you know, the one we decided on."

"Okay."

"Tonight we're technically doing number two *and* number four—staying out all night and sleeping under the stars. But we'll stay out all night tomorrow night too, because it would be breaking the rules to count tonight as two different bucket-list items."

Doubling up would be a freaking crime, I think. But I say, "And we'll be able to tell our new friends in college that we're total party animals and staying out all night is old news."

11

This time Cady nods, but she's serious again. "And then we start the road trip."

"That's number five, right?" I know all of this like I know that in less than eight weeks we'll head in two separate directions for the first time since freshman year. "Where should we go?"

"We need to find a remote spot on the coast because running naked on a beach is number eight. We can't exactly run naked on the Wellington Town Beach without getting arrested for indecent exposure."

"Yeah, a remote coast works best." I want to curl around her. I've done that a time or two, but only when Cady said she was cold. And, since our families and everybody else think I'm gay, our sleepovers are all parent-approved. In the world's opinion, I'm no more than her gay BFF, so they have nothing to fear by letting us sleep next to each other on the two pullout couches in Cady's living room or in my queen-sized bed. But lately, I'm not so sure it was a good idea for them to let us co-sleep; it may not have been quite as innocent as it seemed.

Cady's not sure how she feels about me, either. I'm certain of this thanks to all the staring she does when she thinks I'm not looking. *But, hello—I have peripheral vision!* And the staring disturbs me because we have so much to lose by taking a chance on romance.

"I'm not so sure…" I say it aloud because I hope she'll ask me what the hell I'm talking about. Part of me wants to tell her— maybe Cady can help me figure out why I want to hold her as we fall sleep under the pitch black, very un-starry sky. But I already know I'm not going to spill the beans…. To discuss feelings is risky. And as a result, some people—I hate to name names, but

I'm referring to *Cady LaBrie*—call me "emotionally unavailable." As if she should talk. We're very much two of a kind in this way.

"Hmmm?" I recognize the sleepy tone in her voice because I've heard it so many times before. Cady's about to drift away, and I want to curl around her even more. Or maybe I just want to hang on to her so she doesn't ever leave me.

"It's nothing. Good night, Cadence."

"Don't call me that…"

"Don't *you* let the bedbugs bite."

"Sleeping bag bugs, you mean." And she's gone.

I'm left alone with my thoughts. My muddled, tangled, cloudy, always messing-with-my-head-when-it-comes-to-Cady thoughts. "Freaking mosquitos." I slap at one on my forehead.

CHAPTER 3

"I can't believe we did that, Coop!" She's way too perky for seven a.m.

"Huh?" I don't try to hide my yawn. But Cady always wakes up hot or cold—there is no middle ground. We've slept over at each other's houses one night of almost every weekend since the middle of freshman year, and it was always obvious what mood she'd be in that day the second her eyes popped open. Today Cady's all revved up.

"We slept outside—all night! I wish I could tell Daisy."

Checking activities off our bucket list is working for Cady. In fact, after a night spent beneath the stars, she's already a slightly changed person from the one I bedded down with. More upbeat, maybe even more confident. The list hasn't yet started to work its magic on me—hopefully it will soon. "Daisy's a cat. She doesn't speak English."

"Don't you dare tell me that Daisy doesn't get what I say—she comes when I call her and she understands what 'suppertime, Daisy-girl' means and she knocks it off when I scream, 'enough with the kneading on the bony part of my hip!'"

I'm not up for one of Cady's Daisy-the-cat tangents this early in the morning, especially when I got three hours of sleep, thanks to the mega-ton of bugs buzzing in and out of each of the openings in my head, which sounds like more fun than it was. "I need coffee."

"You look like you have the chicken pox." She sticks the fingers of one hand on the biggest bug bites on my face. "You must taste sweet. Anyhow, we'll get coffee after we take showers at the racquetball club. And don't worry, I already broke down Bradley's tent and stuck it in the backseat of your car."

"Cool."

"So get up. Pretty soon it'll be time for number three on The Weekend Bucket List."

"I'm scared."

"You're supposed to be, dummy."

cadence

ONE OF MY MAJOR FEARS is to take showers in public places without proper foot protection, which I'm forced to do this morning at the club thanks to my inability to think ahead and stick a pair of flip-flops in my backpack. But this isn't the fear we agreed to face together, so I shower quickly, shake the water out of my hair, and meet Cooper in the lobby. As I walk toward him, my feet tingle with the sure knowledge that copious bacteria are multiplying between my toes.

"That lady is looking at me funny," he says the split second I'm in earshot and points with his elbow at the front desk.

"Stop being paranoid." I wave at Mrs. Roper, whose job is to check people in and out of the club and dole out faded pink towels. "Mrs. R is just about the nicest lady in town." I point to his bug-bitten face. "She's probably just worried you're carrying a contagious disease, that's all." My contaminated toes start to itch in my sneakers, so I press my finger hard on the big bug bite under Cooper's right eye to distract myself.

"Stop touching. It makes them itch more." He swats my hand away.

Mrs. Roper's probably also wondering why on earth Cady LaBrie is at the club at seven in the morning on the Saturday before graduation with some random boy. "Let's get out of here. I don't want Mrs. Roper to call my mom."

WE ALREADY KNOW WHERE WE'RE going when we get into Cooper's old Honda Civic. Over the past week, we've invested serious time talking about our greatest fears. And these were intense discussions. At first, we admitted to stuff we already knew about each other, like how I'm freaked out at the idea of getting lice and how he hates having sticky fingers. I then reaffirmed that I'm not much of a spider fan, and he owned up to his severe discomfort with the movie *Jaws,* but soon the discussions shifted to things we'd never confided to each other. He now knows that I would rather endure a twenty-four hour stomach flu than speak aloud in public, and I know Cooper would do about anything to avoid flying in an airplane over a large body of water, which I figure has a lot to do with his shark-phobia. These conversations enlightened me—especially when Cooper disclosed that he can't go number two in a public restroom. Probably TMI, but I tucked it into my memory bank, nonetheless.

We eventually settled on something that would force us to deal with a fear we both need to outgrow and would pull us out of the comfort zones in which we've so far wasted all of our teen years. Conveniently, we can stare our mutual fear in the face at the traveling carnival that is set up in the movie theater parking lot a couple of towns south of Wellington.

"Isn't it handy that a fair's going on in Ellis?" I ask as Cooper drives south on Main Street.

"Yeah, it's handy. Forgive me if I don't jump for joy."

"You can't jump, Murphy; you're *driving*." He sends me a look to kill, but I press on. "We both get that it's vital that we do this. By the way, you know Cecelia Tucker, right?"

"I wish I could say no, but I've had a class with her each year. I'm pretty sure I told you that she harassed the bejesus out of me, like, on a regular basis." He shakes his head and his too-long hair actually bounces on his shoulders. "And I know for a fact that, unlike Daisy the cat, she's not likely to come when you call because she's *all that*. Why?"

"Well, Cece told me in calculus that she's deathly afraid of worms, and so she, Mara Dettoni, and Trish Rickson drank an entire bottle of tequila at Mara's house. Cece was the one who had to swallow the worm!"

As expected, Cooper automatically giggles at the phrase "swallow the worm," and my face gets hot. But his mind swiftly finds its way out of the gutter, and he becomes pensive. "That sounds like numbers three and six on the bucket list in one bottle."

"No, Cooper, *that* is Cece facing her fear of worms." He coughs a few times to cover another juvenile spurt of laughter. This time I ignore it. "And besides, those girls don't need a bucket list, believe me. They've done about *everything* there is to do. This one time, they got naked in the girls' locker room and—"

"Whoa—TMI, Cades." Cooper may have a teen boy's oversexed brain, but he hates to be forced to deal with excessive detail when it comes to girl parts. "When do we eat breakfast?"

A casual look is called for when I face my greatest fear, so I untuck my brother's pale-yellow polo shirt from my khakis. It's soft and wrinkled and reminds me of him, which makes me momentarily nostalgic for the first fifteen years of our lives, when we did almost everything together. But like always, I grit my teeth and thank God that Cooper came along to fill his empty shoes. "Welly Doughnuts is right up the street."

HALF AN HOUR LATER, COOPER'S silver Honda is parked in the movie theater lot. The carnival is set up, but, unfortunately for us and our tight bucket-list schedule, very much dead to the world.

Cooper walks back to the car and leans on the passenger door. "It says on the ticket booth window that the fair opens at noon."

"We can't afford to sit here and waste two hours waiting for it to open its doors. Maybe we should skip ahead to number nine."

We glance across the parking lot at the movie theater. Three cars are parked in front.

"Look, Cooper, they have a morning movie for senior citizens."

"*Driving Miss Daisy…* jeez, Cady."

"I hear it's a classic."

"We're gonna stand out like sore thumbs in there." He does his trademark elbow point in the direction of the theater.

I grab two bright yellow raincoats off the floor of the back seat. "Not if we wear these. We can pull the hoods up to cover our not-gray-yet hair."

"Cady, it isn't raining out."

"A minor detail." I push Dad's yellow raincoat through the open window into Cooper's hands. "Put it on. I'll wear Mom's. Old folks love to dress as twins—have you ever noticed that? And don't you dare roll your eyes at me." I'm the eye-roller in this relationship.

We get out of the car and walk across the empty parking lot toward the Ellis Big Eight Theater. The top halves of our bodies are camouflaged by my parents' lemon-colored rain gear.

"This isn't gonna work, Cady. We can't sneak in anywhere looking like life-sized yield signs."

"Well, I'm up for the challenge, so bend over a little, like your poor elderly back hurts. I'll limp." I continue to walk, dragging my right foot with each step. "Face it, Coop, everybody except us at school has either snuck into a movie or shoplifted. And we agreed that sneaking into a movie seems more ethical."

The yellow hood nods once and then bows down slightly. "I guess we may as well go to the exit at the side of the building and try to get in."

"Shit. It's locked."

"What did you expect—a welcome sign?" I ask. I try to hold back on the sarcasm, but, as usual, fail miserably.

Beneath the yellow hood, Cooper's face is as pink as his belly was just before his naked plunge into Tamarack Lake.

"Should we knock?" I ask.

"You can't knock when you're breaking and entering, Cady." He shakes his head, and I worry that he's no better at criminal behavior than he is at tent erection. "Let's go around back. Maybe we can get inside where they put out the trash."

19

I wrinkle my nose because breaking into a theater isn't half as glamorous as I'd imagined, but I follow him. Behind the theater, we see a dark green Dumpster with a couple of fat black trash bags resting a few feet away on the pavement. Cooper and I study the scene. We must look like we're old folks checking for floodwaters, but we're actually juvenile soon-to-be delinquents sizing up possible points of illicit entry.

"We can't stand here, right out in the open, Cades—it looks like we're casing the joint."

"We *are* casing the joint."

"Come on." He grabs my arm and leads me behind the Dumpster.

Once we're hidden, we peek around the side. And this is when we realize we're not alone. A dark-haired guy about our age—acting at least one hundred times more suspicious than we are, if that's possible—approaches the Dumpster from the other side where the black trash bags are lined up. He looks around and then rips one open, reaches in, and eats whatever it is that he finds inside. After he eats a few handfuls, I decide that he's filling his face with popcorn.

"I think he's eating last night's leftover popcorn," I whisper. Cooper wrinkles his forehead and frowns and then he nods.

The dark-haired guy drops onto his backside and pretty much dives headfirst into the bag, eating so much, so quickly, that he must have popcorn dust stuck in his messy hair and scruffy beard, but I'm not at the right angle to say this for sure.

Cooper and I stay as still as we can to see what he'll do next. I'm sure it's killing Cooper not to scratch at his mosquito bites.

And I can't *not* stare. It's like when I gawk at an accident on the side of the highway. I don't *want* to look, but somehow, I *have* to.

When the guy finishes making a meal of yesterday's popcorn, he brushes off his beard and takes a few seconds to glance around. Once he's sure he's alone, he walks to the big green bin, grabs the side, and starts to climb in—which is when I lose my cool.

"What do you think you're doing?" I demand as I step out of our hiding spot. I stick my hands on my hips because I mean business. "That Dumpster's filthy. If you climb inside, you're going to catch something!"

The guy falls off the side of the Dumpster and lands on his backside on the pavement, but he doesn't turn to look at us. "Wha, what the…?"

Cooper comes to stand beside me. "Hey, buddy, if you need something to eat or drink, just say so."

Although buying this guy breakfast will get us no closer to checking all the items off our bucket list, it's the right thing to do. "Well, are you hungry or not?" I ask.

"It's cool, you guys… and I'm outta here." The popcorn thief gets up and race-walks away.

He doesn't glance at us, even when Cooper calls him back. "Hey! Do you know how to sneak into a theater? If you do, lead us in, and we'll buy you whatever you want from the snack bar."

The guy stops and pats down his unruly black hair. "You for real?"

"Sure, why not?" Cooper replies.

When the kid turns around to look at us, I'm so shocked that I gasp, and it's not because he has a popcorn kernel stuck about an inch below his right eye. He's about the hottest boy

I've ever seen. His eyes and skin are two different shades of tan, and I hate to say it at the risk of sappiness, but I will—the general bronzing effect defines "dreamy." Dark hair, that on first impression I judged unruly, is actually a complicated system of loosely layered curls—ringlets on top of banana curls, each one beautifully liberated and independent—that frame an angel's face. He looks sweet and earnest and he makes me think of a very hot, made-for-TV-movie, *Easter Story* Jesus of Nazareth.

"Then I'll show you how to get in." He flashes a skeptical glance at Cooper. The guy still appears ready to run.

We follow Hot Jesus past a loading dock and to a small gray door with no handle at the building's far corner. He pulls a long, slim metal tool out of his back pocket, which suggests criminal activity is not completely new to him, and slides it into the crack of the door. It opens easily. "And you're in." When he smiles, his teeth gleam so white, and his eyes shine so brightly, I literally swoon. Cooper does too. We collapse into each other like swooning bumper cars.

"Hot Jesus…" I murmur.

Cooper nods in agreement. And then he urges, "You go first, dude." He said the exact same thing to me just before my skinny-dipping striptease. I hope this isn't becoming a cowardly behavior pattern.

Hot Jesus steps through the doorway, and we trail behind him into the back hallway of the movie theater. Once we're inside, he leads us to the central area where the theaters are.

"Go to the restrooms and… uh… maybe you should lose those yellow raincoats," he says, looking at us with sincere regret—as if we're totally fashion-challenged. "Stay in there for five minutes and then meet me in the theater. *Driving Miss Daisy* is the only thing playing this morning. It's in theater three." I swear I see pity in his expression. He obviously thinks we have shamefully bad taste in movies, as well as rain gear. I'm insulted, but I do as he says for the sake of the bucket list.

Five minutes later, we easily find Hot Jesus in the small theater, as only seven elderly people are watching the previews. We sit on either side of him, and Cooper takes our food order. "What do you want from the snack bar?"

"Not popcorn," Hot Jesus replies quickly.

This makes sense; I watched him inhale about half of a tall kitchen trash bag of it in the parking lot. I take charge of the food order. In a loud whisper, I instruct Cooper, "If they have hot dogs or nachos, get him some of them. If it's too early to sell that stuff, find out if they have ice cream or big pretzels. And get a bunch of candy. I'm in the mood for chocolate."

"Water," Hot Jesus adds. "Could you bring me a bottle of water please?"

Cooper glances over my head as he considers Jesus's request. He's putting it together that excessive movie-theater popcorn consumption translates into salt overload, which leads to a thirst equivalent to that of a camel after a desert crossing. He nods and says, "I'll get you a large one. BRB."

Jesus and I sit in the dark, silently watching a movie we don't care about, until Cooper returns with our junk food feast.

As we eat, Cooper asks Hot Jesus questions. "I'm Cooper and this is Cady. What's your name?"

The kid chews happily on a soft pretzel and, after he swallows, replies, "I'm Elias, but most everybody calls me Eli."

mia kerick

"Thanks for sneaking us into the movie, Eli," I say, and mean it. We have successfully completed another mandatory task from the bucket list. *Cha-ching!* I feel jaded, which must be how "normal" kids feel as they walk up and down the halls of the high school on a daily basis. I lean back in my seat and cross my feet in front of me like the badass I now am.

"So, you're into… this kind of movie?" Eli asks.

"It was the only thing playing this morning and…" Cooper starts.

I'm the one to finish the lie, since I'm far better at deceiving people than Cooper—not that this is something to brag about, but, whatever. I yawn widely and drawl, in a whisper, of course, "And we're in *such* a major movie mood." Eli and Cooper stop chewing so they don't miss a word. "I woke up this morning and told my friend Cooper, here, 'I'd kill to see a movie.'"

"And speaking of killing, we're killing time 'til the carnival opens." Cooper looks at me and shrugs. "Right, Cades?" Cooper is compulsively honest, except when discussing his feelings. Naturally.

An elderly woman sitting two seats in front of us turns around, glares, and makes the universal shushing gesture. Not yet my caliber of badass, Cooper emits a noisy gulp.

Eli smiles at the woman sweetly, drops an oversized handful of jujubes into his mouth, and gurgles. "I work at the carnival. I can sneak you in there too." He then shifts his entire effort to chewing the rubbery candy.

Sneaking into a carnival isn't on the bucket list, but it enhances number nine. And I've learned something today: Until now I thought carnies were toothless old men without options, not

24

gorgeous teenage boys who could easily score a modeling gig with American Eagle Outfitters. But I'm not exactly worldly—what do I know?

"That would be great," I reply so quietly I doubt Eli hears, and then we focus on the movie, which turns out to be not half-bad. *Driving Miss Daisy* is a brilliant depiction of blossoming friendship between unlikely people.

Note to self: *Check for the book on Amazon.com.*

CHAPTER 4

cooper

AT FIRST, I'M NOT SURE if I like "Elias, but most everybody calls me Eli."

First of all, Cady's looking at him like, *OMG—he's freaking gorgeous.* And she's drooling. Cady's literally had to wipe the corners of her mouth with the back of her wrist twice in the past sixty seconds. I keep telling myself she's consumed a bucket of seriously salty popcorn and not nearly enough water, but we both know why she can't keep the saliva in her mouth.

Maybe the irritation—that fingernails on a chalkboard feeling—is because I'm jealous that Cady sees him as the perfect specimen of hotness, and I want her to see *me* that way. But I'm more convinced it's from something else. I'm off my game since *I* see Eli *that way* too… because Oh. My. God. He *is* freaking gorgeous.

I plan to reserve judgment on "Elias, but most everybody calls me Eli" until I know him better.

After the movie is over, we follow him out the front door of the theater and across the parking lot toward the carnival. Cady glances my way and grins and then she mouths the words, "Number nine," while she makes a check mark in the air with her finger. Suddenly I'm okay again.

I've got to believe that no matter how much one of us likes another guy's physical appearance, it won't mess up what we've built over the past four years. The problem is, I'm not *sure*. Lately I've been tortured by mental images of Cady entwined with young men more hairy, athletic, and muscular than me. For now, her college boyfriends are still just figments of my vivid imagination. But the truth is, I've never had competition for Cady's attention before. High school boys are unable to appreciate her eclectic appeal the way I can; to them she's just plain weird. I'm fairly certain guys will be more open-minded and observant at Vermont State University. She won't pass by them unnoticed.

"The carnival's just opening. Come on around back with me. Nobody'll care if you come in without paying."

"Are you sure?" I ask. "Because we don't have a problem with the cost of admission." Cady and I saved up our allowances for this weekend.

"Nah, it's stupid to fork out cash for just coming inside the carnival," Eli insists with a wink that makes me melt. Once we get to the entrance, he looks around like he did when he was beside the Dumpster. "Follow me." He jogs toward the back of the fenced-in enclosure. Cady pauses and then follows. I've got no choice now, so I chase along behind them.

The three of us enter the carnival through a narrow alley between two tractor-trailer trucks. Inside the carnival grounds, workers are scattered around getting ready for the day, but they don't seem to care that we're here.

"I'm working at the Tilt-a-Whirl today, I'm pretty sure. I gotta get over there in a hurry, but if you come by in an hour, I'll try to have some ride tickets for you."

Again, he glances around like he's nervous—and nervous looks good on him. Constipated would look good on him.

"Okay, we'll come by and visit you in an hour or so," Cady replies. "Think you can take a break and hang out with us?"

Eli shrugs. "Don't know. Maybe I can, if it's slow."

"Okay, dude." I sense that he's late for work, so I try to cut things short. "You better go."

Our eyes follow Eli as he runs off, and I'm sure Cady's thinking that his ass looks pretty freaking legendary in those faded jeans. And *my* thoughts define screwed-up because I'm basically green with jealousy that Cady could be drooling at his fine jogging ass, while I'm wondering if, beneath his pants, it's as round and cute as it seems.

"If we play our cards right, Eli could be number seven." Cady puts words to the other thing on my mind.

"I guess so," I mumble. This bucket list is taking me to places I'm not sure I want to go, or maybe they're places I want to go too much for my personal health and sanity.

Cady ties both of the yellow raincoats snugly around her waist, one on top of the other. "Let's find the Ferris wheel, Cooper. It's time to look at life from on high."

I gulp so loudly that Eli probably hears it all the way over at the Tilt-a-Whirl.

To FACE A FEAR—AND I mean something you're terrified of right down to your bones—is every bit as crappy as I thought it would be. And for the record, I could have lied to Cady when she first brought up the subject. I could have told her that my acrophobia was a thing of the past, and maybe it'd be more beneficial for us to face our dentophobia instead, since both of us should probably visit the dentist before we leave for college. But I chose to be honest. I leveled with Cady about my biggest admittable fear.

Cady and I met in the fall of freshman year when we'd both opted out of the ropes course in Physical Education class due to an incapacitating fear of heights. For a few weeks, the PE department chairperson came up with no other option to offer us for gym class, so we sat in the conference room in the office and did homework while the other kids climbed ropes that were set in the tall trees behind the high school.

Soon, the PE department chair decided that Cady and I should spend the full hour of daily gym class walking the school grounds. And I knew Cady was special one day when we were walking laps around the school in an early autumn rainstorm. It started with sprinkles, but within a few minutes it turned into a downpour. We were too far from the school building to take cover inside, so we ran for a big oak tree that still held enough leaves to protect us from the rain. But Cady couldn't stay still under that tree for long. She grabbed my hand and pulled me back out into the parking lot, where we jumped into puddles and laughed until Cady said, "I'm gonna pee my pants."

To sum it up, we spent the next few weeks getting better acquainted while improving our cardiovascular health—a win-win situation. This was when we decided life was much improved with each other as sounding boards. We have our incapacitating fear of heights to thank for the birth of our friendship, and now we're going to face this fear together.

As we head across the dusty parking lot in the direction of the carnival's tallest structure, I try to change Cady's mind one last time. "I've been experiencing a recurring nightmare about evil clowns since kindergarten," I say, as I note the brightly colored sign inviting carnival-goers to a one o'clock clown show under the not-very-big top.

My remark doesn't warrant a sideways glance. "Forget it, Murphy. We settled this last week. Today we're addressing our fear of heights."

I sigh loudly enough for her to hear and then I copy her posture—head high, shoulders back, and spine straight; my hope is that appearing brave will provide me with some false courage. We approach the ticket booth beside the Ferris wheel.

"Don't buy too many tickets. We each only need six," I tell her. At the moment, I'm the financial manager of The Weekend Bucket List.

"Not born yesterday," she informs me blandly and buys a roll of twelve.

After the ticket purchase, all we have to do is walk the fifteen feet to the carnival ride that's now causing me to face a different fear—taking a crap in public. This morning's doughnuts don't seem to want to stay put in my gut. I hear that unbridled fear can do this to a person. So, I tighten all the butt muscles necessary to keep my breakfast in its proper place and snatch the string of tickets that dangle from Cady's hand. For no good reason other than self-distraction, I rip the string in half and hand Cady her six. "Time to git'r done."

"I'M GONNA BARF." AT THIS point, my breakfast threatens to make its grand exit through the exact same hole it entered. *Fantastic.*

I'm not alone in my terror. The ride hasn't begun to move, and Cady already clings to my left wrist with a death grip; her closely clipped fingernails stab my pulse point. "We're going to survive this. It'll be a cake walk." Her words are confident, but her voice is shaky.

I, however, don't want to even *think* about cake. I offer a grain of truth. "I'm more concerned about what might eject from my *pie hole.*"

"That's disgusting." She wrinkles her nose. "Now, concentrate on surviving the ride."

Our little chair lurches forward and begins its slow ascent. "Crappity-McCrappington," I utter, clearly not in control of my mouth, which compounds my fear of barfing.

We stop several times on our way up as small groups of fearless preschoolers and their death-defying teachers file into seats. I slide toward Cady, crowding her to the inside of the bench seat.

"Cooper, I can't breathe…"

"I can't either!" I'm too terrified to inhale. I grab my throat and emit a croak.

"*I* can't breathe because you're squishing me into the corner— my lungs have no room to expand."

When she accuses me of intentionally suffocating her, I move over *one* inch, but not a centimeter more. And when the toddlers are finally seated, the ride starts in earnest. As our car reaches the top for the first time, I squeeze my eyes shut and force my mind onto the memory of the tangled beauty of Eli's curls. Somehow, the image soothes me. I'm gratified to hear a pathetic squeak escape from Cady's lips as we begin our backward descent.

And then we're at the bottom again. I crack open one eye, squint to see through my fogged-up glasses, and squelch the urge to scream at the old man who is operating the ride, "*Stop right now and set me free of this death trap!*" Instead, I blow out a humiliated breath between cautiously pursed lips and shut my eyes again.

Even with my eyes closed, I can tell when we're again at the summit. Cady's bony elbow pokes my belly—a risky move considering my nausea. "Cooper, you've got to relax." Her breath is on my face and it smells like coffee. I fight my gag reflex. "Look, I'm freaking out too, but we're going to be better and stronger people for having done this."

I nod. I may not be brave, but at least I'm agreeable.

We go down and then up two more times. Cady still holds my hand, but it isn't a death grip anymore, which unnerves me. "Open your eyes, Coop."

Yeah, right—not in this lifetime.

"I mean it; open your eyes. It's actually kinda cool up here. See the Good Shepherd Church's steeple?"

"You're nothing but a dirty, rotten traitor…" I grumble, my eyes still closed.

"What are you talking about?"

"You're the Benedict Arnold of acrophobes!" I accuse as I jab *my* elbow in her general direction.

"Just because I'm not wigging out to the same extent as you, doesn't mean I'm not scared." I realize she's released her grip on the safety bar when she grabs my shoulders with both hands and shakes me hard. "Open your eyes!"

I'm a guy who, if at all possible, does as he's told. So, despite my terror, I crack one eye open and then the other, and swallow back the two chocolate crullers that have risen to my throat. And I look around. Cady's right. The scenery looks beautiful from up here, in an early summer, pale-green way. The breeze fans my likely also pale-green, sweaty face and I admit the truth: "It… it's not… so bad."

"Check out the church steeple! Over there." Cady releases one of my shoulders to point at the white steeple in the distance. I want to grab her hand and pull it to my chest, but instead I take a deep, calming breath.

I nod again. I'm pretty much an expert bobblehead when it comes to Cady, and since it's not a movement that will rock the gondola, I'm relatively safe—for now.

"Next time around, Cooper—do I have to remind you of what we have to do to fulfill number three?"

"N-n-no. No… I don't need a r-reminder. I'm j-just not r-ready y-yet…"

"Well, I'm going to do it. If I don't do it soon, I'm going to back out and that's not an option."

"Jeez, Cady!" We're already at the bottom, on our way up. "This thing moves at a pretty fast clip and…" Before I finish speaking, we approach the top of the curve. Cady grabs my hand and pulls me to my feet.

"Oh, my freaking word!" I'm not sure if I say this aloud or just think it. I'm not sure it matters. We "stand" in an admittedly hunched position, on top of the whole world. I can't stop staring at the pavement a mere one-hundred-and-fifty feet below, and the likely location of my untimely, brain-splattering death. As I fixate on the ground, we go right over the top, standing—crouching—the whole time.

"Sit in your goddamned seats!" yells the carnival worker as we pass the base of the Ferris wheel, but when I bend my knees in an effort to obey him, Cady pulls me back up.

"We need to stand for a full cycle or it won't count, doofus!" She screams with such wild abandon I have good reason to suspect she's already lost her marbles. I have no clue why Cady's so dang devoted to the specifics of this stupid-ass bucket list. But like her perfect little puppet, I don't sit.

As we rise to the highest point, Cady allows a different sort of scream. "Woohoo! We did it! We can check number three off the list!" And that's when the Ferris wheel slows and comes to a stop. We have to bend over and grab at the safety bar as it jolts, but still we don't sit.

"Get your backsides on the damned bench!" bellows the old man who is in charge of the ride.

"Do you realize what example you are providing to the Morningside Farm preschoolers?" It's an older women's voice. "You teenagers ought to be ashamed of yourselves!"

"Those naughty big kids need a time out, Mrs. Dempsey!"

Cady shrugs and finally sits. "We did it." Her voice sounds smug; she's clearly not experiencing the shame that has shriveled my soul. I sit beside her on the bench, and my cheeks—the ones on my face—burn so much it hurts. Sure, I faced my biggest fear: I stared my acrophobia in the eye and then literally stood up to it. But I'm not proud, and the embarrassment about so blatantly breaking the rules in front of a class of impressionable three-year-olds has turned my face ripe-tomato red.

Very slowly this time, we make our final descent, and, when we reach the bottom, the carnival worker growls a few words into his walkie-talkie. When he's finished, he barks in my face, "I ought to call the goddamned cops on you delinquents!" The man assumes this was my genius idea. "It woulda been my job to scrub yer bloody remains offa the blacktop!"

I swallow hard, though, because he's right about one thing: Cady and I are legit criminals now. Not only have we snuck into a movie without paying, which is technically stealing, but we've also provided a reckless example to toddlers.

Cady doesn't beg or plead, and I desperately want her to wipe the self-satisfied smirk from her face. "Jesus..." she utters.

"I know, *jeez*, Cady, we could have been arrested or fallen to our deaths!"

"No... *Jesus*."

And here he is. Hot Jesus, the food-scavenging, cover-model-carnie, otherwise known as Eli, walks slowly past the ticket booth on his way to the Ferris wheel.

"Throw these delinquents outta here, Stanley!" the old man orders and points at us.

Stanley? Stanley—aka Jesus aka Elias, but call me Eli—comes over to our car, looks at us sheepishly, and says, "Come on. Boss says you gotta go."

"They ain't the king and queen of England, Stanley. Grab 'em by the hair and get 'em the hell outta here!"

Eli lifts the safety bar and helps Cady to her feet. Her eyes are as big as the silver dollars from my coin collection, which I cashed in to pay for this ill-advised adventure. I rise beside her, and Eli takes ahold of each of us by a wrist. "Time to go, guys," he murmurs again.

"Sure thing." Cady uses the haughty tone she saves for the nastiest boys at school. "We were just leaving anyhow; we've had enough of this crappy carnival." I'm surprised to hear the venom in her voice, but at the same time, when Cady gets embarrassed she sets her sharp tongue free to wreak havoc on the innocent—*and* the less than innocent, but that's a story for a different day.

Eli gawks at her as if she sprouted devil horns in her silky brown hair. "*You're welcome,*" he says softly, so only we hear.

He leads us to the front of the fairground. Cady's pissed off and won't look at him, let alone talk to him, so I step up. "Sorry about the Ferris wheel thing, Eli. We got caught in the moment, I guess."

"*I* guess *crappy carnivals* don't deserve any respect." He looks me in the eye, which takes my breath away.

Cady huffs loudly.

"Her words came out wrong, dude. Thanks for getting us in here for free." I glance at Cady, who whistles softly and kicks at the stones on the ground with her sneakers. "Meet us for dinner tonight, Eli. It'll be our treat—our way of saying thank you and sorry." Cady glances at me, but I can't read her dark expression.

Now that he's let go of our wrists, Eli takes a step back so he stands under a big red and white sign that says, "Come one, come all. Step right up and have a ball." He doesn't respond to my offer.

"Can you get out by four?" Cady asks bluntly. "We can't wait around much longer than that because we're going on a road trip."

"I gotta work 'til ten."

"Then it's not going to fly." Cady turns to me and says, "And *he's* not going to be number seven."

Eli seems confused, but he doesn't turn around and leave, which would definitely be his best move.

"Eli, can you get tonight and tomorrow off?" I can't believe I have the balls to ask him this. I must be committed to number seven, and if it's not going to happen with Cady, I want it to go down with Eli. "Because you could come along with us... maybe."

He glances at Cady to check that she agrees with my proposition. After she meets his gaze and gives him a curt nod, he takes a deep breath and says, "I don't know." He shrugs, shakes his head, and then nods, like he's having an internal disagreement with himself. "I, I think maybe I can make it happen. Can you meet me here at four?"

Cady smiles at him, and again I'm jealous. How crazy is it that I'm jealous about something that was all my doing? I can answer that one—pretty dang nuts. In any event, I'm ready to say goodbye to him. "We'll be back. Grab a change of clothes and whatever shit you'll need. And don't forget your swim trunks."

"Will do," Eli replies and turns back to the fairground. "I got a Speedo."

Cady and I study his ass as he trots away. I'd bet money that we're both picturing it in a cherry-red Speedo.

Cady's eyes bulge. Mine do, too.

CHAPTER 5

eli

I GOT A VAGABOND SOUL, so it makes sense that I'm on the road again. I tell myself this a time or two as I head back to Jimmy's trailer and try my best to believe it. Inside my brain, I scream it and I sing it, but the truth is, I'm feeling shaky. So, I say my truth words *out loud* and hope it'll sink into my head. "Dad always said that the souls of the Stanley family men are prone to wandering." I used to think he only said this because he lost his job so often that we never stayed in the same place for more than a year or two, but then he told me Grandpa was a fisherman and he moved around a lot too. "It makes sense that I'm hitting the road."

I climb the three metal stairs to the trailer door and hope like heck that it's not locked. Guess maybe my drifter soul got lucky today, seeing as it's wide open.

Before I quit school, I learned about something in social studies class called *stereotypes,* and I still remember what it means because I'm not one-hundred percent brainless. "A preconceived notion about a group of people." I remember it well enough to say the words out loud in the tiny room and I smile because I'm proud of this fact. I also remember that *productivity* means "output per man hour," so I say this out loud too, even though it seems a little inconsiderate of *ladies'* production levels. It's good to feel smart, though, and it doesn't happen to me all that often.

Anyhow, I'd bet my boots that "all Stanley men got wandering souls" is one of those stereotypes, because I'm Eli Stanley and I'm prone to wanting to live somewhere that's got sheets on the bed and a bathroom with a flush toilet and walls around me that grow out of the ground, not from a trailer with wheels. But I'm not going to cry about it. It's too late. I did the deed—I quit my job so I could head off on a road trip with two kids I don't know from Adam, whoever Adam is.

"If it's not 'cause my soul wants to drift, then why'd I do it?" I ask, as I grab my black duffel bag and fill it with all the crap I got to my name, which isn't much.

At first, all I get for an answer is a shrug. I got to do better. So, I think about it harder and come up with a real reason. "I'm doing it because Cady and Cooper asked me to." This reason works for me, seeing as nobody's invited me anywhere in one heck of a long time and it felt good. How could I say no?

Once my bag is full, I grab a paper plate and turn it over on the tiny counter in the kitchen and jot a quick note to Jimmy to say thanks for all the hospitality. I fork out a few bucks, stick them under the pencil, and shiver because *what-the-heck-was-I-thinking-when-I-quit-my-job?* I throw my bag over my shoulder and go to meet my new friends.

cadence

THE TRUNK IS CLOSED. ALL of our electronics—phones and computers and other gadgets—are stuffed inside double plastic grocery bags and are stowed safely under our backpacks and the tent. "No more electronics until tomorrow afternoon," I announce, although this comes as no surprise to Cooper.

"I hope we can figure out how to get to the coast without the MAPS app on our iPhones." Cooper's eyebrows are crinkled with worry.

"Don't sweat the details so much, Coop." Like I'm one to talk. "The Atlantic Ocean is east, right? How hard can it be to find it?" I step around the car to the passenger seat and get in.

"I suppose…"

"We need to grab some food and a cheap cooler before we pick up Eli."

Cooper hops in the driver's seat and we take off for Shoppers' World. It's notable that we've decided to grocery shop in Ellis. If we shopped in Wellington, people would ask too many questions we can't answer if we want to check off all of the items on The Weekend Bucket List. Besides, sneaking around in a distant town is risky and rebellious, maybe even close to the way playing hooky would have felt, had we ever been daring enough to do it.

"We should have skipped school with everybody else on Senior Skip Day," I say, as if he was the one who stopped us.

Cooper shakes his head. His ginger hair falls a full inch over the collar of his plaid shirt—it has never been long enough to cover his collar before. I fight the urge to touch it just to find out if it's as silky as it looks. "*You* were the one who said, 'No can do,' if I remember correctly, Cades."

This is pure fact. "But I had a homework assignment on *Pride and Prejudice* due that day. If I skipped Lit class I would have gotten a zero on it." I attempt to defend my very limited level of coolness.

"Participating in Senior Skip Day implies that you don't give a shit about school rules or good grades. You were supposed to throw caution to the wind."

"We both would have missed an AP Calc quiz too."

"A zero on *one* quiz wouldn't have changed anything for me," he argues.

He's reminding me that when you have one-hundred percents on all the other quizzes and tests and homework in a class, one measly zero won't affect your grade. You'll still get an A++ in AP Calculus and be Wellington High School's senior class valedictorian. "Must be nice to be a genius."

Cooper turns up the Taylor Swift classic that's playing on the car radio. For the record, we're tuned in to the same local easy-listening pop music radio station that we've tuned in to with our families since we were kids. For the duration of high school, Cooper and I also missed out on the entire Indie music scene because we hit the books too hard.

My partner in crime pulls his car into the grocery store parking lot and finds a spot about as far away from the front doors as you can get, but I manage to stifle my criticism, don't ask me how. "We only have an hour left until we pick up Eli. So, don't dawdle in the chips and snacks aisle," I warn, though we both know that *I'm* the one who lingers over junk food.

"No worries," he replies, obedient as always. I grab a cart and Cooper grabs a Styrofoam cooler. "Don't let me forget a bag of ice."

It doesn't take long for us to push the cart up and down the aisles and pick out stuff for a cookout my mom would be proud to call her own, which isn't saying much, along with snacks and drinks. When we're back in the parking lot, nobody looks at us funny as we load our groceries into the trunk, but I worry that everyone who can see me thinks I'm pregnant. They probably figure I'm a too-young-to-be-married, pregnant high school girl, and this explains why I'm grocery shopping for food with a boy who is equally young. I feel guilty for "getting pregnant" and I've never even had sex.

As we drive back to the carnival, I ask Cooper, "Do you think you're cured of your fear of heights now that you've faced it directly?"

"That's a good question." He doesn't hurry to answer. It's as if my simple question submerges him in an ocean of thought bubbles. I've almost given up on getting an answer from him when he says, "No. I'm still terrified of heights. I'm sure I'll have nightmares about what we did for the rest of my life."

"But we did it, Coop, and we didn't run away." He shrugs. I don't think facing a fear head-on worked as well for him as it did for me. I'm a different person already: more mature and somehow liberated. "We've been set free."

When all he says in reply is "cool," I sigh because I know I'm being selfish.

I'm usually on the same page as Cooper. I don't like to be as far apart in our minds as we've been lately. Something is changing between us, which makes me want him to write an oath swearing that we'll always be friends—in his blood on a square of toilet paper from one of the rolls in the trunk—even if I may want more from him than friendship.

It's ten past four and I'm beginning to have doubts as to whether Eli is going to show up. For exactly thirty-three minutes, we've been staring at the stupid "Come one, come all" sign and the silvery portable fence and all the screaming kids who clutch giant stuffed crayons and the frazzled-zombie parents with hollow "kill me now" eyes exiting the carnival. I'm ready to get this show on the road and I'm not talking about the clown show.

"Eli, *himself*, isn't critical to our plan. I mean, it's not as if he's the *only person* we can do number seven with," I say, resisting the urge to wink. But Cooper's eyes stay glued to the entrance of the stupid little fair. I sigh in frustration; I clearly need to spell it out. "You know, we could even decide do number seven with *each other*."

Now that I've spoken the words aloud, I roll my eyes like I don't care. I can't let him see me sweat when it comes to number seven—the trickiest item on the bucket list, and complicated in ways that make my blood go cold if I dwell on it. But the time has come to figure out what's going on between Cooper and me. Not to mention, time is running short.

"Let's give him ten more minutes," he says in a low monotone.

Again, I sigh loudly. I've been doing this so much it has started to lose its effectiveness. "Whatever you say," I reply with a middle-finger salute, but we both know it's what *I* say that counts most.

Not a minute goes by, and Eli saunters across the parking lot. He looks way too sexy to be a Biblical character, but I still think he resembles a *scorching hot* King of Kings.

"Bless my soul," I mumble as I gawk at the way his snug black T-shirt and snugger black jeans hug his body. And those rugged biker boots.... He's *so* not my type, but my stupid heart goes pitter-patter anyway.

In my defense, Cooper is dumbstruck too.

"Well, stop drooling and go pick him up," I demand. My tone is less-than-sweet, so I add, "'Kay, Coop?"

Cooper pulls his Honda around the end of the long row of cars and right up beside Eli, who hops into the back seat without making eye contact with either of us. "Hey," he says.

"Hey, Eli. How's it shaking?" Cooper turns around to offer Eli a fist bump. He's in super-cool-dude mode. I recognize the tone of voice, as well as his language. It says, *"Follow me 'cuz I'm so chill…. My soul is free and when you smile the sun will shine and the bees will buzz and blah, blah, blah."* Bradley used to have a thing for this singer named Uncle Kracker, and before he left for rehab he played his music—blaringly loud and annoyingly nonstop—in his bedroom, forcing the entire LaBrie family to listen. Cooper's laid-back attitude is like an Uncle Kracker song come to life. *Erghh.*

"Um… well, I'm here, I guess. And I got tonight and tomorrow off work." He clears his throat like he's nervous, and the sound is loud enough for me to hear over the obscenely cheerful Michael Bublé tune on the radio. "Had to quit my job to get tomorrow off, though."

Cooper stops the car, and we all jolt forward. I'm unbuckled, so my forehead hits the dashboard. Cooper, however, isn't worried about my bruised head. "You *quit* your freaking job? On account of *us*?" His voice breaks like a twelve-year-old boy's. The super-chill, come-what-may dude is gone, gone, gone. *Buh-bye, Uncle Kracker.*

"Don't worry about it. I'll find something else to do for work after the road trip. Jobs that don't call for special skills are easy to find, seeing as nobody wants them and they don't pay too good."

Eli runs his slim bronze fingers through his intricate layers of dark curls and then leans back. "Where're we off to?"

Cooper gawks at Eli in the rearview mirror, and his tongue hangs rather unappealingly from the side of his mouth, so I pick up where he left off. I turn around in my seat and reply, "Thought we'd take a trip to the coast."

"You picked a good weekend to do it. Supposed to be clear tonight and sunny tomorrow," Eli informs us and then twirls a spiral curl around an index finger.

This guy can sneak us into places, escort us out of places, *and* predict the weather. Hot Jesus is turning out to be priceless.

"Great," I say, but I refuse to betray my awe at our good fortune. "What do you think is the best route to Rhye Beach?" Maybe he's a directions-whisperer too.

"If it was me driving, I'd take Old Route 92. Not so direct, but real scenic."

"Can you turn water into wine?" Cooper asks, and makes no attempt to hide his awe. I smile, but just to myself, because Cooper and I are back on the same page. "That would come in handy with what we have planned for later on tonight."

"No, but I got a fake ID."

Cooper mumbles, "That works, too." He's seriously impressed. *Whatevs.*

We drive in silence, and eventually Eli drifts off, his curls draped over a corner of the Styrofoam cooler. Asleep, he looks less like Jesus and more like an angel. Maybe he *is* an angel—our guardian angel. He'll make sure we don't get in too much trouble as we check items off the bucket list. My mom can't handle any more trouble from her kids.

I close my eyes, just for a second…

"SHIT, CADY! DO I GO north or south?" We're stopped at an intersection that overlooks the ocean. "Cady—listen up! I haven't been to Rhye Beach since I was seven and I can't flipping remember! And there's a line of cars behind me!"

Unsure of where I am, I jolt upright, but hear a calm voice from the back seat. "Head north, if you're looking for a beach."

After I smooth my hair and untwist my brother's polo shirt at my waist, I turn around to look at Eli.

"I been traveling with the carnival since I quit school when I was seventeen. That was about two years ago, give or take. I been on about every road in this part of the state."

This explains his knowledge of the main streets and back roads of New Hampshire. Cooper obediently heads north, and I ask Eli, "Why did you quit school?"

Eli shrugs. "I saw joining the carnival as better than getting my ass kicked every time I looked at my old man the wrong way."

Cooper proves that, though highly directions-challenged, he's still with the program. "Why'd he beat you up for just looking at him?"

"Long ugly story. I'm pretty sure you two don't wanna hear it."

"Try us." I say it before Cooper can, but he glances at me and nods. Even when competing for the attention of Mr. Wonderful, we think alike.

Eli pulls a purple elastic band from his wrist and ties his hair into a knot on the top of his head. It gives him the appearance of a little girl who's about to step into the bathtub. "Me and my old man just don't see eye to eye. Never did."

I want more info—the hard, cold facts of how somebody so gorgeous got so unlucky. I shut my mouth and listen. Cooper stays quiet, too. He's as curious as I am.

"Dad was on my back to quit school, anyhow, so I could get a job and chip in for rent and stuff. He was done with me riding the gravy train, or so he said. I didn't want to work in the paper factory in town like Dad was doing at that point—it stunk to high heaven and I got a sensitive nose—and seeing as I'm more or less a traveling man, I thought I might just join the army right after graduation. But in maybe, say, April, when I was a senior, the carnival came to town. I stuffed everything I wanted to keep into this very bag…" He points to the black duffel on the floorboard. "…and I joined. Never been back home since."

That's quite a story. I have a sneaking suspicion it's true too. But, if you ask me, he should have stuck it out for the last few months of high school. He was so close to earning his diploma.

"That sucks, man." Cooper coughs a couple times. Fake coughing helps him not cry.

"What are you going to do now?" I ask, practical as always. "You quit your job. How are you going to survive?"

Eli finds this question funny. He laughs, and it's weird because, in all of the made-for-TV Jesus of Nazareth movies, Jesus *never* laughs. In fact, he hardly ever smiles, unless it's at a child or a lamb. But Hot Jesus laughs in the back seat of Cooper's beater Honda because I questioned his ability to get by in life with no family support and no job.

"I don't see what's so funny." I use the tone of voice I reserve for telling Daisy to get her butt off my pillow.

Cooper continues to drive up the coast, but now he's worked up.

"I got some cash saved. I can last on it a while. Don't worry, Cady." It's the first time Eli has said my name. I get goose bumps on my arms.

But my best friend is clearly still worried. "I think we should turn around," Cooper says and coughs again. "Maybe you're missing one night, but you can still go to work tomorrow and—"

"It's a done deal." Eli points to his perfect face. "Mr. Hearn said he doesn't want to see this ugly mug begging for its job back." He stretches, and, when his T-shirt lifts, I spy a narrow strip of tan belly. A thin line of hair leads to his family jewels; Cece calls it a trail to paradise. I wouldn't know, having never been there. "Can we stop soon? Gotta whiz like a racehorse."

Spell it out for us, why don't you, Eli? I face forward to look out the windshield, mostly so he doesn't see me roll my eyes.

"A beach can't be too far from here," Cooper assures him.

It will be dark soon, and Cooper has no clue as to where we are. As it turns out, we only drive five more minutes and the rocky coastline turns into a pebbly beach about a hundred feet from the road.

"We're here?" I ask.

Cooper shrugs. "I should find a place to hide the car."

"I'm good at that kind of stuff. I can help," Eli offers. "But first, I gotta whiz."

Cooper pulls the car onto the side of the road near a path that leads down to the beach, and Eli disappears to "whiz" while we unload the tent and the cooler, the firewood and the groceries, our backpacks, and Eli's duffel bag. When Eli returns, I say, "I'll carry this stuff to the beach while you guys hide the car."

"We should pick up some booze first so we don't have to leave again," Cooper says in his Joe-cool voice.

Once I give my nod of approval, he and Eli climb back in the car and pull onto the road. It takes four trips down the rocky slope to get everything onto the small beach. I dump our stuff in a place that's more sand than pebbles and which is sheltered by a towering rock, and I set up the tent.

cooper

I NEARLY SHIT A BRICK when Eli strolls out of the grocery store pushing a cart stacked with six-packs of various bottled beers. This is so illegal it's not funny. If I get stopped on the way to the beach, I'll lose my full scholarship to Bennigan College, not that I absolutely need it to attend. But losing it would complicate my life and I can't forget about graduation. They wouldn't let a convicted felon give a valedictory speech—not that I'd care, but my parents would.

I hop out of the car and pop open the trunk. "We've got to unload this shit fast—before somebody notices we're underage and calls the cops. Come on! Hurry up!"

Eli's a cool customer compared to me. Then, a pregnant nun would be too. He isn't sweating buckets, but what does he have to lose? He's a homeless, unemployed high school drop-out. College isn't even a distant dream for him.

When my shaking hand reaches for a six-pack, Eli places his hand on mine. "Get in the car and relax, Cooper. I can do this real fast all by myself."

I wipe my sweaty forehead with the inside of my wrist and obey.

Once Eli gets into the car and I start the drive back to the beach, he says, "So, I take it you aren't a big partier."

"Is it that obvious?"

Eli smiles. "You guys seniors?"

"Yeah. We graduate on Monday night."

"You goin' to college?"

I nod and again hope I'm not caught with a car full of booze, suspended from high school graduation, and kicked out of college before I ever set foot on campus. "I'm going to Bennigan College."

"Cool. What about Cady?"

"She's going to state college in Vermont."

He shifts so he can stare out the passenger window. "One of these days I gotta get my GED."

I'm not sure if he says this to himself or me, so I don't reply.

Finally, he asks, "Are you and Cady boyfriend and girlfriend?"

I shake my head. "No, we're just friends." For some reason, I add, "For the most part."

"She's pretty… Cady is," he tells me, as if I don't already know this.

I'm immediately annoyed. "I guess."

We ride back to the beach in silence.

CHAPTER 6

WITH THE BEER AND THE second Styrofoam cooler in tow, Eli and I stagger down the slope to the far corner of the beach where Cady has set up the tent beside a big rock.

"Guess what, Coop?" I know a smug expression when I see it. "No leftover tent poles."

"You suck." I force a smile. "We picked up another cooler and some more ice for the beer."

"We should ice down the beer right now if we want it cold later." Eli stacks the pile of six-packs in the sand. *He* carried all of the beer, but somebody had to get the foam cooler down here in one piece. Those things are freaking fragile.

Cady takes the cooler to a place in the brush where it'll be relatively hidden, in the event our little party is busted. *It's as if she's done this before,* I think, as she casually arranges bottles in ice.

I know for a fact, though, that this is a first for her. She came to my house one night in the spring of sophomore year, when her folks went away to a bed and breakfast to celebrate their anniversary. Bradley immediately invited a bunch of kids to come and party and pressured Cady to have a few beers with them. When I opened my front door to her, she was crying. "I snuck out the back door when Bradley thought I was going to the bathroom. He's probably mad at me that I cut and run! And I wanted to be cool and have a few drinks with him and his friends, but I just couldn't! I can't do that to Mom and Dad!"

I hugged her, and as I pulled her inside my house, she clung to me. I've been with Cady every weekend since, and she's never once cracked open a bottle of anything it takes an ID to purchase.

Once the brews are chilling, the three of us meet in front of the tent for a "now what?" moment.

Cady leans toward me and says under her breath, "We're well on our way to checking off number five." She grins like the Cheshire cat.

And she's right. We have successfully put a road trip into action. But Eli doesn't miss our exchange. "Huh?" he asks. "Number five—what's that?" We pretend not to hear him.

When Cady murmurs, "Now for number eight," I'm uncomfortable because it's not cool to talk about the bucket-list numbers when Eli has no clue. Our opportunity to run naked on the beach fast approaches, though, so I'm complicit.

Maybe I'm getting pulled into the spirit of The Weekend Bucket List, because Cady's enthusiasm is contagious. And then there's the fact that I'm a consummate follower. So I suggest, "Let's go swimming." Cady and I exchange glances before I pull off my glasses and stick them on top of the big rock.

Cady heads to the tent to change into her swimsuit. She's not a bikini type, and comes out of the tent wearing a sensible one-piece, her navy blue Speedo.

And she's not the only who wears a Speedo.

I'd tried not to gawk when, beside the big rock, Eli stripped off his biker-dude clothes, and then, completely naked, bent over, stuck a hand into his duffel bag, and pulled out black

Speedo briefs. I'd expected red. And to be real, none of the guys I know would be caught dead in a Speedo, unless they were on the Wellington High School Swim Team, if we had one. But Eli pulled his speedo briefs over his strong thighs and round ass, turned around, and stood there looking at me—lips parted and hair blowing in the sea breeze—completely unaware that he had just fulfilled one of my most secret fantasies. So, I'd grabbed my backpack and gone behind the tent to change into my oversized swim trunks. It wouldn't have been a good moment to be caught naked by the subject of my… interest.

Cady shoves a towel into each of our arms and runs to the water. She has barely dipped one toe when she announces, "The water's frigid."

Eli and I join her. I suddenly feel virile, and brave the freezing water to my knees before I stop short. After twenty seconds, I no longer have sensation in my feet.

Eli shouts, "Only one way to get this done!" And he plunges headfirst into the water, clearly demonstrating who has the nerve at this small party.

When his head pops through the water's surface, he shakes the wet curls off of his face and exclaims, "Refreshing!"

I can't hold back a scowl.

Naturally, Cady is next to demonstrate her willingness to brave the icy Atlantic. She takes a few steps, sinks to her neck in the water, and allows an adorable shriek followed by a spurt of frenzied laughter. I am the lonely wimp who is still bone-dry from my knobby knees on up. At this point, I really have no choice, so I grit my teeth and dive—straight into a rock. My chin takes the brunt of the impact.

When I stand, Cady says, "Your chin's bleeding, Murphy."

Eli's at my side in a split second; his perfect brown hand is placed lightly on my chest, and he studies me with deep concern. "Cooper, are you okay? I think you dove into a rock."

I simultaneously fight the urge to call him a freaking genius *and* get hard from his closeness, which is quite a trick considering the frigid water and abundant humiliation. "I'm fine." I dive back in. Thankfully I don't come face to face with another boulder. Or a bloom of jellyfish. Or, with my luck, a great white shark.

We splash around in the water for two minutes, not a second more, because it's actually painful. Cady beats us to our campsite. She pulls a towel around her shoulders and sighs at the warmth. Eli and I saunter slowly up the beach, as if we wouldn't kill to be wrapped like babies in our towels too. I glance at Eli's Speedo with new confidence, expecting evidence of the serious shrinkage I'm currently experiencing, but I see nothing of the sort. Shrinkage or not, Eli is hung like an Argentine Lake Duck… Mom and I watch a lot of nature documentaries.

And then Cady proceeds with The Weekend Bucket List. Beneath the towel she somehow manages to pull off her swimsuit, and then flings it with her foot so it lands on top of my glasses on the big rock. She now has our undivided attention.

Next thing we know, her floral bathroom towel is on the sand, and skinny, naked Cady sprints across the beach in a zigzag pattern like she's dodging machine gun fire. It takes me a few seconds to realize that she's trying to avoid the larger rocks in the sand.

"Number eight!" She yells into the wind, and even without my glasses it's clear to see that her tiny ass is pink from the chill of the water. Eli stares in her direction and grins. He has noticed the splendor of her rear end too.

When his fingers slip beneath the low waist of his Speedo, I decide I can't allow him to complete number eight before I do. I mean, *I* am one of The Weekend Bucket List creators, and he's a mere participant. Though I would like nothing more than to stand here, cozy in my towel, and stare from Cady to Eli and back, I yank off my trunks, kick them onto the rocky sand, and sprint toward Cady. When I glance back to assure myself that Eli is naked too, I realize that he had merely been adjusting the tie inside his bathing suit. Still wearing his itsy-bitsy bikini bottom, he stands as still as a deer caught in headlights and takes in the bare-ass eye candy darting this way and that along the rocky coast.

I'm certain that, in my birthday suit, I am the freaking whitest creature ever to come in contact with this sand, unless a baby beluga has beached itself here. But it's too late for self-consciousness, so I push awareness of the abundant freckles that cover my pale skin from the forefront of my mind and grab Cady's hand. Together we run to the shore and kick our feet in the water. Well, technically, we flick the waves with our toes, because the ocean *is* cold enough to stop profuse bleeding from the chin.

"We're wild, Murphy! Nobody at Wellington High is as free-spirited as us!" She shouts into the wind with a new confidence in her tone.

I want to correct her by yelling, "No one at Wellington would risk frostbite by swimming in the Atlantic Ocean off the United States' northeastern coast in early June!" But I just shout, "Yeah!" so as not to burst her bubble or appear uncool.

mia kerick

eli

I NEVER GOT TOO MUCH good advice from the grown-ups in my life. Take this example: before Mom took off, she told me it was fine to go to school wearing Band-Aids on my zits. Not a good choice. Got me beat up for looking like a dork, but, since I learn quick, I only made that mistake once.

Dad's advice wasn't real helpful either: "Never use your blinker when you're driving, boy—it ain't nobody's business where you're going." That advice got me stopped by the cops a couple times before I wised up.

I got other pieces of crappy advice from Mom and Dad before our family fell apart:

"If you pretend like you got balls, you won't get bullied so much, Eli." *So, I fake cool.*

"Nah, son, permanent marker ain't actually permanent." *Um, it kinda is.*

"The best cure for poison ivy? Definitely bleach." *Ouch, you know?*

"I told you already, Elias, don't smell it; just eat it real fast." *Hello, barf-city.*

But nobody ever told me to steer clear of folks who stripped off all their clothes and ran along the beach in their birthday suits. So here I am, building a fire that'll toast Cady and Cooper's frozen buns, or their cute-as-heck, rosy, frozen buns. I know this, because I took a good long look at both sets of cheeks.

Truth is, I like these kids a lot. It's stupid how much I want them to like me back. If someone was to ask me which one of

56

them I was hot for, though, I'd have to shrug and walk away. I haven't got a *good* answer to that question, but I got an answer.

I like them both. They make me smile, and I haven't done too much of that for ages. The thing is, I never *did* figure out how I could dream all night about Patriots' cheerleaders and wake up to pop a woody at the sight of the dude on the Abercrombie & Fitch shopping bag on the chair beside my bed, but it's how I roll. Hot is hot. I get into curves on a girl as much as muscles on a guy. And I like muscles on a girl and curves on a guy too—just saying. I never knew the right question to ask myself about how this could happen, so I just told me, "Eli, some folks like steak *and* chicken. And I see no need to choose one flavor of meat right yet."

It's like Cady mind-reads my thoughts about meat. "I'm starving," she says and plops beside the fire. She's comfortable now, dressed in gray sweatpants and a State University of Vermont sweatshirt. "When do we eat?'

If I didn't know better, I'd say that Cooper timed his return to the fireside just to answer her question. "Anytime we want, now that I found these perfect hotdog-roasting sticks." He holds them in the air to show them off.

Nobody asked me, but Cooper looks way prouder than a dude who took *twenty minutes* to find three almost-straight sticks ought to, but still I say, "Way to go, Cooper. You found some fine sticks."

"Damn straight," he says, and I'm not sure if he's talking about the sticks or something else. And by the way Cooper stares at the campfire, I suspect he's a little scared of it. I tell him, "Why don't you grab the hotdogs and buns; that way we can start cooking? I'll tend to the fire."

"Don't forget the mustard and a bag of chips." Cady's a little demanding, but she wears it well. "And the jar of pickles."

Within a couple minutes us three are roasting wieners.

CHAPTER 7

cooper

WE SIT BESIDE THE ROARING fire that Eli built. Cady brought a big stack of wood from her backyard, but I had no clue how to turn it into an actual campfire. Eli, however, cleared an area on the beach, and in it made a circle of rocks, gathered pine needles and dry brush from the hill, and then got all set up with Cady's dry wood. He even arranged it from small pieces to large ones. Then Eli built the fire as though it was as simple as applying deodorant. Plus, he was the only genius to bring a lighter.

Cady and I are not what you'd call survivalists. Eli clearly is. And it's possible that I'm too impressed. Or maybe I'm slightly envious of his Dora-the-Explorer proficiency, but I'm proud to say that *I'm* the guy who found three long sticks across the street in the woods, *and* I didn't break them on my way down the slope to the beach. We stuck our hotdogs on the ends and cooked them until they weren't cold in the middle, and when we put them in buns and squirted on mustard, I felt a different type of satisfaction than I get from completing advanced math problems faster and with more accuracy than anyone else in the class.

And Eli knows how a beach party operates. He grabs three beers and uses the bottle opener on his pocketknife to pop the caps off. I imagine Cady and I trying to open beer bottles with twigs. We completely forgot to take along a bottle opener, and my mother has warned me to *never* use my teeth to open anything, as she spent eight thousand dollars on my Invisaligns and doesn't want me to mess with her investment.

I hope we would have had the sense to buy cans of beer instead of bottles.

"You guys graduate high school soon, right?" Eli looks like he was born to lounge on this beach. His curls have dried into dozens of tiny, salty ringlets that bob on his bare shoulders. All he wears is a pair of ripped and faded jeans that I'm pretty sure got "destructed" by Eli *actually* doing hard physical labor while wearing them, rather than purchasing them that way as an I'm-rugged fashion statement. No belt, bare feet… just nature-boy Eli in the great outdoors. *Nice.* "Is this weekend a private graduation party?"

"Yeah… it's kinda like that—in advance, though," I reply.

"We both did well in high school," Cady offers, and she isn't bragging. Her tone is more apologetic. "We missed out on all of the fun stuff the other kids were doing. So, before we start our summer jobs—they begin right after graduation—we're doing some of the recreational things we've never done before."

Sure, if by *recreational*, she means *rebellious*—and in some cases, *illegal.*

For four years we've never once stepped outside the lines, mainly because of the way it was at home for Cady. She knew with certainty that her parents would fall overboard and drown if she rocked the boat even slightly, since living with her substance-abusing brother was like surviving a tropical storm at sea for the LaBries. Being her best friend, I stuck by her in this straightlaced lifestyle. But the truth is, I never experienced much of an urge to test the limits. I'm not wired that way. I am, however, wired to please people, and Cady's on the top of that list.

I'm glad Cady doesn't spell out the whole bucket-list thing to Eli, though. He wouldn't get it. I'm not sure *I* get it.

Eli places a log deep in the flames and doesn't burn his fingers, which is quite a trick. "And you guys are letting me join in your special weekend?"

Cady and I look at each other. I don't know about her, but I'm guilty as hell, which is not surprising because I'm also wired *this* way.

"We never went out and met kids from other schools. We just hung together and studied," she explains. Technically, this isn't a lie. For the past four years, all we did, night after night, was sit in my room or her living room and study. And once in a while we volunteered our free time. We fed the elderly and entertained little kids at charity events and shoveled snow on sidewalks, but we never left Wellington.

Being a "good kid" and never breaking out of the mold for the entire span of high school took a measure of creative effort. We weren't exactly sought-after at school, unless somebody was in need of a math or English tutor. Other kids looked at us and saw nerdy brainiacs, which was okay with us because we made our own fun. I'll never forget this time we held a karaoke night for the old folks at the senior center. Cady borrowed a karaoke machine from the middle school, set it up in the lounge, and the elderly people filed in. At first, nobody volunteered to sing, so we had to show the seniors how it was done. We sang an off-key version of "I Got You Babe" by Sonny and Cher. Got a standing ovation. It was unforgettable.

"So, you fit into our weekend plans, Eli. Just perfectly," she concludes.

Cady's careful not to mention number seven. I mean, why would she? The fact that we need to each experience our first kiss to complete the requirements of the bucket list isn't exactly need-to-know information for Eli. When the time comes, he can decide to go with it or not go with it, *if* he ends up directly involved in number seven. "Eli, you're in a win-win-win situation here with us," I tell him, but still I feel like shit.

Eli scratches his head and says, "Tell me about your families. I bet they're *real* families, like with moms *and* dads. Tell me…"

Again, Cady and I catch eyes because his request is odd; most families have moms *and* dads, even if they aren't together. She quickly glances away, studies the bottle in her hand, peels off the label as horny people are said to do, and then sucks down as much beer as she can swallow. After she wrinkles her nose, Cady says, "My family isn't as picture perfect as you may think."

"Really?" he asks.

"Really." Cady takes another long swig, and the bottle is empty. The consumption of her very first beer in two long gulps is pretty impressive. And like the gentlemanly cabana boy he seems to be, Eli jumps to his feet to replace her beer. She continues. "We were *supposed* to be the perfect family. Dad has a good job as an accountant at a law firm, and Mom used to work at the front desk of a doctor's office, but now she stays at home to cook and clean… or try to."

An image of a bread bowl filled with SpaghettiOs forms in my mind.

"That sure sounds picture-perfect to me." Eli hangs on her every word. "Keep going with your story."

"Well, it was like that until the end of sophomore year, when Bradley—he's my twin brother—started to associate with the wrong crowd."

Eli sniffs. "He probably started hangin' with guys like me."

Cady studies him. "No. I don't think they were much like you at all."

"What happened with Bradley?"

"I guess the long and short of it is, drugs happened. It started with drinking, but soon went to marijuana and moved on from there. At the end of last summer, he OD'd on prescription painkillers. Got carted off to the ER." She sucks down a large portion of her second beer, burps without excusing herself, and continues. "Mom and Dad were forced to take a hard look at his life and our lives too. That's when Mom quit her job so she could be a more hands-on mother, which made no difference with Bradley."

Cady never gets into much detail about what went down with her brother. I'm surprised at her relative openness tonight. She probably figures Eli's a safe person to confide in, since we're never going to see him again.

"I stuck to the straight and narrow... until now." Cady stands and takes a few steps toward the shore. "You know, until this." She holds up her beer and studies it rather than us.

Clearly worried, Eli glances at me. Our potential first-kiss-guy wears his heart on his sleeve. "That must've been rough, Cady."

"Yeah, it sucked, but Bradley's in rehab now, so it's all good." She digs her toes into the sand and then adds, "Hopefully."

Eli nods and focuses on me. "What about *your* folks, Cooper?"

Cady answers for me. "Cooper comes from a family of geniuses."

"They simply possess limited talent and have been relatively lucky in life," I argue. This is not a new debate for us.

"Go ahead; tell him about their utter amazingness, Murphy," Cady demands, and I, as always, obey.

"My father's sort of a famous chef. He spends most of his time at his restaurant in LA, though. He comes home about one long weekend a month, I'd say."

"Seriously? Did they make a television series about him?"

I laugh because Eli's not too far off the mark. "Not yet, but some big-business types have approached him about it." I'm inexplicably proud of this fact and I don't even watch much TV. "When he comes home it's super cool. He cooks with me pretty much nonstop, and we go to concerts and bookstores and do all kinds of fun shit."

"He must be smart."

"Not as smart as Cooper's mother. She's an online college professor. Advanced mathematics." Cady freely shares *my* personal info. And Eli's eyes have grown large.

"Mom's always been able to help me with my math homework. So, I got pretty good with numbers too."

"Cooper's the class valedictorian, Eli. He has to make a speech at graduation on Monday night."

Eli's quiet for a minute. "I'm a dummy. But Mr. Hearn says I got a good work ethic. Well, he said it up until I quit my job. Then he told me I was a no-good, lazy loser."

A heavy pile of guilt drops on my shoulders. Soon I'm drowning in it. All I can do is cough to stop tears from rolling down my cheeks and I end up doing a pretty decent impression of Daisy when she's hacking up a fur ball.

"A work ethic is as important as talent and brilliance." Cady's about to go all preachy on our asses. I recognize her righteous tone. "My twin brother is every bit as smart as me, but he got nowhere fast because he couldn't find the discipline to work hard and stay on the right track. What I'm telling you is, you don't have to be the next Albert Einstein to make something of yourself." Cady steps over to Eli and offers him her hand. He takes it and stands in front of her. "And besides, you don't seem like a dummy to me."

They study each other. This intimate scene reminds me of postcards I noticed on my family trip to the coast of Maine last summer. I searched all week for the perfect postcard to send Cady, but the only ones I could find depicted silhouettes of loving couples gazing into each other's eyes with the ocean rolling behind them—way too romantic for us.

I find myself moving between them, inserting myself into their postcard moment. "And who's to say you can't get your GED and then further your own education if you want?"

Cady steps back and stares at me, like she's surprised that I care. Where was she when I was hacking up the emo-hairball two minutes ago?

Eli mumbles, "I guess I could." As soon as we finish our beers, he shakes his head and grabs our empties. "Time for another brew."

CHAPTER 8

cadence

"TIME FOR ANOTHER BREW" GOES on for the next two hours. Having never before indulged in so much as a sip of beer, Cooper and I are, by now, quite intoxicated. Or as Cece so often said when she bragged to me in Honors Lit about her Saturday night antics, "totes bombed."

Eli doesn't seem to be as impaired as we are, but judging from the way he just stumbled back from the hill where he went to "whiz," I wouldn't get in a car if he was behind the wheel.

"So hungry. Wanna make s'mores, you guys." Cooper slurs. The word for him is *wasted.* Last year, Bradley demonstrated that one nightly.

"This girl I know, Cece Tucker, told me about the 'drunken munchies,' and I think Cooper's got 'em," I ramble.

"I'll get the fire going again so we can cook." Cooper and I are pressed against each other in front of the fire. It's the first time tonight we've stopped force-feeding ourselves bottles of beer. We watch as closely as dive judges while Eli stands, grabs some wood from the pile beside the tent, and bends to place it on the fire.

"He does gots a nice ass, don't he?" Cooper asks me, and his head slides to my lap.

I take my time as I study Eli's backside. "Yeah, Murphy, it's a fine ass," I declare, intentionally loud enough for Eli to hear.

When he turns around and looks at me, I wink at him. Maybe I assume—even in my sloppy state—that it'll be easier to get from nowhere to number seven, if he understands that I like what I see—or that *we* like what *we* see.

Eli returns his attention to the fire and magically makes the flames roar. When he stands, he takes a few steps, sits on the other side of the fire, and gazes at us over the flames. "Thought you guys wanted to toast marshmallows," he says and sounds defensive. "But it seems more like you wanna mess with my head."

"What do you mean?" I ask, although I know exactly what he means. I'm not dumb, despite the fact that, when necessary, I play I am.

"You guys are all cuddled up like lovebirds and then you start talking about *my* butt. What's the deal with that?" We've already blown his mind and we haven't even gotten started on the real deal. This is not a good omen in terms of accomplishing number seven.

I slide away from Cooper, and his head drops to the ground. "We're *not* a couple, Cooper and me. We're just good friends." I pat the ground as an invitation for Eli to come sit with us, but he doesn't move.

Cooper lifts his head from the sand and says, "We're… us two are like *really* good friends."

"*Okay…*" Eli tilts his head, thoroughly confused. I'm confused too.

It's obvious that Cooper will not be much help in accomplishing number seven. He's drooling on himself. I'll have to do it myself. "Maybe we're such good friends that we don't have a problem sharing," I say in a voice that drips sweetness, like it was dunked in a big bowl of honey.

"What stuff do you guys share?" Eli asks.

I sigh. *Looks like I'm going to have to spell it out again.* "Let me put it this way, Eli. Cooper and I share our calculus notes and rides to school and our beer tonight and… we want to share, well, you know…" I stop and hope Cooper will step up and finish my very obvious thought.

He doesn't. But Eli does. "*Me?* You guys wanna share *me?*"

"Bingo!" Cooper shouts. "We sure as shit do!" He snickers rather lasciviously.

Again, I sigh, but go with a subtle nod instead of more explanation. The damage has been done; all I can do is act like I don't care.

"Let me get this straight—"

Before Eli's mind goes to places it shouldn't, I decide it's time to explain. I sincerely wish Cooper would stop licking his lips, though, because it makes me look like his horny co-conspirator. "I can only speak for myself—" I begin.

"Speak for me, too, Cady, the way you always do. I mean, why stop now?"

I should be insulted, but I focus on the challenge at hand. "All we want from you is… something small."

Cooper giggles. I roll my eyes.

"Yeah?" Eli's eyes are as huge and round as the Ferris wheel. "Like what?"

"We just, we just want to kiss you." When Eli's eyes pop open wider, which I would never have guessed was physically possible without his head exploding, I add, "It's not exactly a crime."

Eli paces in front of the fire. When he finally stops and faces us, he asks, "Why?"

"We have our reasons." I may seem mysterious, but I'm actually quite desperate.

It's chilly, but Eli still hasn't put his black T-shirt back on, so Cooper and I are compelled to stare at his muscular chest, with that trail to paradise leading south to… to paradise, I guess.

And then I'm momentarily distracted from my distraction. This situation would be so much simpler if Cooper and I simply shared our first kiss with each other, alone in the tent, the next time Eli goes to whiz. We'd find out a big part of what we need to know: whether a certain *zing* in our kiss tells us there's more to "Cooper and Cady" than best buds. But we wouldn't learn the *other* part of it—the thing about Cooper. The thing about my pal Cooper, who appears simultaneously giddy *and* guilty.

Uh-uh-uh—you can't change the rules now, *buddy,* I tell him with my eyes and then refocus on that hairy path to supposed ecstasy beneath Eli's belly button.

Last week, Cooper and I banged out the gritty details. To count as an official kiss, the lip lock will have to last three full seconds. We didn't specify details about who it could happen with. We can kiss anybody who isn't related to us—male, female, young, old… or each other. *On the lips* and *for three full seconds* are the only requirements. The prospect of Cooper kissing Eli works perfectly. In fact, it doesn't sound too bad at all, but this could be the beer talking.

First of all, Eli is hot, which is nice. And he's here, which is mandatory. Plus, we may not have another chance like this over the weekend. Next, Cooper is buzzed, so his inhibitions, which normally rule him, are relaxed. And last, Cooper *must* kiss a boy.

I need him to experience a boy-kiss as much as I need to find out how it feels to kiss Cooper. With this second part, comes danger: If Cooper and I lock lips, will it change things between us? And by change, I mean ruin, destroy, *completely obliterate.* I'm not sure if it's worth the risk of wrecking the best friendship in the history of the world for a chance at love.

Nonetheless, I ask, "So, are you in?" My impatience is easy to pick up on; I have a bucket list to complete.

Eli glances at the ground. I sincerely hope he's mulling over our offer.

I tap my foot. Then I hear myself bark, "Well, maybe it doesn't even matter." For a hot second, I pretend that I don't care about his decision, though Eli's answer matters more than ever.

The boys gawk at me.

I focus my wild eyes on Cooper. "*We'll* get it done no matter what," I hiss. For just a moment they both seem frightened.

Eli squats in front of us and smiles the sweetest smile ever. "Are you guys saying that *both* of you like me?" He looks from Cooper to me.

Cooper answers for both of us, which is usually my job. "What's not to like? Heeheehee…"

"My God! It's just a damn kiss!" I reply so sharply that it echoes off the hillside. "We're not proposing matrimony."

Eli ignores my outburst and looks at Cooper. "Are you gay?" he asks. "I mean, it's not a big deal to me. I just wanna know."

"It's possible… that I'm… like *halfway* gay," Cooper replies slowly and then adds, "You know, maybe."

Eli catches my gaze and then points at Cooper with his thumb. "And he's not your boyfriend? For real?"

"Not at this point." An honest response. I have no idea why a sizeable drop of perspiration trickles from between my boobs into my belly button.

"So, you're saying that nobody's gonna go home all bent outta shape on account of getting cheated on? Because, I'm thinking maybe I want to do it. Kiss you… you know?"

"It's only a stupid kiss, not a declaration of undying love, for crap's sake!" I push myself to my feet. "And what *is* this—twenty questions?" I step over to Eli and hold out my hands to him. He grips them, and I pull him to his feet so he stands in front of me. Then I toss caution to the ocean breeze, completely forget my plan to share my first kiss with Cooper Murphy, stand on tiptoes, throw my arms around his shoulders, and press my lips to his.

One one-thousand, two one-thousand, three one-thousand.

My first kiss, and just like that, my part in number seven is finished. Closed mouths, dry, and indescribably awkward—not exactly the stuff dreams are made of. But a very done deal.

Side note: While I was locking lips with the most gorgeous guy I've ever seen, Cooper mumbled something about how he's *still flipping starving*, but is willing to wait to make s'mores until after he and Eli get busy. *Erghh.*

I take a step back from Eli, whose eyes are now the size of Oreo cookies, glance at Cooper, who is studying us as carefully as he can in his condition, and I say one word. "Tent."

IT'S A GOOD THING THAT I was the one to set up the tent rather than Cooper, because the prelude to Cooper and Eli's kiss is what I'd call *lively*. In other words, if I hadn't built a sturdy tent, the three of us would be wearing it. After we roll around on top of each other in our effort to get reasonably comfortable, we lie shoulder-to-shoulder-to-shoulder, like three little monkeys on a bed, which is clearly not a sober thought. Poor Eli is the defenseless monkey in the middle.

When Cooper and I stayed at my house, we each slept on one of the two pull-out couches in our living room. God forbid our feet would brush together in the middle of the night. Mom once told me that if that happened the whole town would consider me compromised. Cooper's parents are more liberal and let us sleep together on the big bed in his room. And maybe we were technically in the same bed, but we never cuddled. We always built a tower of Cooper's old stuffed animals in the space between us, because it made us feel like we were at a slumber party, since we were never invited to *real* parties with actual human beings.

A mere two monkeys away from me is a sloshed—yes, another Cece word—Cooper Murphy. Over the past four years, I've spent more time with him than anybody else in the world. He's made me laugh and he's made me want to strangle him. I've admired his brilliance and pondered his stupidity. Lately, I've spent way too much time wondering if he's always going to be my friend or if he could be much more. Now, he needs to kiss a boy he hardly knows to find out whether or not he can fall in love with me. And I need to orchestrate it.

This is a real-life test.

My blood goes cold, and I need to change this test's direction. So, I make an impulsive decision, one that runs contrary to the precisely planned items on The Weekend Bucket List. The thing is, *I* need to kiss Cooper right now so I can find out for sure what he means to me, before my hopes and dreams and fantasies of a different way of being "us" carry me to a place I can't return from.

I dive gracelessly over Eli's still-bare chest, grasp Cooper's face between my palms, and lower my lips so that we breathe the same air. Then I close my eyes and lose myself to Cooper's sloppy lips, complete with the pungent smell of beer and the click of tooth enamel. But if I expected the clouds to part in my head and for everything to be clear in this kiss's aftermath, I'd have been deeply disappointed.

Yeah, I'm deeply disappointed.

Maybe it fell short because a kiss should be a two-way street, or *maybe* the big blank space in our relationship will remain blank until Cooper kisses Eli.

Everything is moving so fast, I almost miss it when Cooper says, "It's done now, Cady."

I flop back to my spot beside Eli. I know exactly what Cooper means: Number seven is complete. We have each kissed a human being unrelated to us on the lips, so we can check *first kisses* off the bucket list. Cooper has no official reason to kiss Eli now.

"No, it's not! Our kiss didn't last three seconds. I, I was counting." This is a straight-up lie—the duration of our sloppy lip lock was five seconds, minimum.

Eli looks from Cooper to me and back.

"But Cady—"

"Just do it, Cooper." I turn my back to them promptly. "Just. Do. It." The Nike slogan that erupts from deep in my throat is hoarse and raspy and frightening, sounding like the thing in a horror flick that beams in, brainwashes you, and then demands that you eat your best friend.

It's silent in the tent. Eli moves against my back as he turns toward Cooper. The last thing I want to do is witness what's about to happen, but somehow I need to. I flip onto my belly and army-crawl to the back of the tent where my view is unobstructed: Cooper and Eli, lying on their sides, staring at each other, panting like they're on the verge of emotional breakdowns.

And other than the heavy breathing, that's *all* they're doing—gawking at each other, like neither has ever seen a trembling, terrified teenage boy. So, I take it upon myself to encourage the kiss.

"Take a deep breath and do it, Cooper. You know you want to."

My voice is shrill and insistent, but quite effective. Cooper nods, because a big part of him actually *does* want to do this and the rest of him is, as always, obedient. Eli nods too, but seems detached. And then Cooper touches Eli's chin with a shaky fingertip—just like he once touched mine—and moves forward to press their lips together. He shudders at the initial contact, which tells me a lot about how intense this experience is for him. I'm not sure where that detail should go in my mental file cabinet, and it hits me that Cooper and I are testing ourselves with a person who isn't in on the secret, but who seems pretty into kissing us, nonetheless. They close their eyes, bob forward, and then pull back, but not enough to come apart.

They share a sweet, three-second kiss. For Cooper, it's the simple act of kissing that's new. I'm not sure if kissing, itself, is new for Eli, but kissing another boy probably opens a whole new chapter in his life.

I'm not drunk anymore, or maybe I'm not drunk enough. I just watched Cooper close his eyes to kiss a guy who resembles Disney's Aladdin and then submit to a full-body shudder. So sue me if I found that sobering.

Maybe this whole kissing thing is so profound because of the sheltered nature of our lives. I understand the enormity of what's happening to him, because it's also happening to me. And when they pull away from each other, I realize that Cooper is still wearing his glasses. He stares at me from within the thick, black frames, and I see resignation, as though he's saying, *I did what you told me to do. Are you satisfied now, Cady?*

I shake my head and look away. I've pushed my nose where it doesn't belong by visually sharing in their kiss. Maybe I even pressured them to kiss. And nothing is clear to me, the way I thought it would be. If possible, my feelings for Cooper are more jumbled. I wonder if the clouds in Cooper's head have parted with regard to his sexuality, with regard to how he feels about me. And then there's Eli, who willingly, if not enthusiastically, offered his lips. I'm not sure of his motivation, but he seemed to enjoy himself.

This situation is a mess, so I cling to my insignificant remnant of a buzz. *I'm still drunk, aren't I?*

If I'm still drunk, whatever I conclude tonight will be meaningless, which is a relief. But avoiding *this very moment* is one of the reasons I never wanted to drink with Cooper. When you're drunk, things that aren't real seem real, if only for a few minutes.

I'm clearly overthinking this situation.

I crawl back to my place beside Eli and I force a smile that turns into a shit-eating grin. The most important thing—the fulfillment of number seven—has been accomplished.

My gloating is interrupted when Cooper asks in an anguished tone I don't recognize, "Why's everything spinning?" He burps loudly enough to make me cringe and cover my head, squats, and fumbles for the tent's vertical zipper. Then he scrambles out of the tent. A few seconds later the distinctive sounds of vomiting come from about ten feet away.

Cooper is too drunk. I'm not drunk enough. I'm not sure how drunk Eli is, and I'm not sure I care. Number seven is a done deal. Strangely, I don't feel more mature, liberated, or ready for college with this one. I just feel confused.

CHAPTER 9

cooper

BARFING ACTUALLY HELPS A LOT. It's not the same as when you're a kid with the flu and you hurl, feel better for twenty minutes, and then a ball of lead in the pit of your stomach tells you, "Get ready to hurl again, kid, because, like it or not, it's coming." Tonight, I ran behind the tent, tossed my cookies, brushed my teeth with water from our gallon jug, and got back to being my regular self. *Sort of.*

Maybe losing everything in my belly cleansed me of my post-lip-locking stress. My two first kisses were equally amazing and awful. The amazing part: finally acting on my growing attraction to Cady and to my physical desire for a boy—it was relief mixed with *hell, yeah*. Plus, I enjoyed the closeness to other human beings—the goose bumps and the thrill.

The awful part? This is much easier to explain. Awful is the lingering uncertainty about who I am that I'd expected to disappear with at least *one* of the two kisses. But seriously, *nothing* has changed in me—I liked and hated both. Equally. I'm still not ready for the sexual challenges in my future because I'm *still* unsure of my own sexuality. And vomiting all my confusion into the brush and stones behind the tent cleansed me of my need to dwell on that, at least for the time being. It changed my internal mantra from "who do you love?" to "barfing *so* sucks."

So I'm still hazy about whether I want an intimate relationship with a boy or a girl. Maybe my sexuality is somehow too deeply divided for me to ever figure out. This possibility makes me feel like barfing again.

I'll operate on the theory that I'm still drunk, and this is a satisfactory reason for not analyzing what went on with Cady's, Eli's, and my lips. All I know for sure is that I'm not more sexually connected to either Cady or Eli since we locked lips. It *is* possible that kissing a boy *and* a girl was too much like conducting a human sexuality experiment to let me feel anything at all.

When I stumble around the side of the tent, Cady and Eli are sitting by the campfire toasting marshmallows. "I shoulda worn flip-flops. The rocks are tearing up my toes… Uh, so where's the chow, dudes?" I'm definitely not sober.

Eli replies. "You should have a graham cracker, Cooper, before you eat anything else. It'll be a test to see if you can keep food down."

This sounds like reasonable advice, so I grab the box of graham crackers, open an inside package, and stuff one in my mouth. Cady has another beer in her hand. I hope like hell she isn't drinking to forget what just went down in the tent.

"Can I use one of you guys' cell phones? I want to make sure the dude whose trailer I been staying in knows I'm not coming home tonight."

Cady answers before I can. "We didn't take our phones with us this weekend. We're off the grid."

I'm astonished. Cady would normally give the shirt off her back to somebody who needed it, but she won't mess up number ten to let Eli use her phone. "Cady, don't you think—"

"No!" She cuts me off before I finish my question. "No, I don't think that."

"It doesn't matter. Jimmy probably won't even notice if I don't come home." He places his perfectly toasted marshmallow between two graham crackers and a piece of chocolate. "This one's for you, Cooper. You seem okay to eat now."

I sit beside him and take the s'more from his outstretched hand. "Thanks."

Cady stares at her marshmallow, which is now fully engulfed in flames. Then she drops her stick and stands. "I'm cold. I'm going to grab my fleece vest," she tells us and climbs into the tent.

"The breeze picked up, for sure," Eli agrees, although she's already gone. He walks to his duffel bag and pulls out a dark-colored sweatshirt. When he pulls it on and stands in front of the fire to toast another marshmallow, his dark curls blow around his handsome face, and he doesn't look like a carnie *or* a high school dropout *or* a homeless dude. He looks like a teenager having fun in the summer before he heads off to his big future—but maybe ten times more gorgeous. I'm as guilty as sin and I'm not sure why. *I'm* not the reason Eli quit high school. I *am*, however, part of the reason he doesn't have any future prospects.

"You got halfway through senior year before you quit school?" I ask him.

"More than halfway," Eli answers.

"It shouldn't take too much work to get you back on track, dude." I watch the tent until Cady climbs out. "You, know, Cady and I would be the best GED tutors you could ever want. I'm an ace in math and science, and Cady got the Senior English Award at the school assembly last week. We could help you get your GED if you stick around Wellington this summer, right Cady?" She nods, but her eyes are bugging out. She's noticed how incredibly generous I'm being to this perfect stranger we're supposed to leave in our bucket-list dust tomorrow morning.

"But I need a job and a place to live, so it probably can't happen…"

As much as I'm in shock that Cady and I—well, mostly me—have just offered to ride in on our academic white stallions to save Eli's hot ass, I can't believe he's actually considering it. He's supposed to say, "No, I could never ask that of you."

Cady surprises me even more. "Old Route Eleven is lined with restaurants. They're always looking for help." Apparently, she's okay with this *very* tentative plan too. "Every summer I go back to the same waitressing job at this place called Mad Eats and I could ask if they need help."

"I could check with the home store I'm starting at later this week. I'm pretty sure they need help delivering furniture, at least every once in a while," I offer.

Maybe it's because we're buzzed that we're so generous. Maybe what we say and do tonight isn't real because it's just a "crazy Weekend Bucket List moment" that will disappear, as though it never happened, when the weekend is over. In any event, Eli pulls Cady to where I'm sitting, squats, and throws his arms around our shoulders. "Maybe today was *my* lucky day. And maybe I was meant to meet you guys behind the theater. Because for real, I almost gave up on getting my high school diploma and now I think maybe I'll try for it."

"Cool." I say, and what's weird is I *do* think it's cool, even if it's not real.

Cady takes a few steps away from us and gazes at the ocean; her expression is a cross between pleased and shell-shocked.

"The thing is, I got lots to worry about right now—no job and no place to live. Maybe for tonight I'll just forget about everything. I sure don't wanna drag you guys down on your graduation party." He concentrates on making another s'more as if it's the job he doesn't have and places it on the empty hot dog plate Cady left on the rock. "Cady, I made you a s'more. I stuck it on a paper plate on that ginormous rock!" He points. When she doesn't move, he adds. "I'll go get it."

"Thanks, Eli. You don't have to."

"I know, but I want to."

She sends him a sheepish half-smile, finishes her beer, and tips the bottle upside-down in front of her. "This was the last beer. Now all we've got to drink are the water jugs."

"That's okay. Beer doesn't go too good with s'mores, anyhow." Eli hands Cady her s'more and gets back to work. "Want this one to be for you, Cooper?"

"Nah, I'm all set."

"Okay, then, I guess this one's mine."

I watch his hands as he works. They're slim and graceful. After he finishes eating, he runs to the water to rinse his fingers.

"We should've let Eli use one of our cell phones, Cades. I could've walked him to the car so he could use it." I'm growling, and my pissed-off tone surprises me.

"You heard what he said—it's no big deal. So just forget about it."

"Cady, that's not cool."

"If he broke his leg or something, I'd have used my phone to call an ambulance. But this *isn't* a big deal."

I want to tell her what I think about her attitude, but Eli comes back. I'll never know if I would've actually stood up to her, because I'm distracted by his smile. It's adorable—a kid's kind of smile.

"I got an idea," he says.

Cady's eyes widen, like she's *so* sweet and innocent, when we both know she's not. At least, she's not *tonight*.

"How about we make a giant sand castle?"

Cady's eclectic; she doesn't get into shopping at the mall or playing competitive softball or taking selfies with her cell phone like most other girls I know. But she's into stuff like drawing dead body chalk outlines all over the sidewalk in front of the school early in the morning and baking chocolate chip banana bread in plant pots. Eli's idea of building an enormous sand castle will surely spark her interest.

"It's pretty dark, but we could build it close to the fire so we'll be able to see what we're doing." For the record, she's more breathless than when we kissed in the tent.

"I got another great idea. How about we build it in the shape of a pyramid from… say… Egypt?"

"Well, I know what a pyramid shape is, but not the details of a specific pyramid," Cady says. "Let's just make a regular castle shape. We can stick shells all over the outside of it."

"Uh, Cady, every time I get a chance to go to a library, I look at the books about pyramids. Did you know that Egypt and Mexico and Guatemala and Italy *and* Sudan all have pyramids?"

"Well, I knew about the ones in Egypt, Mexico, and Guatemala." Cady sounds defensive.

"My favorite one is called El Castillo in Mexico. You got paper and a pencil? 'Cause I can draw it for you real good."

Impressed that this kid has a passion for pyramids, I jump up and grab my backpack. I pull out an old AP Calc quiz and a black pen and bring them to Eli. He puts the paper on the graham cracker box and goes to work on a sketch.

"It's made out of all these square terraces, and on each of the four sides it's got wide stairways. And then on the top is a temple."

Cady comes to check out the drawing. "That's gonna take some serious time to build." Disappointed, Eli looks down at the sand. "We'll need to put more wood on the fire if we want to be able to see what we're doing," she adds.

He grins. "We can build a sand El Castillo?"

"Of course." Cady's gaze lingers on his face as she tries to come up with a reason that this is a dumbass idea, but can't. She finally smiles and says, "I'll grab some wood."

Cady was right. Our sand El Castillo took almost two hours to build.

She and I needed a few breaks because our backs got stiff, but Eli was like a man possessed. As he worked, he told us about how the real El Castillo pyramid was built by a pre-Colombian Mayan civilization, and how, at spring and autumn equinoxes, when the sun hits a certain spot, it creates triangular shadows and makes the serpent sculpted on the side of the northern stairway seem to crawl down the pyramid. To sum it up, Eli knows about the El Castillo pyramid the way most seven-year-olds know dinosaur facts. He didn't slow down once—talking or working—until it was finished.

My fingers tingle with a need for my phone. I'd love to snap a few pictures of the sand castle, because, even by the light of the dwindling fire, it's pretty awesome. The three of us spend at least fifteen minutes admiring the pyramid from different angles and listening to more of Eli's stories about pyramids of the world. He ends the dissertation with, "I sure gotta whiz."

"Well, if I were you, I'd go behind the rock instead of behind the tent, since you've got bare feet." I make the universal gagging gesture.

"God, Cooper." Cady rolls her eyes. I'm sure of this, although it's too dark to see.

"I catch your drift," Eli says and heads to the rock.

After private visits to Mother Nature, we each brush our teeth and decide it's time for bed—or time for tent.

CHAPTER 10

cadence

NOBODY SCRAMBLES TO BE THE monkey in the middle. The guys expect me, the female "glue," to move straight to the center, as if it's my rightful position. But I don't. I just kneel by the tent door and wait for what happens next. Finally, Eli flops onto his back on top of Cooper's sleeping bag.

This cuddling-up-in-tight-quarters thing is virgin territory for Cooper and me, and I mean that literally. We catch eyes and shrug before we lie down. When we stretch out on either side of Eli, he sighs loudly and sounds satisfied. He doesn't have to weigh and measure the significance of every move he makes the way Cooper and I have been lately. I drag my sleeping bag over the three of us and wait for the King Kong of awkward of silences to barge into the tent.

"This tent feels more like home to me than I felt in Jimmy's trailer for the past six months," Eli murmurs.

Cooper gulps. None of us can miss it. He always swallows noisily when he's nervous, guilty, or otherwise emotional. Take the time junior year when a bird flew into his windshield on Main Street: As soon as we heard the loud thunking sound and the bird disappeared from sight, we knew it had been the thunk of death. Cooper took it to heart. After he uttered, "I murdered a pigeon," he gulped audibly every five minutes for the rest of the day. At least he's not coughing. Or crying.

"I don't think it's just the tent," Eli adds, and wraps his arms around our shoulders.

Cooper emits another loud gulp.

"It's the whole night we spent together that makes it seem like I'm at home here. We went swimming and got loaded and ate cookout food. Then you guys promised to help me study for the GED, and we built the best sand castle ever." His voice grows softer with each phrase. Almost too quietly to hear, he adds, "I like having friends." Eli leaves out how we kissed, and I wonder how much that meant to him.

This time I'm the one who swallows hard. Eli deserves more out of life than to be a homeless high school dropout. Maybe he even deserves to be more than the fulfillment of number seven on the bucket list of two privileged high school students. It's sappy, but I say, "I had a great time too, Eli."

"Me too," Cooper agrees quickly and he coughs. When he sniffs, it's clear he lost the battle with tears.

"You never told us your last name," I say to Eli. I'm not sure why I want to know this. Maybe I don't want to know—maybe it's just something to say to fill the dark.

"Stanley. I'm Elias Stanley." He speaks with pride. "And I'm a wanderer."

"A wanderer, you say?" I can't miss the what-the-hell in Cooper's voice.

"Yeah, that's what Dad told me. Well, he actually called us vagrants, but I like to think of myself as a wanderer, or a globe-trotter, even though I haven't left the east coast of *this* country

86

yet." He pauses and pulls in a deep breath. "Yup—*globe-trotter* sounds way cool for somebody who can't stay in one place for too long. Don't ya think?"

I glance at Cooper and he shrugs, so I'm left to scramble for something reasonable to say. "One time I watched Harlem Globe-trotters videos on YouTube for three hours straight," I offer. Coop's jaw drops with surprise because I'm *so* not sportsy. "Don't look at me like that—maybe I'm not much into basketball, but Bradley was watching Harlem Globe-trotter videos on his computer in the recreation room when I visited him at rehab over winter break. So I sat there and watched with him all afternoon. Those guys have some serious skills."

"Well, I'm not that kind of globe-trotter 'cause I got no real skills—I just move around a lot," Eli concedes. "We moved every couple years from the time I was in kindergarten—I went to six different schools, but I liked it best when we lived near Mom's sister and my cousins in Maine." Eli kicks at the sleeping bag until it falls more evenly over us. "Mom took off on us when I was twelve; she'd had it with traipsing across the countryside."

I listen for Cooper to gulp or cough again, but all he does is say, "Shit." Neither of us question Eli about why his mother left.

"What are you guys' last names?" Eli asks.

It's so weird that Cooper and I have kissed this guy and he doesn't know our full names. "He's Cooper Murphy and I'm Cady LaBrie."

"Her real name is Cadence. I love how it sounds, but she won't let me call her that 'because it's pretentious.'" It's too dark to see if Cooper made air quotes, but I'd bet my life he did.

87

"Not sure about how pretend-us it is, but the name Cadence is real pretty." He sighs and pulls me in so my head is on his shoulder. "So is the name Cady, though."

And then, the talking is over. Nobody says goodnight, but we know it's time to sleep. I'm left alone with my thoughts and a slight headache.

eli

CADENCE *IS* A REAL PRETTY name. And Cooper is a happy, perky one. I like both names.

I like both.

But I'm super-glad that one or the other of them didn't paw at me before we fell asleep, because I'd have hated to say, "Keep your paws to yourself; I'm not doing it with you." I would've told them no, though. It's not that I'm a cold person, but tonight I just want to shut my eyes and be close to Cady and Cooper—close, but not *too* close. You know, I just want to enjoy the not-aloneness and still keep myself to myself.

Sounds dumb, especially since I kissed them. The thing is, I was curious about what it would be like to kiss, but I'm not one bit curious about sex.

It's nice here between them. Haven't felt this tight with anybody for way too long. Even when I lived with Dad, I never fit with him. And it's hard for me to remember any details about Mom. Once I got to about the age of ten, she never was around much, although technically she *was* still around.

Cady's hair rubs against my nose. It smells fresh, like the beach and the salty air, and a little bit sweet, like a girl. But she's a different sort of girl than most of the ones who came to the carnival, all decked-out and glossy and spicy-smelling. Different in a plain way—and in a good way. She seems more real.

I let my fingers draw lines on her bare arm, and when little goose bumps rise, I think about how pretty she is. Cady's tiny and fragile, but how she acts is large and in charge, like the way Mr. Hearn is—or how he used to be.

She isn't asleep yet, I'm pretty sure. I've had to bed down beside lots of people since I ran off with the carnival. Some of them were strangers, and others I called friends, at the time. Some wanted to get into my pants and others lay beside me, scared I'd want to get into theirs. So, by now, I've learned how easy sleep feels against my shoulder and how restless sleep feels too. I also know how staring into the dark, wide-awake and scared as heck, feels when it happens right beside me.

And right now, it's Cady who can't fall asleep. Her problem is she wants too much control over the stuff that's not controllable. She's lying beside me, trying to puzzle it all out, but coming up empty.

Cooper is softer than Cady, and I'm not talking about the lines of his body. He's just a softer sort of person. And soft works for him, but it's not better than Cady's sharp edges. I got opposites on each side of me—warm and cold, hard and soft, sweet and sour.

I fit in the middle, like I was made to be here.

Cooper is snuggled close against my side, fast asleep, like I knew him forever and a day. He trusts I won't mess with his body or his head. I make a circle on his shoulder with my finger, because it's not right that I only rub on Cady's arm.

mia kerick

These two balance each other. They could keep me balanced too.

I like hard and soft ice cream…

I like hot and cold showers…

I like Cooper because he's sweet and Cady because she's sharp.

I like to fit in the middle of my friends, I guess.

cadence

HERE IN THIS TENT ON the beach, it's much darker than in my bedroom. And it's cooler, although the tent is a little stuffy. It's damp too; when I open my mouth, I can taste the salt water in the air. The quiet is a different kind of quiet than in my bedroom. Sometimes, when the house is dark and still, I can hear my mother cry. And I know exactly when Dad can't take it anymore—the floorboards creak as he heads to the stairs so he can go to the living room and sleep on one of the couches. Instead of the soft hum of the fan in my window, I hear the rhythmic pounding of waves on the shore. I wonder if Daisy has realized that I'm gone.

Though I notice the familiar sound of Cooper's sleep-breathing and let myself ride the even rise and fall of Eli's chest beneath my head, I'm still all alone.

The bucket list pops into my mind. We've nearly accomplished all of its items and have actually done a few things that should have been on the list but weren't. These are items that Cooper and I never even considered, like making a waist-high, work-of-art sand castle with a stranger on the beach, who isn't so much a stranger anymore.

We made a temporary friend.

We also completed what I thought would be the hardest item—number seven, the first kiss. It was relatively easy, although we *were* pretty drunk. It happened naturally, like stuff the birds and the bees just instinctively do.

Okay… that's a complete lie. I pretty much landed awkward kisses on both boys' lips, surprising all three of us. I hate to admit that I manipulated Cooper into kissing Eli for *my* personal reasons, but I did that too. In my defense, we both needed to learn the truth of how Cooper felt with his lips pressed against another boy's. I'm pretty sure Coop was into it. And Eli wasn't complaining either.

I always figured my first kiss would be with Cooper, but I shared it with Eli Stanley, the gorgeous drifter who gave up everything to come here with us tonight. For me, though, tonight is really all about Cooper. And what's so weird is that, if he asked me how I feel about him right now, I'd have to plead the fifth. I don't have a clue what it is I want to share with Cooper, although I'm sure I love him. We're best friends, maybe even soul mates.

Do soul mates have to be lovers? Or can they be best friends?

I throw my hand across Eli's waist and it lands on Cooper's back. He's shifted onto his side in his sleep and faces the wall of the tiny tent, turned away from Eli and me—somehow alone, but also with us. I think Cooper wants it this way.

I stare into the darkness and note how the rise and fall of Eli's chest matches Cooper's breathing. And I'm more confused than I've ever been. What I've long thought was me falling in love with Cooper may simply be my fear of losing him when we separate to attend different colleges.

I'm going to continue to throw myself into The Weekend Bucket List, as it's a safe place to focus my mind. The list comforts me. It binds me to Cooper and distracts me from him at the same time.

CHAPTER 11

cooper

I WAKE UP WITH ONE hell of a nasty headache. If I didn't know better, I'd think that my forehead is trying to secede from the rest of my head and has met with military resistance. *Ouch.* Eli, however, expects this. As soon as I crack open a bloodshot eye, he climbs out of the stuffy tent to grab a jug of water.

When he climbs back in, he says, "I always got a bottle of Advil on me," and he hands me a small pile of tablets with the water. "Go ahead and take three, 'cause my prediction is that you got a headache that could bring Sasquatch to his knees."

"I thought fortunetellers were female," I quip.

"It wouldn't take a fortuneteller to predict that you were gonna have the hangover from hell this morning, Cooper."

My next couple of heartbeats go faster than they're supposed to. The raw awareness in the sober light of day that he and I kissed in the tent last night has my heart racing. "Yeah, whatever."

It takes less than a second to figure out if Cady's mood is hot or cold this morning. She opens her eyes with serious difficulty. "Sucks to sleep without my pillow," she groans.

Eli's lips twist to the side. "I thought *I* was your pillow." He taps the spot on his chest where her head had rested.

"I'm used to *my own* pillow," Cady explains. We definitely woke up with the hard, cold version of Cady this morning.

Grumpy-bedhead moments are part of her quirky charm. "But it's time to get up; we've got stuff to do today."

I'm not a fortuneteller either, but I'm somehow certain that Cady's already obsessing about completing numbers eleven and twelve on The Weekend Bucket List.

"Doughnuts…" is Cady's next word, and she fumbles with the door flap to get outside. I hear her moan and say, "Oh my God, this is sooo good."

She sinks her teeth into a Boston cream as I climb out. I challenge her. "They're just doughnuts."

"Wait 'til you taste one. I promise you, it'll be the best thing you ever ate."

I grab a chocolate cruller and take a bite. Cady's right. "Oh, man…"

"Everything tastes better in the morning when you got wasted the night before," Eli says as he pops out of the tent. He grabs a honey-dipped.

"We're gonna need coffee soon," I inform them.

Cady replies, "Well, then, we'd better pack things up and get a move on." She hasn't made eye contact with me. *What is she hiding now?*

Eli stuffs the rest of the doughnut into his mouth, grabs the sleeping bags, and pulls them out of the tent. He carefully folds and zips them and starts to roll one. "Could you drop me off back in Ellis, maybe at the town library?"

An image of Eli sitting in a standard wooden chair in the town library and poring through books about pyramids flashes in my mind. Even in terms of mental images, it's pretty pale and pathetic. "Sure, I can drop you off anywhere you want."

He finishes rolling the sleeping bag into a perfect spiral. "Great. I'll be able to check out the help wanted section in the newspaper. And then I'll go online and find a cheap motel that takes cash."

We are two royal pieces of shit. His situation is all our fault.

"Are you sure the Ellis Public Library is open on Sunday?" Cady asks, and I can tell by her tone that she's up to something. "Spend today with us and do your job search tomorrow."

Eli's gaze wanders up to the soft blue morning sky. Then his lips move as he counts to himself. I feel certain that he's considering his budget—figuring out how long he has before he's out of cash and shit out of luck. "I can manage that, if you *both* want to put up with me all day." In search of my approval, he glances at me.

I guess shit outta luck is another day away for Eli. "Sounds good to me," I assure him.

"Maybe Jimmy'll let me stay in his trailer tonight, seeing as the carnival's not supposed to leave Ellis 'til tomorrow morning. As long as Mr. Hearn doesn't find me there, 'cause he'll boot me for sure. He owns all of the trailers."

I should offer to let him use my cell phone so he can call Jimmy and find out for sure if he has a place to sleep tonight, but Cady would have my head. She won't let me near my phone for four more hours, thanks to number ten.

Eli ties the first sleeping bag and moves on to the second. Homeless and jobless, with absolutely nobody to depend upon, he just hums and goes about the business of life.

"Perfect," says Cady and she smirks in the way that seems to be a new part of her. "I've got big plans for today."

WE STOP AT A McDONALD's for coffee and to use the bathroom sinks to wash. When Eli's in the bathroom, I say to Cady, "The poor guy has zero options."

Cady covers her face with her hands; only her nose pokes out from between her fingers. "I'm aware of that." Her voice is sharp, but then she sighs, and I'm glad to know that she's experiencing some pain on his behalf. I'm not used to the version of Cady who sizes things up, but doesn't put herself in other people's shoes. "Life's not fair, I guess."

I'm not sure if I appreciate her remark, but I agree. "Yeah, and it sucks for Eli."

"Then let's make today the perfect day for him," she suggests with unexpected brightness, and our gazes meet for the first time this morning. I have no idea why I'm so suspicious of her motives today. I'm not used to second-guessing Cady, and the worst part is that I suspect she knows how I feel. Our friendship has never involved so much analysis.

Still, I nod, and, before I have a chance to say anything, Eli approaches us; his dark curls are wet, and his stubbly cheeks are scrubbed to the point of pinkness.

"We got you a large coffee, Eli. Hope you take it regular." Cady hands him the cup.

"I take it however I can get it," he says with a grin—and then a wink.

Cady and I gasp, caught off guard by his unknowing innuendo. I fight to not catch her eye again, but fail.

"Well, let's get going." Cady's in a hurry to complete the list.

"Get going where?" Eli asks, after he sips his coffee.

"I'll explain in the car." Cady surprises me. She winks back at him.

"It's our treat," Cady argues.

"This is *our* graduation party, so you've got to let us do it *our* way!" I press further. No way will we let Eli spend his last few dollars to complete *our* freaking bucket list.

We're parked in front of a run-down tattoo parlor, where a hand-painted sign over the door declares it, "NEEDLE SLAVES: The Home of Custom Tattoos." Against the right side of the storefront window is another sign, this one on ripped cardboard, handwritten in black Sharpie marker. It says:

"IF YOU ARE

under 18,

drunk,

stoned,

dirty,

rude,

or broke,

come back when you

ARE NOT."

I'm not quite sure how we ended up at *this* particular tattoo parlor. If Cady allowed me to use my cell phone I could have done a little research on the topic and found one that suggested more sterility. But using the sophisticated system of *driving around until you come across a tattoo parlor*, this is what we get.

"Okay, then, if you guys are sure about it." Eli finally gives in. We sigh. We're on the same page even if Eli has no clue what page it is.

Until now, Eli insisted that he'd hold our hands as Cady and I got tattoos, but wouldn't get a tattoo himself. He told us he couldn't spare the cash. But Cady and I had arrived at a mutual, silent agreement that Eli was in this with us. If we have our way, he'll live with a permanent reminder of *our* bucket list. He'll wear it on his skin.

The three of us get out of the car and walk across the parking lot to the shop. "Here goes nothing." I pull open the door.

We step to the counter, where a tiny, very tattooed lady with a platinum buzz cut sits and waits for customers. "IDs," she demands. We fumble a bit in our rush to pull our licenses out of our pockets. She examines them and says, "Sit down and fill out these papers." Then she flings several stapled packets in our direction.

This is not a warm and fuzzy tattoo parlor.

Eli and I follow Cady to three plastic chairs in the corner that comprise the Needle Slaves Tattoo Parlor's bad excuse for a waiting room. We fill out the papers, and, since a few tattoo catalogs are scattered on a nearby card table, Cady picks one up and starts to leaf through. It doesn't shock me that she doesn't come across a tattoo of a bucket, which I know she's looking for.

I'm not in the market for a bucket tattoo, though. Since I kissed a girl and liked it and a few minutes later kissed a boy and liked it, something inside me has changed. Overnight, my deep confusion gave way to limited clarity, and I *know* something about my inner core that I wasn't sure of before. I'm not sure I fully accept it yet, but at least I know it.

Maybe—I hope this theory is correct—if I make a permanently inked statement about who I am on my body, I'll be able to move into the future without beating myself up so much.

Eli gives us no indication of which tattoo he's interested in. He studies the pages of the catalog over Cady's shoulder, but doesn't say a word.

"Okay, one of you come on over to the chair. Leave your paperwork on the counter." Cady goes to the chair first. We start to follow, but she puts out her hand to stop us.

"I want to surprise you guys." As she says this, she only looks at me.

Eli and I again sit on the plastic chairs. Neither of us lifts a catalog.

Cady and the tiny tattoo artist exchange a few words. They seem to come to an agreement, and then it's quiet again. We hear nothing more except the buzz of the needle. About forty-five minutes later, Cady calls us.

On the inside of her right wrist is a two-inch long, black outline of a girl wearing an oversized shirt and a short skirt, as Cady is right now, with a bucket over her head.

I get it and nod. She has memorialized The Weekend Bucket List in ink. Eli, to his credit, doesn't ask, "What the hell is that supposed to be?"

"I think it's cute, Cady," he says.

Cady's eyes widen before she blinks.

Then the lady points to me. "You're next." As she creams and wraps Cady's tattoo, Eli goes back to the plastic chairs, and I take my shirt off. I've decided to get a bowtie on the base of my neck, which was one of the tattoos I saw in the book. But I want my bowtie to be striped: pink, lavender, and blue.

When Cady sits, the lady focuses on me, and it's time to talk business. "What do you want, kid?"

"A bowtie. I want a bowtie on my neck."

"You want color?"

"Yeah, I want it striped pink, lavender, and blue?"

"The bi flag?"

"Uh… yeah. Like that. Maybe it could be a little bigger than the one you gave Cady." I show her how big with my finger and my thumb.

"It'll be a buck-fifty. Take just over an hour."

"Fair enough." I sit in the dentist-style chair and experience a surge of what could be dentophobia, but is more likely just plain old fear of pain. "So, um… what's your name?" I can't see any harm in making small talk with my torturer. It might distract me.

"Tina." I nod again, and she says, "Quit moving." Tina washes my neck with rubbing alcohol pads and then opens a plastic package and takes out a brand-new razor. "You aren't exactly a gorilla, but even tiny hairs can screw it up." She shaves the cleaned area. I'm surprised when she grabs a marker and bends over me.

"I'm way into doing freehand. Using stencils all day drives me to drink," she confesses. If I had to describe Tina the tattoo artist in three words I'd say, "bored with life," but when she starts to draw, an expression of deep concentration comes over her face, and it's not all business anymore. She smiles a little and says, "I think you're gonna get into this shit."

She hands me a mirror. I see the reflection of a neat bow tie that is better than the one in the book. "Sweet."

Tina takes a few minutes to prep her ink and needles. I'm comforted by the attention she pays to the little things—such as cleanliness. When she's ready to start, she rubs some ointment on the spot and says, "This ain't gonna tickle. Your neck hasn't got much fat on it, so buckle up…"

She called it right. A neck tattoo is very painful. Over the course of the inking, I question the wisdom of what I'm doing here and I curse the goddamned bucket list—more than once.

"Take a deep breath," Tina instructs, once I've survived the first half hour. I do as she says, but I'm already used to the tiny needle that pierces my skin. I don't exactly *like* it, but I can deal with it. I guess Tina just doesn't want me to pass out or barf on her chair.

"Outline's done. Now color and shading." She switches needles and the next part seems to go by much faster. When it's finished she cleans the area and applies a hot towel. "If you want your buddies to check out my artistry, now's the time."

I take another deep breath and shout, "Cady, Eli—come here!"

When they stand over me, Tina lifts the towel like she's unveiling a work of art.

Cady studies it and nods once; her face is like stone. The tiny bisexual-flag bow tie serves as a confession, or maybe a confirmation, on my part. She gets it.

Eli says, "Your tattoo is cute too."

He doesn't have a clue what my tattoo means, which is ironic, since he was instrumental in my decision to get it.

Tina points at him. "You're up, kid."

Eli immediately starts to unbutton his faded jeans. Cady rushes back to the plastic chairs as if she's never seen a hipbone before, but I have to wait as Tina puts the cream on and bandages my neck. I get up, and Eli sits on the dentist chair. He pulls down his jeans, exposing his right hip. He's going commando today, so it's easy access.

I stare at his left hipbone until Eli says, "It's a private place for a private kind of tattoo."

"Oh, yeah… I gotcha. I'll go take a seat." I'm curious about what tattoo he plans to get, but I don't ask questions and join Cady at the plastic chairs. The burning on my neck easily distracts me.

"You're going to have to wear a turtleneck jersey to graduation," Cady mutters as she taps on my bandage.

"Funny," I reply, but I refuse to smile. "My shirt and tie will hide this. Not that I necessarily *want* to hide it." But, yeah, I'll definitely need to hide it. Everybody at school would freak out, and I'd pay the price with a bloody nose or a black eye.

"It's still going to be all gooey tomorrow. And you aren't supposed to wear anything tight on it."

"I guess I'll have to loosen my tie," I say, my voice sharp. I honestly hadn't given the practical considerations of a neck tattoo any thought.

We sink into awkward silence because we have so much serious shit to talk over, and it can't be done here. There's an elephant in the room, and it's sitting in the third chair in the waiting area, holding a sign that says, "I'm with him, and he's *bisexual,*" with a little finger that points at me on it. At least now I have admitted who I am. And Cady knows too, which is only fair. As for Eli, he knows because of last night's kisses.

Time passes slowly, more slowly than when Cady got her tattoo, more slowly than when the needle pierced my skin. But in reality, Eli's tattoo takes less time than Cady's did.

"You guys wanna see what you're paying for?" he calls out. We walk over as if we're cool customers when all we are is…

customers. And I don't have a clue why I'm so nervous, but my belly is twisted in knots. Probably I'm just hungry.

Cady's eager too. She tries to push in front of me, but today I'm quicker. She stands a half-step behind me as we look down at Eli's six-pack, which is impressive, and then lower, at the tattoo on his right hip. A single row of words.

Cady reads it aloud. "One friend can change your life, and I found two."

After a few seconds of silence, Tina asks, "Well?" She's insulted at our silence, but it has nothing to do with a lack of artistry.

"It's nice. Simple." Cady eyes the tattoo as if it's a jumping spider, poised to spring from Eli's spectacular hip, land on her chin, and take a big bite.

Tina says, "It's a minimalist font. Less is more, right?"

I nod, although I'm clueless about minimalist fonts. And then I do the last thing I want to do. I let go one of those noisy, sob-preventing gulps, because Cady and I have been permanently etched on Eli's chiseled hipbone. The real estate is nothing to sneeze at, but we don't deserve to be there, even if it's in name only.

"Yeah…" Eli utters, wearing nothing but torn jeans and a dreamy expression. Literally. "Last night changed everything for me."

"Shit." *Did I say that out loud?*

Eli glances from Cady to me. His lips twist to the side. I hurt his feelings.

"I like it, Eli, I do. We… we just haven't known each other for very long and…" I'm babbling nonsensically.

"What Cooper means is, last night meant a lot to us too." Cady steps in and saves my ass. I could kiss her. Well, I *have* kissed her. But I'm not in the right state of mind to dwell on it, or to do it again.

Seconds later, Tina applies the hot towel to Eli's side. "His tattoo is eighty bucks. Twenty bucks off the top of the whole bill if you pay me in cash." Tina smiles broadly for the first time since we arrived at the tattoo parlor. "I like me some cash."

Cady smirks at her and says, "So Eli, after you get bandaged and button your fly, meet us by the door."

At the cash register, we count out the money for the tattoos. "Ink ain't cheap," I joke, trying to make light of my new bisexual bow tie and Eli's tattooed true confession, but she's not interested in silliness.

"Are we supposed to tip a tattoo artist?" she asks, all business.

"I'd say so."

She pulls a couple more twenties from our pile of cash, which has shrunk noticeably. "We still have enough for piercings. And lunch." Still no smiles or eye contact. Looks like I'm in the pink-, lavender-, and blue-striped doghouse.

Eli meets us by the door, and Tina hands Cady a notecard with tattoo care instructions. "Take those bandages off after a couple hours. And keep the wounds clean, or you'll pay the price." She smiles for the second time—this time it's more of an evil grin—and then points to the notecard. "Don't forget to read that."

"Thanks." Cady hands Tina the pile of cash without another word and turns toward the door.

Eli lingers behind. "You're a real good tattoo artist, Tina. Maybe I'll come back sometime and get a globe done on my belly beside the words. And don't worry, it doesn't have to be too fancy—I know globes can be real hard to draw." Tina stops counting her cash to listen to the rest of what he has to say. "I'm a globe-trotter, you know. I'm a non-stop world traveler." His face turns pink, probably because he hasn't actually traveled beyond the east coast of the United States. "I'll bring a library book with a good globe picture for you to look at, 'kay?"

"You do that, kid. And it'll be on the house." She returns her attention to the money.

CHAPTER 12

"WE'VE GOTTA EAT SOON, CADY." My belly is screaming at me. "You must be starving too, Eli. You hardly ate anything for breakfast." I steal a glance at Eli in the rearview mirror. He's looking down; his eyelashes rest against his skin as he checks out his ink.

Our gazes connect in the mirror. "I'm good. We can eat whenever." He glances out the window.

"We should go to the Rustic Valley Mall. It has a jewelry store that does piercings and it has a pretty decent food court," Cady suggests.

"Piercings?" This catches Eli's attention. "What about piercings?"

Cady turns around in her seat. "Cooper and I made a deal. We promised each other we'd do a few things this weekend that would be lasting, even permanent. We're doing them to celebrate high school graduation and to remind each other of our friendship when we're away at college."

With a tilt of his head, Eli takes in her message. These aren't the *actual* reasons we've decided to get tattooed and pierced, though. They're simply Cady's cheap explanation to Eli.

It has started to feel a lot like we're on a crazy and unscrupulous two-day dare.

"Just because you guys are going off to college doesn't mean your friendship's gonna change and that your lives are gonna be different. All that'll change is *where* you are, not what you guys mean to each other."

My loud swallow makes them jerk their heads toward me. They probably think I'm choking on my tongue. In my defense, I have to do *something* to keep my emotions in check, because Eli just put words to a major truth that Cady and I somehow missed.

Cady turns her head to stare out the passenger window. She has no clue what to do with Eli's brilliant sentiment. She puts everything she thinks and feels in separate boxes in her mind and she doesn't have a box for us being apart.

I squeeze her knee to let her know that I'm worried too. When she looks at me, I see a spark of fear in the back of her eyes—more fear than I knew about. I have a few suspicions as to why she's so flipping scared, so I don't let go of her knee. I leave my hand on it until we get to the mall.

Cady doesn't place her hand on mine, though. She just stares out the window.

cadence

AT LUNCH, COOPER EATS AS much as I do, which rarely, if ever, happens. He and I put down three-quarters of a pizza each. Eli finishes them off and insists that he pay. He isn't in a position to spend his money, but it's a pride thing because we paid for his tattoo. After we eat, we go to the restrooms in the food court and take off our bandages and then we clean our tattoos and slime them with more antibiotic ointment.

I meet the boys by the water fountain in the middle of the mall. "Time to get pierced." I tell them. Eli glances at Cooper in search of an explanation, but I'm in too much of a hurry for that. Certain that they'll follow along, I turn and head toward the Piercing Pavilion. "We don't have all night."

I march inside to talk to the lady at the cash register, who assures me that as long as we're eighteen years old we can get our ears pierced, but the ear lobe *only*. This severely limits our choices. No belly button, eyebrow, or nose piercings will occur today. My disappointment is outweighed by my relief.

More eager than scared, I sit on the high stool that's next to a tall desk with a jar of cotton balls on top. I've never been into jewelry; this will be my first experience with a piercing gun. And I want to get it done.

I select sterling silver stud earrings, and the worker draws two dots on my ear lobes with a felt-tip marker. Eli steps directly in front of me, so close his breath wisps across my lips. "Let me take a peek, Cady. I wanna make sure they're even."

When he places his fingertips on my chin, I lift my head, and he studies my ears. I get chills from his innocent touch and ask myself why it affects me so much when I've already admitted that I'm interested in Cooper.

"The dots seem even to me, Cady." He winks, and I can't help but shiver.

Then Cooper steps beside Eli, nudges him out of the way, and examines my ears for himself. "I think they look even too."

This scene is weird. It reminds me of the weekend last summer when Cooper rescued me from visiting Bradley at rehab. He invited me to stay at his house out of a sense of duty—it was what I expected him to do—but he'd really wanted me to go see my brother. Sometimes Cooper does things just because he thinks he's supposed to.

After cleaning my ears with alcohol-soaked cotton balls, she pierces my ear without too much fanfare. "It burns." My eyes water. I'm not looking for pity, so I add, "Your turn, Cooper."

Cooper wants to get only one ear pierced, and, when the woman marks his right ear with a tiny black dot, Eli shows the same interest in its placement. He touches Cooper's chin exactly as he'd just touched mine. At first, Cooper refuses to look at Eli, and his eyes drift off to the left. But when Eli says, "It should be just a tiny bit lower," Cooper meets his gaze. And then they smile at each other—just small smiles, but it's an unspeakably sweet scene.

"Any time now…" I tap my foot.

Cooper chooses a black stud, and three words later—"shit, that hurt"—it's done. It's Eli's turn to sit on the high stool and be physically altered according to the requirements of *our* bucket list.

"I'm not gonna get my ears pierced today," he says.

"If it's about the cash, no worries, dude. We got it," Cooper replies, but Eli shakes his head.

"That's not the whole reason."

"Then what's the problem?" I ask. It doesn't affect the bucket list if Eli gets pierced or not. In fact, we don't need him at all to finish our weekend challenge. But for some reason I want him to do this with us. It's fun to do stuff as a team rather than always as a couple.

The piercing woman says to Eli, "Think it over, son, and let me know when you decide," and she goes back to the cash register.

"So why don't you want to get it done, if it isn't the money?" Cooper's more patient than I am.

"It's like… like I'm afraid it'll be harder to get a job if I got pierced ears, you know?"

Eli is stunningly beautiful, but he doesn't have the slightest clue about this. And right now, he doesn't seem to know where to focus, so his long, dark lashes brush his cheeks as his eyes move from side to side, scanning the floor. I have a bizarre urge to place my hand on the side of his face and encourage him with the softest words to settle down, but I don't.

Instead I say, "Believe me, Eli, an earring will not stop any employer from hiring you. They'll be able to tell just by how you act that you're a good person and will be a hard worker." Honesty and earnestness are written all over his face. Any employer with an ounce of sense will recognize this.

"You really think so, Cady?" Eli lifts his gaze and looks at me. In his wide eyes, I see trust.

"Yeah, I really think so." I push the thoughts of Mom and Dad and how they also trust me from my mind. We're still in bucket-list mode, and my mother is not part of this, although she's part of the reason that there is a bucket list to begin with.

"Then I'm gonna do it." He smiles, and I remember how his lips felt on mine.

Cooper walks over to the worker to inform her of Eli's decision, and Eli says, "I want to get my ears pierced with those sparkly diamonds in the case."

"You mean the cubic zirconia?" I ask.

Eli seems confused. "No, the diamonds."

He points to the gaudy fake diamonds under the glass that he wants to wear in his ears, and I say, "Good choice." "Diamonds" are the perfect choice for him.

When the lady pierces his ears, Eli doesn't flinch. He doesn't even blink. And when she holds the hand mirror to his face, he turns his head from side to side to examine the way his earrings look. "These jewels are too fancy for a guy like me."

He's so incredibly wrong. Clearly in agreement, Cooper and I shake our heads in unison.

"Do you guys like how they look?" he asks, and in similar unison, we nod.

Spiral curls and feathery eyelashes and sparkly gems—Eli is delicately pretty, which should seem all wrong because he's also muscular and manly. But something about him is undeniably sweet and soft.

Why shouldn't he be a sweet and soft boy? I'm a hard and tough girl. Of course, he has every right to his sweetness, but a big part of me wants it to vanish. The same part of me wants him to be less alluring, and be just an ordinary, run-of-the-mill guy, so Cooper will stop looking at him the way he's looking at him right now. The rest of me wants to hug him.

Before I've resolved my conflict, Cooper lets out a loud gulp, coughs a few times, *and* sniffs. "Well, it's time to pay," he squeaks and follows the woman to the cash register.

Eli is close on his heels. "I can pay for my own earrings, Cooper."

Cooper places his hand on Eli's chest. "No, please consider it a thank you." He glances at me.

I know exactly what's on his mind. "Number twelve," I utter. The only item on the bucket list that we have not accomplished is to thank someone in our lives who deserves it. I'm still not sure why we put this one on the list; it doesn't prove that we're cool enough to go to college or that we're as deviant as the rest of the senior class. And it does nothing to help us figure out what we mean to each other. Maybe we just stuck it on the end of the list to assure some small measure of meaningful human growth this weekend.

And I figured that Coop and I would do this last one independently. I'd finish off the bucket list by going home and thanking Mom for absolutely everything she has done for me, and Cooper would go home and do the same. *See universe—not only are we cool, but we're also self-aware.* Thanking Eli works better, so I stand beside him on my tiptoes and kiss his cheek. "It's our way of saying thank you for hanging out with us this weekend. Please accept it."

eli

"I GOTTA MAKE A PIT stop," I tell Cady and Cooper when we get to the big fountain in the middle of the mall. "Be right back." I don't ask them if they gotta whiz, too. Instead, I press a couple of pennies I found deep in the pocket of my jeans into their hands and mumble, "Toss them in and make a wish," and then I race through the narrow hallway and into the men's room. I sure don't want to keep Cady and Cooper waiting on their special weekend, but I need a minute alone to get my head together.

First, I step over to the urinal and unbutton my jeans. And when I glance down, I'm stunned to see the string of words about friendship I got inked so close to my junk. As I stare at the raised, reddened sentence, hope and fear race through my veins.

I think I found my people. At least, I hope I found them.

Dad once told me, "Nothin' ventured, nothin' gained." Good advice, I'd say. And I took it this weekend. I went on an adventure, for sure. I took a chance and hit the road with Cady and Cooper. I kissed each of them and I liked it. I can't wait to find out what else I gained. They think I want their help to study for my GED, and I do, and they promised, but mostly I want to be friends with them.

After I whiz, I carefully button my fly and tug my jeans below my hipbone so nothing rubs on my sore tattoo. Then I head to the sink to rinse off my hands. In the mirror over the faucet, a new me looks back—a me with sparkling diamonds in his ears and a gleam of hope in his eyes. It's a good look for Elias Stanley, the globe-trotter who hopes to stay put until he gets his GED.

I wash my hands real fast and head back to my new friends to see if I'm in or I'm out.

cadence

IT'S A FEW MINUTES PAST six when we come out of the mall, and nearly time we clean our tattoos again. I'm not sure which hurts more, my wrist or my ears. "We have a lot of infection-prevention to do over the next few weeks," I say, and the guys mumble "mmhmm."

But Eli has lost his happy-go-lucky spirit. "I gotta figure out where I'm gonna sleep. Think maybe you guys could drop me off over by the carnival so I can see if Jimmy'll let me crash with him tonight?"

"You have to go already?" Cooper asks.

I'm not sure if I want Eli to stay or go, so I don't say anything. The truth is, I'm thoroughly confused about more than just Eli. The Weekend Bucket List is now a done deal. I should be reveling in the glory of liberation from nerd-hood, but I'm feeling surprisingly unchanged—like maybe I'm the same mixed-up, sheltered geek I was on Friday afternoon before I stripped off my clothes and jumped in the lake. This possibility is hard to swallow.

Eli's reply brings me back to the mall parking lot. "I should, or else I could end up sleeping on the street tonight."

Cooper shoots me a glare that clearly says, "Maybe it's time to break out our cell phones so the guy can call this 'Jimmy' person and avoid homelessness."

I shoot a look back at him that says, "No way. If we do that then Eli will realize we *do* have cell phones that we could have let him use yesterday and didn't." As always, I get my way. It's just not as satisfying as usual.

We pile into the car and head to the movie theater parking lot.

"Shit," Cooper says as we stare out over the vacant parking lot.

"Eli, I thought you said that the carnival wasn't leaving town until tomorrow." My words sound like an accusation.

Eli gets out of the car, dragging his duffel bag behind him like a security blanket. His face is blank. He drops the bag and touches his "diamonds" with both hands and then takes a step toward the place where the carnival once stood. "Guess they closed up shop early. Must've been a slow weekend. Mr. Hearn probably figured they were losing money here."

I don't need to hear Cooper's coughing fit to get that he's stressed out about Eli's predicament.

"Um… could you drop me downtown instead? I saw one of those motels for travelers there. If it's cheap enough and they take cash, I can book a room for the next few days while I… while I figure things out." He's homeless and jobless and alone, but the kid doesn't show a single sign of cracking. His steeliness in the face of what Cooper would call an "impending shit storm" is admirable.

We pile back into the car along with the duffel bag containing all of Eli's worldly possessions and head to downtown Ellis.

"Go in and find out if they have rooms available and then check the price. Ask if they take cash. We'll wait in the car with your bag," Cooper tells him. Eli goes into the Travelers' Haven Motel. He's been very quiet since he discovered that the carnival left town.

"He's up shit creek," I say to Cooper.

"No paddle," he adds. He removes his glasses and rubs his eyes hard with his thumbs.

"I don't see how we can help him." It isn't lost on me that this is what many casual observers have said about innocent victims throughout history.

"Me neither," Cooper agrees, but I'm not convinced he means it.

I sigh, and it's loud.

Cooper adds, "This seriously sucks."

Within five minutes, Eli is back at the car. He opens the passenger door and says, "I'm all set. They let me pay cash for a basement room 'cause they have trouble getting people to stay in it. I got it for the next four days."

"That's good news." I can't muster up much enthusiasm.

"So, are you going to try to find a job tomorrow?" Cooper asks.

"Yeah. I kind of got to." Once his duffel bag is beside him on the sidewalk, Eli leans his elbows on the passenger window. "It was real fun, you know, hanging with you guys for the weekend. Hate for it to be over."

"It was great," I say, still without passion. I'm careful not to give him any reason to think that it's *not* over. Weekend flings aren't meant to last.

My partner in crime may as well be a gulping/coughing/ sniffing machine. First, Cooper swallows loudly enough to wake the dead and then he coughs up a lung. His persistent sniffing is frosting on the I'm-a-piece-of-work cake.

"And… um… you guys know how to find me because I'm gonna be here 'til Thursday morning." He looks so hopeful, even *I* feel guilty. "Like I said, downstairs in the basement room. They only got one room down there, so it's easy to find."

"Right." My gaze is fixed on the dusty dashboard.

"We're graduating from Wellington High School tomorrow night, so we're gonna be pretty busy, at least until Tuesday," Cooper informs him.

Eli nods. "I hear ya."

"Don't forget to keep your piercings and tattoo clean." Everything I say sounds more feeble than the thing before it. I should just shut up.

116

"I won't forget, Cady." Eli slings the duffel bag over his shoulder. "Can't wait to start studying for my GED with you guys. And if we study at the public library, maybe I can show you some of my favorite pyramid books."

"Maybe," I say.

"Maybe," Cooper agrees and starts the car.

"I guess I'll see you around." Eli winks and smiles and then he scratches his hip on the spot of the brand new tattoo that describes how he has found two life-changing friends. He turns slowly, as if he's waiting for us to call him back. But we let him walk away.

PART TWO
CHAPTER 13

cooper

MONDAY IS AS BUSY AS hell. Thankfully, Mom doesn't demand I remove my new black stud earring. But she *does* force me to go with Dad for a haircut. I manage to keep my tattoo covered all day—even at the barber, which was a trick—with a linen scarf that Cady gave me for my eighteenth birthday. I've never worn it before, because I doubted I could pull off such a hipster look. I'm still not sure if it's cool to wear a scarf with a suit and tie, but the need to conceal has overruled my fear of committing a fashion faux pas.

Cady calls about an hour before we have to be at The Wellfleet Pavilion where the Wellington High School graduation ceremony is to take place.

"Mom saw my tattoo. She freaked!" Cady is hyperventilating. I recognize her stressed tone from having been by her side while she did everything humanly possible to avoid disappointing her mother over the past four years. Time to engage in emotional breakdown preventive measures.

"Look, Cady, you're eighteen years old and it's *your* body. You didn't do anything wrong." Even though I speak slowly and calmly, she's beyond listening to reason.

"Mom's crying, Coop. She says I ruined graduation for her."

"It's *your* graduation, not hers." I need to calm her down, and this can only be done in person. I don't want her to pull her eyelashes out, which she admits to having done quite frequently as a child. "Get your dress on and—"

"Skirt. I'm wearing my blue skirt."

Right. Cady wouldn't be caught dead in a dress. I sigh. "Get dressed and grab your cap and gown. I'll pick you up in ten minutes. We'll get to the school early and chill in the parking lot."

"Okay… okay. I'll be waiting for you on the sidewalk."

I take a deep breath to stifle how pissed off I am at Mrs. LaBrie. Throughout high school Cady's been the perfect kid. As far as her mother knows, getting a tattoo on her wrist is the only thing Cady has ever done to rock the I'm-a-model-child boat. And since last fall when Bradley went to rehab, Cady has been under more stress to make up for the pain her twin brother caused.

I put on my suit and my *very* loosely knotted tie. I plan to wear the scarf at graduation and every single day until I leave for college because I'm not sure I'm ready to explain the bisexual bow tie to my parents or anybody else in this town.

From the bottom of the stairs, I shout, "Mom, Dad—I'm gonna go pick up Cady and drive over to the school!"

"Okay, Cooper!" Mom shouts back from the master bathroom, where she's getting ready. "Good luck on your speech. And remember, if you speak too fast the audience won't be able to understand you!" This may not be such a bad thing. I'm not sure my speech is monumental in any way. I'm more of a numbers guy.

"Don't worry, I won't rush it, Mom!" Little does she know how often I've practiced my slow talking technique with Cady—every time I needed to walk her off a mother-induced ledge.

Dad steps out of the kitchen dressed more like he's going for a hike than to his only son's graduation. Upscale camper/mature hippy—thanks to his grayish-red hair and flowing beard—is his personal style when he's not in a commercial kitchen wearing chef's whites and a hairnet. But even when sporting a hairnet, the man is intrinsically cooler than me, and everybody knows it. "You know that we're very proud of you, Coop?"

"Uh-huh."

"Have you practiced your speech?"

"I practiced last week with the principal. First time I'd ever been in his office." I smirk because I'll be reciting a different speech tonight.

"Well, relax and breathe. And Coop…"

"Yeah, Dad?"

"I'm looking forward to checking out your tattoo, whenever you're ready to show it to me."

My cheeks burn, because my secret tattoo isn't so secret after all. Our gazes meet, and, at exactly the same time, we each ruffle our own freshly cut red hair. "I'll show it to you when it heals."

Dad smiles and says, "Go have fun."

BY THE TIME WE SET foot on the stage, Cady has calmed down enough to *appear* as if she's enjoying graduation. And I'm not overly nervous. Everybody knows I'm a math guy, not an eloquent writer, so the expectations for my speech aren't particularly high. In April, I discussed my original idea for a speech that would be acceptable, yet incapable of knocking the socks off anyone in the audience, with Mr. O'Leary, the high school principal. The concept he signed off on and I practiced in his office was pretty basic, in the manner of a traditional valedictory speech. It could easily have been summed up by its conclusion, which went something like this: "In closing, fellow classmates, I hope you remember that nothing we do is worthwhile unless we're challenging ourselves by taking risks. If all we do is focus on the things we have mastered, we will end up running in circles, like hamsters on wheels."

Ho hum. That speech has been delivered, in slightly different versions, by more high school graduates than there are grains of sand on the town beach. And my perspective has changed since I wrote those words. So last night I sacrificed sleep and came up with a new speech, a better one. *This* speech, I wrote for one person—Cady—and today, I will deliver it to her alone, even if I gaze out at the crowd in the stands. It's quite possible that Mr. O'Leary will have a litter of kittens when he realizes I'm going maverick.

I clear my throat and begin. "You've all heard the expression 'to kick the bucket,' right? And you know it means to die." A collection of wide eyes, all of which appear perplexed at why the hell I started my speech of future hope with the concept of death, studies me. "It's widely agreed that the idiom 'kick the bucket' comes from a historical method of execution—to be specific, a hanging. The person to be hanged was made to stand on a bucket with a noose around his neck. The executioner kicked the bucket beneath his feet and, you know... it, well, it killed him."

I risk a glance to the right at Mr. O'Leary, who is seated between the vice principal and Mr. Ortiz, the football coach and adult commencement speaker, and shrug without apology at his shit-a-brick expression.

"And so, it makes total sense that a bucket list is a list of things to do before you croak. Are you all still with me?"

It's the audience's turn to offer me a collective shrug.

"But why would a person create a list of things to do before he kicks the bucket? *I* think creating a bucket list is a way to set goals. And writing things down, as we learned in sixth grade when we were issued assignment notebooks in homeroom on the first day of school, is mandatory to achieving them. The written list turns a vague wish into a true goal. So, yeah, I'm urging you all—fellow graduates and parents and friends and family—to sit down somewhere quiet, brainstorm what would make your life more meaningful, and write it down."

A few audience members are now nodding, which gives me a surge of confidence. So I take a deep breath and go on.

"Here's what I've come up with so far for my lifetime bucket list; it's kind of like my top ten. And keep in mind, my list isn't finished. It takes time to focus on the purpose and direction of your life. You guys will find this out when you try to make your own bucket lists.

Number ten: Donate blood regularly. It's just the right thing to do.

Number nine: No more procrastinating. Staying up all night sucks—take it from the guy who came up with this new idea for a valedictory speech last night at eleven.

Number eight: Speak on a stage in front of a thousand people. It will force you to come out of your shell. Um… I can now check that one off my list.

Number seven: Volunteer your time. And never be stingy with it because karma is real.

Number six: Take action to fight climate change, you know, if you care about the future of our planet and the lives of your future children and grandchildren.

Number five: Learn conflict resolution skills and use them. In other words, always fight fair.

Number four: Figure out what makes you happy. Then, as the Nike slogan says, just do it.

Number three: Forgive those who ask. Remember, forgiveness is a gift to yourself, too.

Number two: Care less about what people think and just be yourself. For obvious reasons.

Number one: Inspire others to create bucket lists of their own. I hope I can check this one off too. And I'll fill you in on something that comes from the wisdom of an eighteen-year-old who has experience with the topic, you *will* thank me one day."

I turn around to look at Cady, who seems slightly puzzled, since I practiced the old "take risks" speech for her last week. But she's laughing. And if she's laughing, it means she's listening, so this is the perfect opportunity to deliver an additional, and essential, personal message. Ever since our co-ed kisses on Saturday night, I haven't been able to relax when I think about what I have with Cady and what I want with her in the future, which has led me to obsess over the difference between romantic love and friendship.

"In closing, fellow classmates…" And by this, I mean Cady. "… I'd like to quote one of my heroes, with regard to another, unrelated topic that's important to me at this time in my life. Elie Wiesel, a Holocaust survivor, global activist, and Nobel Prize winner, who lived his life as if his bucket list for personal growth was always in the forefront of his mind, said, 'Friendship marks a life even more deeply than love. Love risks degenerating into obsession, friendship is never anything but sharing.'"

One more time, I turn and glance at Cady. She isn't laughing anymore and, when I catch her eye, she slowly shakes her head. I'm not sure what she's trying to tell me, so, again, I do what I do best: I shrug. Right now, we're on totally different pages, maybe different chapters, in our lives. I just hope we're still in the same book.

THE PROCESSION OUT OF THE stadium is bittersweet. I experience the typical graduating senior's mixed emotions—a combination of excitement for the future splashed against nostalgia for the past. I have a perfect view of Cady, as she is four people in front of me in line, and when she passes her parents, they smile at her. I breathe a sigh of relief that they aren't still pissed off, which is cut short when I notice an unexpected face in the crowd.

Eli sits three rows behind Cady's parents. He waves wildly and grins at us, expecting that his new BFFs will be totally cool with his presence at this transitional moment in their lives. Cady waves half-heartedly at him and then turns around to gawk at me. The panic in her eyes is more striking than it was when I picked her up on the sidewalk in front of her house.

When Eli meets my gaze, he winks and then he waves. I half melt and half freeze, which isn't an easy thing to accomplish, especially in public. It all happens in a blur, and I'm not sure if I wave back at him. However, I *am* sure of one thing: He *can't* approach Cady or me when we greet our families at the conclusion of the ceremony.

Eli can't approach us here, in our real lives, when he's nothing more than human fallout from the only time we ever stepped out of our responsible teenager roles, the weekend we proved we were "normal" kids by the fulfillment of our mutinous bucket list. Cady and I haven't yet had a chance to talk about the *real* meaning of the bucket list—why we put so much pressure on ourselves to spend a weekend impersonating the kind of kids we aren't. We haven't yet decided if we actually intend to contact Eli and help him study for the GED, as we said we would. Plus, Cady's mother would chew off all of her fingernails if long-haired, diamond-pierced, and inelegant Eli gave her precious daughter a hug and a second kiss at the end of the recessional. She'd assume that Cady now associates with the wrong crowd, like the kids who "dragged Bradley into addiction," when Bradley went willingly.

I smile at Cady and call, just loud enough for her to hear, "No worries—I've got this!" In other words, I'll get rid of him.

As soon as the graduates have marched out of the pavilion and the families mill around under the open roof, I make a beeline for Eli. I find him standing alone by a column. He holds two bouquets of daisies, each tied together with purple hair elastics, and is looking around for Cady and me. When he sees me, his eyes light up, which causes my heart to harden out of pure necessity.

I know damn well what I need to accomplish. "Eli, what're you doing here?"

His smile falls, as this wasn't the greeting he expected. "Your speech was good. And you're right—I ought to write down my own bucket list sometime soon." His grin both charms and disarms me, but I'm a man of steel. "I already did one of the things that'll be on my list. I took a risk on you and Cady."

Eli is clearly not a hamster on a wheel, which I respect, but still I ask, "You also took a risk by coming here tonight, huh?"

He rubs his face with his palm and then scratches his hip. He wears pants with the wrinkles from the package still evident. His dress shirt also shows crisp folds. It's clear that he bought brand new clothes for our big day. My hard heart has no alternative than to shrink, as Cady has been everything to me for the past four years, and I will do whatever is necessary to protect her, *to protect us*. I'm the Grinch who stole Christmas, with a two-sizes-too-small heart.

"What do you mean?" Eli hides his face behind one of the flower bouquets. When he lowers the daisies to his chin, he seems to have found new hope. "What do you mean, Cooper?" he asks again, in a brighter tone.

Here's where I plug my ears to the screaming of my conscience. "Well, graduation's a family event, so Cady and I can't hang out with you tonight."

Eli nods. "I… I get that."

I swallow hard. "So, um… maybe you should, you know…"

"I guess I'll take off now."

"Okay." Not a gulp or cough or a single sniff. I'm made of stone.

"Tell Cady I said congratulations and give her these for me, 'kay?"

"I will." I do my best to keep my face blank and my voice flat as I take the flowers from his outstretched hand.

"And these other ones are for you."

I'm careful not to brush his fingers when I accept the second bunch of daisies.

"And... I, you know, I guess we'll talk to each other soon." It sounds like a question.

I don't want to look at him, but I do. I'm aware of the strong possibility that I'll never see him again. And Eli Stanley is seriously beautiful. Tonight, his curls are held off his face neatly with a soft, black headband, and his earlobes sparkle with the cubic zirconia studs he loves so much. I'm relieved that I'm unable to read the expression in his dark eyes, as they're fixed on the cement beneath our feet. His bright white teeth sinking into his bottom lip are evidence that Eli is doing his best to stay in control.

"You guys know where to find me: at the Travelers' Haven Motel in the only basement room until Thursday, and then I'm hopefully gonna be someplace more permanent. 'Kay?" His voice cracks three times in this short reminder.

"Yeah. We know where you're staying." Still I don't gulp, which is a minor miracle.

Eli nods again and then turns and starts to walk away, just as my father grabs and hugs me. "Cooper, my boy, you hit it out of the park with your speech!"

Eli glances behind him and our gazes meet one last time. And then I let myself be led away by Dad.

eli

I DON'T *WANT* TO RUN out of that fancy pavilion place and I try hard not to. But I can only walk like I'm cool with what went down between my new friends and me as far as the stone pathway that leads to the exit and then I bolt. I race down the rest of the pathway, out through the gate, across the parking lot, and down the road. And I run alongside the main town road, cars whizzing past, until my new clothes are stuck to my body and my curls stick to my neck from sweat.

I'm alone, all alone. Cady and Cooper aren't gonna call me or come find me. I already know this. I'm alone the way I was when Mom left and alone like when I knew my best choice was to run off with a traveling carnival. My thoughts race as fast as the rest of me books it down the main street of Cady and Cooper's pretty town.

I need to get control of myself—and I'm not talking about all of the control in the world, but just enough so I don't come apart at the seams. Nobody's around to pick me back up and set me on my feet if I fall. But this scene's not new to me. I been down and out before. I been alone; I know how it's done better than anybody. I got this… I got my own back.

Friends aren't everything, like I thought yesterday. They're just not. Ten minutes ago Cooper proved that he didn't mean what he said at the end of his speech. So, friends are nothing.

Finally, I slow down so I seem like I'm just a dude jogging to keep in shape, not a kid running away from everything in life that's aiming to pull him apart at the seams, even if I *am* dressed like a TV lawyer.

When I'm far enough away for my heart's safety, I let myself walk. I'm steady on my feet now as I head back to the place I'll call home for the next couple of days—to the place where Cady and Cooper know they can find me, but won't—the only motel room The Traveler's Haven Motel has got that's underground, where it's damp and dark and a little funny-smelling, but is cheap as heck and good enough for me, and better than most of the many places I slept in my life.

CHAPTER 14

cadence

I couldn't meet Cooper on Tuesday night or Wednesday because I was serving food at Mad Eats, the restaurant I've worked at off and on since I was old enough to have a job. It's a cool place: a little retro and a lot quirky, and it serves both comfort food like Grandma makes and newfangled stuff you've never heard of. I like my job here. The staff is liberal, and the diners are eclectic. Cooper has been busy, too, training for his job at the Sugar Street Home Store in the Rustic Valley Mall, where he'll be a stock boy this summer.

As we planned, Cooper shows up at Mad Eats when I'm off the clock at four. We sit at a table in the bar that's empty because it's too early for happy hour and sip on a couple of lemon-mango-mint iced teas I made for us.

"You know what we need to talk about, Cades—it can't wait any longer."

I have avoided the topic of Eli since we returned from our weekend adventure. Honestly, I've avoided *all* conversation beyond, "The weather is freaking fantastic, huh?" with my best friend. I have a strong feeling that I don't want to hear what he has to say. He dropped a bomb on me at graduation with his personal growth bucket list and the "let's just be friends" quotation. I figure that as soon as we have the discussion about whether or not we should contact Eli, it will be the end of us. I'll be out, and Eli will be in.

I'm not all broken up over the lack of a budding romance with Cooper. Maybe I don't want us to be a loving couple, either. But nothing's worse than being the powerless victim of somebody else's decision to reject me. So, we've settled into a period in our relationship where silence is golden.

Who can blame me? I'd prefer to move on without having the "big talk" that will change everything between us without my permission. And maybe they don't write country songs about it, but broken friendships cause broken hearts too.

"Eli's only staying at the Travelers' Haven for one more night. We have no clue where he'll go after that and we won't be able to get in touch with him." Cooper makes ignoring a subject extremely difficult when he addresses it so directly.

I snap into human-lie-detector mode and conduct a spur-of-the-moment analysis on Cooper. I size up the tone of his voice and his facial expression and search for evidence of excessive perspiration. I easily arrive at the conclusion that Cooper is under serious stress and badly wants to reach out to Eli.

"We said we'd help him study for his GED, Cady."

"I *know* what we said." I practically bite his head off. "But you know as well as I do that we were in bucket-list mode that night."

"So what we said didn't mean anything?" Cooper looks at me as if I'm the greenish-black scum that grows under the toilet bowl rim. "We were just *lying* to him for the sake of the blessed bucket list?"

"Well, I don't think we were *lying*. We meant those things when we said them."

Cooper sucks down the rest of his iced tea and then spits a lemon seed into the glass. "Cady, I can't come up with a legit reason why we shouldn't help him study this summer."

I'm well aware of what is making me sweat in the deep freeze of Mad Eats' commercial AC: I'm scared. But worry and guilt are mixed in with my fear, a toxic blend. "Let's just drop it, okay?"

"Are you saying you don't want to help Eli study?"

If I can't control a situation, I want out of it. This is a sad fact of my life, despite Cooper's lofty graduation speech suggestion that we should always fight fair. I can't exactly spell out my fear *and* hold onto Cooper's respect, so I just shake my head. "I don't think either of us should contact him, not that you'd understand." How can he understand when I hardly do?

"Oh, I think I get it." Cooper's voice is laced with a bitterness I had no idea he was capable of. "You're saying that Eli served his purpose and now we're done with him."

I shrug. "God, Cooper, I'm… I'm just confused about what happened on Saturday night with Eli and you and me."

"The kisses?" Cooper replies quickly. "Did it ever occur to you that I'm confused too?"

"So maybe it's for the best that we let the whole thing with Eli drop."

"Don't you think we should talk about this a little more before we write him off?"

I shake my head. When I spit out, "Nope," my relief is sufficiently profound to ease my guilty conscience.

Cooper's jaw drops; he's seeing a side of me he's not familiar with. In his defense, I'm not accustomed to this shallow version of myself either. He pulls off his glasses and rubs his eyes with his thumbs. I've surprised him and not in a good way. "Okay, then, Cadence."

Ouch. "Okay?"

"Yeah. You mean more to me than Eli does." These are the exact words I've longed to hear. I should be over the moon, giddy with glee, but it's hard to miss that Cooper is backing away from me, as if I've got a contagious disease he'd like to avoid. "Listen, I've gotta get to work. I'll call you tomorrow." Cooper doesn't suggest that we go out for ice cream later tonight or hit a movie that's more current than *Driving Miss Daisy.* He doesn't even wait for me to say goodbye.

Cooper turns and walks away. He leaves me with more questions than I had when he got here.

Cecelia Tucker calls when I get home from Mad Eats. She invites me to go to the Rustic Valley Mall to shop for dormitory room stuff. Mara and Trish must not be available.

"I have tons of gossip to dish about the party on graduation night at Billy Starr's house!" she gushes.

It is an established fact, in my mind, at least: Cece's far more excited about what goes on in this town than I will ever be. And although it was a party that I wasn't considered cool enough to be invited to, I say, "Sure, why not? But I'd rather shop for clothes than for dorm stuff, if that's okay."

We're both surprised to hear me say this, since I'm a girl who wears strictly solid colors—a white T-shirt and tan pants is the most creative I get with clothes. Lately, I like to wear shirts I steal from Bradley's room: his old golf shirts and button-downs. Whenever she notices that I'm wearing his stuff, Mom insists that

I must miss my twin brother dreadfully. But I ask myself, *Why should Bradley's perfectly good clothes go to waste?* It's nothing more significant than that. And you'll never catch me in floral prints or sparkles or, God forbid, ruffles. These styles are not welcome in my plain-Jane wardrobe. No scarves or heels or jewelry, either, aside from the new silver studs in my ears.

Sure, I'm a girl, but I'm just not girly. I pity women who wear high heels to look sexy. Makeup, in my opinion, makes girls look like circus clowns. Clothes should be comfortable and neat, and should cover the body sufficiently for public viewing. Glitzy mall clothing stores are foreign territory; the L.L. Bean online store works just fine for me, thank you very much.

I'd rather swim with piranha than spend an hour in Forever 21, but I nonetheless suggest clothes shopping tonight because Cooper's working at the home store where all the dorm essentials can be found, and I'm not in the mood to see him.

CHAPTER 15

cooper

I NEVER FIGURED I'D SEE the day when I'd think, *Cady has changed, and not for the better.* And I surely never thought I'd discuss the topic with Dad, but that's what is happening. We're on the couch in the living room with snack tables in front of us, watching baseball, which isn't interesting enough to fully hold *my* attention. But the omelet he just made me is delicious, so I'm not in a huge hurry to go anywhere until it's gone.

"Coop, looks like you got a tattoo of a bow tie on your neck." He takes a bite of his omelet and closes his eyes because it is so damn good. Must be nice to appreciate the product of your own effort so thoroughly. "A fashion statement?"

"I guess," I reply, fully aware that this could be the start of something big.

"Why isn't it *rainbow* striped? If you're going to make a statement about who you are, why not go all the way with it?"

"Dad, I *did* go all the way with it." I pick up my phone and search for the bisexual flag. When I find a decent image, I hand the phone to my father. "Look."

Dad studies it and nods. "Bisexual, huh?"

I shrug because it's weird to hear my father say the word out loud and then I nod reluctantly. "I'm pretty sure."

"You don't have to answer me, but… do you have feelings for Cady?"

I stand and grab my empty plate with the fork from the snack table. "I think so. But I also like, well…"

"Boys?"

"Yeah. It's pretty messed up." I walk into the kitchen and go straight to the dishwasher.

"I imagine it must seem that way to you." Dad follows me into the kitchen and passes me his plate. "You don't have to make a decision about the rest of your life right now. You have plenty of time to live and learn and discover who you are." He folds his arms across his chest and studies me.

Once I've loaded the dishes and forks, I turn around and prop my ass on the counter. "Dad, I know who I am. It took me a while to figure it out and even longer to accept it, but I don't think it's going to change."

"You could be right about that, and I'm happy that you've given this some serious thought." He opens the fridge to put away the ketchup. "What about Cady? How does she fit into your life?"

This seems to be the question of the summer. "I thought Cady wanted to start a romantic thing with me. And for a while I thought maybe I felt the same way."

"What happened?"

Eli happened, and Cady changed. And maybe I'm just not ready to be in a romantic relationship. I close my eyes and shake my head. What happened is still too raw to put into words.

"If you and Cady decide not to become lovers, you can still be the best of friends. Maybe even soul mates. And I agree with Elie Wiesel. Friends have the most profound effect on your life." Dad is so perceptive. He caught that small detail from the ad-lib addition to my graduation speech. "Coop, the basis of my relationship with your mother is friendship. That's how it started with us and it's why we get along so well."

For the first time, I admit to myself that the pain of losing my friendship with Cady is killing me. I'm heartbroken in a way I thought could only happen when you lost a lover. I try to explain, but all that comes out of my mouth is a croak.

Dad's cool and acts as if he doesn't hear. "If you were asking for advice, Coop, I'd tell you that friendship is the deepest form of love. But society deems the love between friends less important than romantic love. Friendship is highly underrated." He smiles. "Not that you're asking for help with this."

"Thanks, Dad." I'm not into heart-to-hearts, but this one-sided conversation Dad just held with mostly himself actually helps. "I've gotta get to work, but I'll definitely keep what you said in mind."

What confuses me more than anything is that regret about losing Eli drags me down too, and we only knew each other for a few days. But it's there—regret that I skipped out on a friend who needed me. And regret that I didn't pursue a relationship with a person I connected with, regret that I can't turn back time and do things differently.

* * *

This room ain't too bad.

137

It's got a window with curtains on it—yellow ones—and I'm into yellow because it's a cheerful color. And I got my own bed, even if the room is jammed full of beds for other dudes too. My bed has got a pancake mattress, but it's way better than the floor, and I got the bottom three drawers in a scratched-up white bureau. Plus, we got a bathroom to share down the hall.

And this place gets bonus points because it's not on wheels. I tuck my new sheets in around my mattress and then spread out the wool blanket that I found folded on the floor beside my bed. No pillow. Must've got snatched by one of the other guys.

An old dude named Harold rolls over onto his belly in the bed next to mine. He could be sleeping off a buzz, or maybe he works the night shift and daytime's when he gets to crash. It could be that he's in bed because he's depressed, and I get that too. So as not to annoy him, I try to be quiet as I toss the blanket over my bed. When my bed is made, I flop onto it and try hard to imagine that I'm home, but it isn't easy.

My mind goes *there* again. So, I tell me, *Eli, don't think about that anymore.* This is hard to do, but I have to try to block them out of my mind because when I spend all my time asking myself why Cady and Cooper blew me off, I don't end up anywhere good. The way I see it is that I fell into friendship too quick, the way some folks fall in love at first sight. I let myself hope that I found a couple of real friends. But nope, I was wrong, so I had to pack my duffel bag and keep on going. And that meant I needed to head out into the world to find a new place to live and a job. Good thing I'm a globe-trotter.

The Ellis Crossing Over Project for Men is where I live now.

Home Sweet Homeless Shelter.

I pull a folded envelope out of the pocket of my jeans. Written on it in my messy handwriting is a list of all the job opportunities I found when I did an online search on the library computer. I plan to walk to these places and knock on their front doors to ask about work, because I still haven't got a cell phone. Lucky for me, most of the addresses are in the downtown part of Ellis, so I should be able to cover the spots on the list in one day. And that day has got to be today, seeing as I got nothing better to do and I need cash quick.

For a moment, I close my eyes. Hopes and dreams aren't ever too far below the surface of my thoughts, and Cady's and Cooper's faces slip into my brain before I can boot them out. I liked Cady's prickly, "do what I say" way. I admired her. She was smart and brave enough to take on the hard stuff. Cady was a mystery that I wanted to figure out.

Cooper had a big heart—too big, maybe. He tried to make Cady and me happy because how we felt meant everything to him. I knew I was safe with Cooper, but also, he thought I was special. Even when we said our last goodbye, he still wanted to be my friend. The caring was in his eyes. If we met in another life, I bet we'd be impossible to split apart.

I hop off the bed, kick my empty duffel bag under the bureau, and head down the hall toward the stairs. It's time to find a job. I can't sit here on my bed, daydreaming about what's over with.

✿ ✿ ✿

cadence

I HATE TO ADMIT IT, but I'm struggling.

I can only think this, though, as I have nobody left to tell. At least, nobody who cares. And it's not that I'm actually alone, because I'm not. I've been officially "adopted" by Cece, Mara, and Trish—three popular girls who had no time for me in high school. Strangely, we've become inseparable.

The most obvious question is, where's Cooper? For four years I shared *almost* all of my innermost thoughts with him. But I never shared the most important stuff—the thoughts that put me at risk for embarrassment or rejection. Nonetheless, it's clear that I'm suffering from Cooper-withdrawal symptoms when I realize I'm nostalgic for the lame way he points with his elbow.

And then there's the Eli factor. I think about him and feel heartless. I totally screwed that boy over when he deserved support—and a huge hug.

"What's the matter, Cady? You look like you're carrying the weight of the world on your shoulders." Mara is slightly more tuned in to human emotion than Cece, but I wouldn't exactly call her empathetic. "And your sighing is bumming me out."

Nope, not empathetic at all.

Trish hands me a glass of wine. "Here you go. Suck that puppy down and you'll feel better."

That'll solve it, Trish, I think. *Just like drugs made everything better for Bradley.*

"Chug it, sista," Trish insists.

"Yeah, wine is just what I need," I reply. "Thanks." And I drink about half of what's in the goblet in a single gulp. It's easier to drink alcohol since I've done it once before.

Thank you, Weekend Bucket List. I guess…

"Drink up, girls, because we're going to a party on Dave Benardi's boat. Word is his family has a private dock in the backyard of their lake house on the Wobego River and the parties are famous for getting over-the-top sick."

"OMG—it's gonna be a full moon tonight!" Mara, number three on the mean-girl totem pole, bubbles over with enthusiasm. I fake a smile, but… *erghh*. "That means it's gonna be insane! And *everybody's* supposed to be there!"

Wrong. Cooper won't attend. He's not cool enough, but I am. Apparently, I'm cool enough now. *I hope I can contain my excitement.*

We suck down our first glass of wine, which leads to a second. And the weirdest part is that we're drinking booze at Cece's kitchen table and Mrs. Tucker hasn't tried to stop us. She's been here in the kitchen making BLTs for the past fifteen minutes and knows exactly what we're up to. After she places a plate of sandwiches on the table, she reaches into Cece's purse and snatches her car keys. "Don't even think you're going to be driving anywhere in your condition, young lady." Mrs. Tucker giggles without a smile, clearly nervous to lay down the law in her own house.

Cece's older brother walks to the kitchen table and grabs a sandwich. He's tall and blond and Ken-doll cute, if you like the plastic type. "I've been on the Benardis' boat a few times," he brags. "It's a rocket."

"Are you worried about us, Marty? Scared we might fall off the boat?" Trish asks, snapping into flirtation mode. "Why don't you come along and be my personal lifeguard?"

Cece's brother shrugs, stuffs half the BLT sandwich into his mouth, grabs a second, and leaves the kitchen. Trish blushes and finishes her drink. I try not to gag at the stupidity of it all, and, for the most part, succeed.

A few minutes later we stumble out the door without Marty, Trish's human lifejacket, and get picked up in front of the Tuckers' house by a boy I vaguely recognize from Wellington High School who's driving his family's minivan. He's another total player—the type of boy who only knew I was alive in high school when he needed to copy my homework.

I don't much care if I go for a ride on David Benardi's ridiculous rocket-boat or if I pick up extra hours at work. As long as I don't have to sit around and wonder why Cooper never texts or calls me anymore. As long as I don't have to dwell on how empty my life is, I'll be fine.

It's as if Cooper died, and, after skipping the funeral, I refuse to mourn.

CHAPTER 16

cooper

IT SUCKS WITHOUT CADY AROUND.

"Home again today, Coop?" Mom asks, tying an elastic into her always-messy dark hair. "Is Cady working tonight?" Lately, she's constantly digging for info about my missing-in-action BFF. "That girl sure works a lot, hmm?"

I'm not inclined to share the tangled mess in my head with my mother. I have strict rules of non-engagement in my life: If someone hurts me, I keep my distance from that person. And maybe sometimes I get mad, but I never get even. If I want something to improve in my life, the most I'm willing to do is hope for change. So, I don't rat out Cady on her questionable behavior.

"Uh, I *think* she's working... maybe."

Mom comes to the recliner. She is pretty in the way of a teenage girl—always wearing sweatshirts and tight jeans and a loose bun directly on the top of her head. But Mom is nothing like most teenage girls I know, at least, not on the inside. She's a total brain when it comes to math and she's incredibly wise about life. And she's every bit a mother. "At some point, you've got to trust somebody, Coop." She bends over a little and places her index finger on my bow tie tattoo. "Why not me? Why not right now?"

I have no idea how I turned out to be such a closed-off person. My parents are cool and open-minded. I have no real reason to fear they'd reject me for being bi, just like they never rejected me for being just plain weird—socially awkward and geeky and out of step with the rest of the kids at school. "Spilling my guts isn't easy, Mom."

"Your father and I never tried to force you into 'be normal' mode." She gulps as noticeably as I do. "Did we somehow make you feel that our acceptance of you was conditional, Coop?" Mom's eyes are already wet and puffy, and I feel like shit on wheels. I pull her down beside me on the arm of the chair. "We've always loved you just as you are, son."

"I know that." I really do.

"Then trust me now. Talk to me, Cooper. *Please.*"

Lucky for Mom, worse than my fear of whatever it is that keeps me all clammed up is my fear of hurting someone I care about. "Mom, I really do trust you."

She leans hard against my shoulder and issues a dare. "Then prove it and talk to me."

Mom doesn't make avoidance of my problems easy. "It's just that Cady's changed a lot."

"How has she changed?"

I betray my best friend when I reply, "Cady's been acting selfish lately and she's not as caring about people as she used to be." I literally sweat with guilt as I say this, so I'm surprised when relief rushes in as soon as the words are out.

Mom straightens and stares directly into my eyes. My instinct is to glance away, but, for once, I don't. "That girl has been through a lot at home over the past several years, what with her brother's addiction and her mother's desire to control her every move."

"Mrs. LaBrie expects Cady to be the perfect child. And Cady's Dad is the king of avoidance."

Mom nods. "That must put a lot of pressure on a teenager."

"Yeah." Poor Cady. Without me, all she's got is Daisy the cat. "She's scared, I think."

"Scared of what?"

Cady's scared of change. She's terrified to lose someone else she loves, the way she lost Bradley. In particular, she's scared to lose *me*. But I don't answer my mother's question. I shrug as if I haven't got a clue.

"Well, maybe you should think about it, Coop. It may help you to understand where Cady's coming from." Mom stands. "I'm sure she's anxious about leaving home *and leaving you* when she heads off to college."

I'm relieved that Mom didn't ask me if I'm in love with Cady. Because I *am* a little bit… or I was. But it's complicated. Maybe it's easier to let her go than sort through the complications.

"Have you ever considered that she's worried to lose you in the very way she *thinks* she wants you—in a romantic way—to a boy?"

Mom touches my tattoo again. I gulp and then cough, because a vision of Eli's earnest dark eyes rushes into my mind. I'm mad at Cady and I'm mad at Eli and I'm mad at myself too. "Well, I'm not waiting around for Cady tonight. I've got to go to work." I hop to my feet and tuck in my shirt. "I have to get going."

After she sends me one of those meaningful motherly glances, Mom turns around and leaves the living room. My stomach churns. But now alone in the room, I speak aloud to myself. "And *that* is precisely why I don't talk to my parents about personal shit." I know better, though, so when I lie to myself, I don't believe it.

What I neglected to tell Mom is that I hurt somebody. I didn't explain to her that I left the world's kindest boy high and dry after using him as a human guinea pig in our twisted sexual orientation experiment. That I gave him empty promises, and no explanations. And that I offered him no real goodbye. I was just a big freaking no-show, and I'm certain that I'm not forgiven. Because even if Eli has forgiven what Cady and I did to him, I can't forgive us.

❊ ❊ ❊

eli

DAD USED TO PLAY A certain song on the boom box in the kitchen as he fried hot dogs for supper when I was a kid. And the words to the song said, "alone again, naturally." This might be *my song*, because here I am, living in the homeless shelter, keeping to myself for the most part, and hoping I can find a job where I don't have to talk to anybody too much.

Alone just works for me. It's simple and it's easy. When I'm alone, I don't have to slow down to wait for anybody to keep up. I don't owe anybody a thing. My brain can always stay quiet because nobody else's problems are swirling around, pestering me.

"Alone again, naturally." I tell myself stuff like this until I'm blue in the face, but that doesn't make me believe it. Truth is,

I'm lonely as heck. And sometimes, as in, *right now,* I say things out loud.

"Stop your mumbling, Stanley, and tell us, you got yourself a job yet?" asks Henry, the old dude who sleeps in the bed beside mine during the day. He's awake now because it's time to make supper. All eight of us guys at the shelter usually work together to fix a simple supper, like the spaghetti and salad we're having tonight. And then we all sit down at the scratched-up, secondhand table, say a quick prayer, and dig in. But I still feel like I'm eating alone.

Usually we don't talk too much at meals, but we're always polite to each other. It's kind of a rule here. If somebody asks me a question, I do my best to answer. "Uh-huh. Found a job landscaping for Baron Brothers Lawn Services," I reply to Henry and anybody else who's listening.

I start my job tomorrow. Hated to do it, but I had to spend a pile of my saved-up carnival cash to buy the right sort of boots to work in and a tube of sunblock and some food for lunch and a cooler to stick it in. The cooler doesn't make me think of that night with Cady and Cooper too much because it's not Styrofoam. It's the type of cooler you take on real camping trips, not stupid road trips with strangers who say they're going to come visit you and help you study for the GED and don't.

"I know this kid who worked at Baron's last summer," says the other guy who's around my age and down on his luck enough to be living at a halfway house for homeless men. I don't know his name and don't plan on asking. People never stick around in my life long enough to make learning their names time well spent. "He said they work you hard, but they're stand-up guys, those Baron brothers."

"Cool." I shovel in a forkful of spaghetti.

Henry grunts, "That's a good job for somebody young like you. I got to find me a job that won't break my back."

"Be a Walmart greeter, then," one of the guys wisecracks, and after a few others snicker it gets quiet again. *I'd* really like to be a Walmart greeter if it paid enough.

I get up from the table before everybody else is finished eating, which is against the politeness rules of the group home, but I can't avoid it. I wash my bowl and fork and then sip some water right from the faucet. "Sorry, everybody. I gotta cut and run seeing as I start work tomorrow and I forgot to pick up ice packs for my cooler."

Everybody at the table nods, and a few of them grunt. I don't think they much care what I do. They got worries of their own.

"Leave the sauce pot soaking in the sink and I'll scrub it when I get home from the store." I'm not a guy who shirks his duties. *Some people* do what they say they're going to do.

Again, my housemates nod and grunt.

As I head out the back door of the kitchen, I decide that life is a lonely place. It's about time I got this fact through my thick skull.

cooper

"COOPER, CAN YOU DO A price check on an item in the Children's Department?" The headphones I wear may look goofy, but they come in handy. If not for them, all of these messages would be broadcast over the store's intercom and it would be noisy as hell around here. "We have a customer at the register with several strawberry- and banana-shaped icepacks that have no price tags on them."

"I'm on it." I put the beach towels I'm stacking back in the shopping cart, head over to the kids' area, grab a few different fruit-shaped ice packs, and then jog to the front of the store. The second I catch a glimpse of the back of the customer's head, I know who these ice packs are for. Nobody else in the world has curls that amazing.

I step to the counter so that our shoulders touch. His skin is sticky, as if he jogged here. It brings me back to the night we spent at the beach, when we lay close beside each other in the tiny tent.

Eli turns and, as soon as he sees me, he says to the cashier, "I changed my mind on getting these cooler packs, ma'am. But thank you for the help." He heads straight for the exit.

I drop the fruit icepacks on the counter and follow him out into the mall, not caring that I'm supposed to be working. I have my priorities set correctly now, where I made such a mess of everything the last time I saw him. "Hey, Eli! I want to talk to you for a minute!"

He stops, but doesn't turn around. "You want to talk to me *now?*"

I scramble to him and grab his arm so he can't take off. "Eli, dude, I'm sorry about not coming by the motel last week. I totally screwed up." It's a relief to admit this to him.

Eli stares at my hand on his arm. "I stayed at the Travelers' Haven Motel all the way 'til Sunday. *Sunday!* You and Cady never came for me." His voice cracks the way it did when he spoke to me at graduation and again it guts me.

"I'm sorry." And since it's the beginning and end of what's on my mind, I say it again. "I'm sorry as… as hell. You have no idea."

He finally turns and looks at me. Eli's eyes are, as always, easy to read, and right now they tell me he's hurt and a little dazed. Then I notice that his diamond earrings are gone, and I stare at the puckered pink dots on his ears where they used to be. This is all wrong, and it's my fault.

"I want to explain what happened, Eli. Can I meet you after work tonight?"

Eli doesn't shake or nod his head, but he seems to notice I'm staring at his ears. He tilts his head and tugs on his right earlobe. "I took out the earrings. I threw 'em away."

"They looked perfect on you. Eli. I wish you hadn't done that."

"It was all I could think of to do when Sunday morning came and you and Cady still hadn't stopped by the motel."

I close my eyes and see a vision of Eli's sparkling earrings rolling around in the bottom of a plastic motel trashcan. "I get why you did it. Just let me take you to dinner to explain."

"I can't tonight."

I have absolutely zero problem with begging. Pride is overrated. "Then meet me tomorrow, Eli. *Please.*"

"Will Cady come too?" he asks and again tugs on his earlobe, like a kid with an ear infection.

I shake my head. "Cady and I… we haven't seen too much of each other lately."

"That's too bad."

I shrug, because at the moment all I want is to fix things with him. "Will you meet me?"

"Where?" he asks, clearly wary.

"How about the Seafood Shack? Tomorrow at five." I'm ready to drop to my knees, if necessary.

"Six… Let's meet at six. And if *I* say I'll be there, Cooper, I *will* be there."

"Ouch." I deserved that.

"And I'm saying I'll be there."

Although I haven't smiled in way too long, it's easy to do.

CHAPTER 17

cadence

PARTYING IS MORE THAN JUST a bad habit; it has turned into my greatest escape, and sadly, the aspect of life I most look forward to. I read somewhere that certain families have hereditary tendencies toward addiction. I think that I may belong to one of those families, because, since the first time I got drunk on the beach with Cooper and Eli, it's become my favorite thing to do. Getting bombed takes me away from my problems, even if the headache makes me regret it the next day.

I'm parked in Mom's Volvo wagon outside of the Bodies in Motion Racquetball Club where Cece serves protein shakes at the juice bar. I'm waiting for her to get out of work. She's my main accomplice in the ruination of my life. It helps that her mother actually buys our booze for us, so we always have a generous supply, and we have a place to drink because Mrs. Tucker is one of those parents who says that she'd rather have her teenager drink at home than go do it somewhere else. But I suspect she'd much rather that Cece not drink at all.

"Hey, girl." Cece hops into the passenger seat. "I got some sick news."

"Yeah?" I start the car. "Well, don't keep me in suspense."

"Party at Julie Carrington's house. It's on Old Wagon Wheel Drive—let's head over." When I don't pull onto the road as instructed, she stares at me. "What are you waiting for?"

"Cece, I can't drive there. I'm in my mother's car. She'd have my head if I crashed it or got stopped and arrested for DWI on the way home."

Cece sighs noisily as she pulls her brush out of her purse and starts to primp for the party. "You won't get stopped if you just get buzzed, not wasted."

I fight not to roll my eyes at her stupidity. I've broken the rules right and left since the bucket-list weekend, but getting an underage DWI crosses a line I'm not okay with. The not-so-slight possibly that I could kill myself or, worse, somebody else gives me pause. "Let's just go to your house and get drunk, the way we planned. I have all my stuff to sleep over."

"We aren't exactly gonna meet guys at my house, are we?" When Cece's hair is arranged artfully on her shoulders, she opens her makeup case and pulls down the mirror on the visor. "Just get us there, and we'll figure out how to get home later. Or we'll crash on Julie's couch. She won't mind." Cece glides some gloss on her lips. "But shit, you are such a goody two-shoes. Loosen up, girl!"

I shake my head, but still pull onto the road as instructed. "I can't drive us home tonight. No matter what."

"I should have invited Mara tonight. At least she's chill," Cece mumbles, but I know I'm supposed to hear.

WHEN WE GET TO THE party, I drop Cece off in front of the house and park the car alone. Instead of sticking my car keys in the pocket of my jeans, I hide them behind a back tire. Cece can't force me to drive later tonight if I "accidentally" lose my keys. I text Mom and let her know that my plan is to sleep over at Cecelia Tucker's house tonight, and naturally, she doesn't question her model child.

Just have the car home before noon so I can grocery shop, dear, she texts back.

Grocery shopping is Mom's biggest concern when it comes to her only daughter's use of her secondhand Volvo. She's still as naïve as when Bradley was a high school sophomore and existed only to party it up with anybody who had what it would take to get him wasted.

I hike up the street to Julie Carrington's house, where Cece stands in the front yard, already chatting with a guy who was on the Wellington High School football team, which in some people's minds makes him royalty. She sends me a "get lost" glare and presents me with her back.

As I scan the yard for someone I recognize, a well-used cliché pops into my mind—one that I never considered before because my only pal was Cooper: With friends like these, who needs enemies?

CHAPTER 18

cooper

HE'S WAITING FOR ME WHEN I arrive.

Eli sits on a leather couch in the front lobby and studies the menu. The first thing he says to me is, "I can't pay this much for dinner, Cooper, but I saw a Wendy's down the street we can go to instead."

"*I'm* taking *you* to dinner. And believe me, money's not a problem. I've saved every penny I've made this summer and I have a scholarship to college."

Eli stands. "Okay, I guess. But Wendy's works for me, too." He's aloof, which is an unfamiliar look on him. Eli is the essence of an accessible person, so when he acts like a classic movie mean girl, it throws me.

The hostess seats us across from each other at a small table in the corner, which couldn't be more perfect. I don't plan to wait until after we order to explain myself. As soon as we're served tall glasses of water, I get right to business. "There's no good reason for what Cady and I did—telling you one thing and doing another."

"Lying," he says. The candle flickering between us on the table emits a subtle light that makes Eli look as if he's the romantic lead in an old black-and-white movie. His face is striking, but somehow tragic, even when he tells me things I don't want to hear.

"Yeah, right. *Lying.*" I take a breath to clear my head before I try to explain. "We lied to you, but the lie happened after the fact."

He glances at me over his water glass. "What do you mean?"

"It's like this, Eli: When we told you we were gonna help you study for the GED, we meant it."

He doesn't smile as I'd hoped. "So, what went wrong?"

"This may sound crazy, but it didn't have as much to do with you as it did with Cady and me. Things just went off the track with *us*, and so we never got in touch with you."

Eli's expression softens. "Is it because you love her?"

I hadn't expected this question, but I owe him the truth. "I think so. I love her as..." I've never expressed this before, not even to myself. "I love her as a close friend, a *precious* friend."

He nods. "Does she love you as a precious friend too?"

"I don't have a clue how she feels, Eli. Maybe she does." I shake my head. "I don't know."

"What was the problem between you guys?"

"I can only speak for myself."

"Then go ahead and speak."

"Our problem was that we were both too scared to talk to each other about how we felt." This was, at least, the biggest part of the problem. "We hid too much."

"It wasn't because of me? Because of how I kissed you *and* Cady that night... and because of jealousy."

"Maybe it was a little."

"I knew it." His smirk is smug and adorable. It reminds me of Cady. "I just knew it."

"Maybe the kissing we did that night broke the rules for friends."

"Then maybe something's wrong with the rules, not with you and Cady."

"You could be right about that."

When Eli smiles at me, wide enough to flash his mouthful of gleaming teeth, I'm convinced that I've triumphed, if only in a small way. I return his smile with one of my own, but our grinning contest is interrupted by the waiter who approaches the table to take our order.

While we wait for the food to be served, I ask, "Where have you been living since graduation?"

"I was lucky and got a bed in a house for homeless men. They say I can stay until I get on my feet." Eli seems happy about this, but the words are like a punch in the gut. Life can be very hard for some people.

"And what do you do for work?"

"I got a job landscaping. It pays even better than the carnival." He sucks down his entire glass of water and grins. "I'm real thirsty because today was my first day on the job and I worked my butt off."

"I'm glad you found a job." I'm glad, but I know how I can make his life better—better for both of us. I swallow hard, throw caution to the wind, and ask, "Would you consider coming to stay at my house for the rest of the summer?"

"I can't do that." And with those words, he stands. "Meeting up with you was a bad idea. I'm not here to get stuff, Cooper."

I jump to my feet, grab his hand, and pull him back into his seat. "I, I just want you to know you can lean on me—that I *want* you to lean on me. I told you I was sorry for what I did and—"

"Listen, Cooper, I made a mistake too. I thought we were friends, but we were strangers. Except for one weekend, a couple of drunk kisses, and building a super awesome sand castle on the beach, we don't know each other at all."

"Maybe you're right, but sometimes you just click with a person, and I click with you." I appreciate the way Eli focuses on friendship, yet I can't deny that I'm as attracted to him as I am to Cady. I blow out a breath, because this suddenly makes sense. All of it—friendship and romance—falls into the category of love. And we can choose in which direction we want to take our love for each other.

"I used to call it 'falling into friendship,' back when I first met you and Cady."

"That's a perfect way to say it."

"That's why I said it." He runs his fingers through his amazing curls. "But now I think friendship might need to build up a little slower."

"Maybe." I smile. "You don't have to answer me now. Just consider staying at my house. That's all I ask."

Eli doesn't nod or shake his head. He looks at me with a sweet expression until a few moments later when dinner is served.

I MUST BE AN EXTREMELY impatient person because, as soon as Eli takes his last bite of surf and turf, before we even stop to put down our forks, I ask again. "Will you come and stay with me until the end of the summer?"

We had a nice dinner. Except for the first few minutes, conversation was light, but it was pleasant enough. In other words, Eli didn't fling accusations or hurl insults in my face, which I would have deserved.

"What about your folks? They aren't gonna want some stranger living with them."

I'm one step ahead of him, as I figured he'd ask me this. "My father spends most of his time on the West Coast. And my mother would love to have you stay. Cady used to sleep over all the time and Mom couldn't get enough of her; Mom's a people person." I experience a momentary sting in my throat when I speak Cady's name. I miss her so much. Sometimes I wonder if she's changed as much as I think she has, but the girl I knew would never have left someone like Eli hanging.

"Are you sure?" His question brings me back to the here and now.

"I'm positive."

When he nods, I'm surprised at what I've done. But I'm not disappointed.

cadence

I PLAY MOM'S WORDS OVER and over in my head as I lie in bed.

"I have wonderful news, dear. Bradley is coming home."

She sounded giddy when she said it, as if she couldn't believe the absolute awesomeness of her own words. Mom actually giggled after she told me. I wouldn't have been surprised if she'd broken into song and dance.

I pull the sheets over my head, but the worries still roll in. Dad is bent out of shape at the "wonderful news." Why else would he have snuck down the stairs a few minutes ago to sleep on the couch the way he used to when things were so out of control with Bradley? He remembers that when his son lived at home, he couldn't maintain control of his domain. And as a dominant guy, this fact irks him royally. Dad doesn't have a clue whether everything will spin out of control again when Bradley comes home—neither do I.

"Bradley's coming home," I repeat. No one is listening because I'm alone in my bedroom, but I have nobody to tell big news to anyway—my new friends Cece, Mara, and Trish don't care, and my old friend Cooper has given up on me. Even Daisy shuns me lately.

When Mom told us the big news over dinner, I quickly made my move. I crawled into my shell, although I was sitting at the table with Mom and Dad. In other words, I slipped into my private headspace where I'm safe and asked if I could be excused; my bad excuse was a nasty headache. My protective shell works better when I'm alone, which defeats the purpose of protective shells.

My life is already ninety-five percent ruined. I made my best friend hate me because I was jealous and insecure. I turned my back on Bradley, the only person other than my best friend I've connected with since middle school, and I did it when he needed help the most. And it seems I've turned into a total alcoholic who would have driven Mom's Volvo while intoxicated on several occasions had I not hidden my own keys from myself. I've turned into what I despise. Why not add my prodigal brother's joyous return to my dysfunctional family home to the equation and flush the remainder of my life down the toilet?

I'm still mad at Bradley. He tore Mom and Dad apart and forced me to be the one on whom they hang all of their hopes and dreams. And he left me here alone. I'm angry at him, even as I worry that I might be turning into him. I can't survive more drama like what went down last summer. I'm certain I can't do it without Cooper.

I'm also certain that I'll never fall asleep tonight. I wish I had a bottle of vodka. But all I've got is Daisy, who skulked into my room during my worry fest. She kneads my hipbone mercilessly, and I let her because it's better than nothing.

eli

AFTER DINNER AND HANGING OUT in the restaurant parking lot in his car until late, Cooper dropped me off at the shelter. He wanted to come in and check out my room and say hi to the other guys, but I said no. I don't want him to think of me as a homeless dude—not that I'm ashamed I'm in this situation, because I'm not. But I've bottomed out in life and I don't want Cooper to think of me at my lowest point every time he looks my way.

I should pack my stuff, because we decided that I'll move in with Cooper's family over the weekend, but I don't. I'd wake the other guys for sure. Instead I lie on my bed and relive tonight. It was one of the best nights in my life for one simple reason: Cooper proved I'm worth fighting for. I take a long sip of the bottle of water I took to bed, tuck it under the T-shirt I'm using as a pillow, and close my eyes, expecting to see Cooper's smiling face from when I told him I'd come to stay with him. But instead, I see the face of the person who could make it all perfect, because the three of us fit together like we're the last three pieces in a "kittens in a basket" puzzle.

I see my friend Cady's smirk.

CHAPTER 19

cadence

MOM FLUTTERS AROUND THE KITCHEN, wiping and polishing everything as though Barack Obama is coming to visit. *No, Mom. Your prodigal son returns today from an extended stay at A Better Future Rehabilitation Center of South Florida.*

"Go take a peek at Bradley's bedroom, Cadence." Mom says as she sprays a coconut scented air freshener in the entryway. "I bought him new bedding and curtains—all of it with a tropical theme to remind him of the changes he made at A Better Future Rehab."

"Yeah, I checked it out when I passed his room." I would have needed sunglasses if I'd actually entered his room because the bed set is *bright*. "Way to go, Mom. It will bring him right back to sunny Florida."

She smiles and says, "Dad and Bradley should arrive home from the airport any second now. You'll be here, I hope."

"I have to work at eleven-thirty, so if he doesn't get here in the next ten minutes—"

"Oh, Cadence." She sounds so disappointed, and that's just too damn bad. I'm the one who lived through all the late nights when my frantic parents had to go out searching for Bradley because he missed curfew. And I dealt with all the other kids at school who harassed me because my "loser brother" used illegal substances on school grounds and got caught skipping class on a regular basis. Students and teachers alike would ask me, "Are you *sure* Bradley LaBrie is related to you?" And finally, I suffered when he was carted off to the ER after I found him unconscious in his room one night last August.

I clearly hold some residual resentment toward my twin brother.

"Mom, I'm going to college in a few weeks. And we have tuition to pay, *remember*? I need every hour I can get at my job."

Mom sighs as if I've let her down, which I probably have. After a monumental eye roll, I go to brush my teeth with high hopes that I'll be able to make my sneaky exit before Prince Bradley makes his royal entrance.

It's not my lucky day.

"Oh, Bradley! Welcome home!" Mom exclaims. "The flight from Florida was early? How nice!" *An early flight? When does that happen?* "It's so good to have you back, dear!"

I expect Bradley's voice to sound subdued, maybe even depressed, but he's very upbeat. "I'm glad to be home because I missed drinking coffee and sleeping late and hanging with you guys. Where's Cady?"

"She's brushing her teeth. She has to work today."

My brother is quiet, and then he says, "Work is important. She's got to help earn her college tuition, right?" It could be my imagination, but he sounds disappointed. *Well, that's a crying shame.* "Rehab was a good experience for me. A great one, really. All of us did so much stuff together—lots of physical activities that pushed my body to the max. And we talked about *everything*."

Bradley is rambling. *And* he's absolutely glowing, which I notice when I step into the hallway. Looking at Bradley is like looking in a mirror. We're the spitting image of each other. We're small and, as Cooper used to say, skinny, and we wear our light brown hair exactly the same way—chopped neatly at our matching chins. The big difference between us is that he's tanned and healthy and appears happy, while I'm pale from a long winter and chilly spring, and am very sullen. Although I get how hard rehab must have been, I spit out, "Better Futures Rehab sounds like summer camp."

Mom and Dad gasp, but Bradley pulls me in for an awkward hug. He's not much bigger than me, and for a guy, this makes him tiny, but he's clearly in great shape. "Hey, Cades. It's been a long time, huh?" He kisses my forehead and says, "I missed you too." And then he glances up the hallway. "Where's your other half?"

I don't need to be given the third degree about where Cooper is by my long-lost brother. "Some of us have to work, bro, so if you're in the mood to eat the best meatloaf and mashed potatoes in town with an apple sauce chai, drop by Mad Eats tonight."

I walk out the door without a backward glance. Before I get to the car I hear Bradley inform Mom and Dad that long-distance cycling is his new addiction.

As I WALK FROM THE parking lot to the restaurant, I get a call from Cece. "Big plans tonight, girl. Party at the quarry in Rockland."

"I have to work until four."

"Meet me at The Burger and Dairy Bar at four-thirty. We'll grab a bite to eat and then pick up Mara and Trish and head to the quarry."

"See you then," I say with false enthusiasm. Guilt swells in my chest because I should spend Bradley's first night home from rehab with him. Good thing I keep my swimsuit and a towel in my backpack. I won't have to swing by our house and be reminded by Mom of my callousness.

I'M TOTES BOMBED. *THE LAST thing I should do is jump into a rock quarry filled with water, but somebody's got to do it, right?* I take a running leap off the cliff and am completely shocked by the icy water when I break its surface. I guess I forgot about the water below while I was midair, which sums up the essence of a drunken Cady LaBrie.

As soon as my head pops up, I hear Patrick McCormack's voice. "Did you borrow your grandmother's swimsuit, LaBrie? And like… who even invited you here?"

Drunk or sober, I'm the same girl who has never been comfortable in her own skin, and who chooses to cover up with a one-piece navy blue athletic bathing suit instead of a tiny, polka-dot bikini like all of the other girls wear. And I'm the same social outcast I was in high school.

I swim to the edge of the quarry, find a rock to sit on that's as far as possible from everybody else, and plant my butt until it gets dark. No one comes over to say hello, or ask what's wrong, or anything at all. My new "friends" are too busy laughing and drinking and rubbing shoulders with the other cool kids to notice that I sit alone. Most of me is glad to be alone because these are not my people, anyway.

I have no clue how we'll get back to The Burger and Dairy Bar where I left my car. My only option will be to get a ride with another sloshed partygoer, and this spells S.T.U.P.I.D. Despite the fact that I'm drunk, I know this. And then I'll have to somehow get home from there. I'm screwed in so many ways it isn't funny. On top of all that, I'm going to catch hell from Mom and Dad when I get home because I avoided Bradley when he needed me most. I don't much care—Mom, Dad, and Bradley aren't my people either.

I used to have a person, and he was the perfect best friend. He was my soul mate. I thought we would last forever. And I had a brief, but super-sweet, connection with another boy on a certain well-planned weekend. Maybe he wasn't a soul mate, but that sort of thing takes time.

I blew all that sky-high.

The result? I sit shivering on a rock in my damp, out-of-style swimsuit, enduring sporadic harassment from the *real* cool kids, while trying to figure out how to get back to my unhappy home in one piece.

cooper

MOM WAS INCREDIBLY COOL WHEN I brought home a stranger with a big black duffel bag, totally unannounced, who I referred to as an "old friend," and announced that I'd invited him to move in. Luckily, she has a good sense of people and she could tell that Eli is as good as gold.

The first thing Mom, Eli, and I did was wash, dry, and fold all of his clothes, because they seriously needed it. In other words, everything in his black duffel smelled like a well-used gym bag. We washed the duffel bag too. Then Mom changed the sheets on my bed while Eli and I took turns showering. To cap off the night, the three of us hung out in the living room and watched *Naked and Afraid* on the Discovery Channel. Before we went upstairs to go to bed, Mom hugged Eli right after she hugged me.

He came dangerously close to crying. And so did I, but a convenient coughing fit prevented it.

It was a good night. The only thing missing wasn't a thing at all. It was a person.

It was Cady.

"THIS IS WAY MORE COMFORTABLE than when we slept in the tent," I say when Eli and I are stretched out side-by-side on my bed staring at the solar system stickers I stuck on the ceiling when I was seven years old.

"No doubt. But think of those folks on *Naked and Afraid* sleeping out in the open in the woods with all of those bugs." Eli shudders enough to rock the bed, and then I do. I have experience surviving hungry bugs—from the first night of the bucket-list challenge, when Cady and I slept under the stars. He adds, "I'm happy it never came to that for me."

"Me too. And I wish Cady could be here," I admit. "I don't know why she's not. We're just *apart*, you know?"

"Not really. Maybe we should try to figure out why she's gone."

"Maybe tomorrow... or the next day." I still get tired when I think of Cady. I get pissed off and confused and worn out—just plain tired.

And anybody would figure I'd be horny as hell, lying in bed beside the most gorgeous guy I've ever seen. But instead of grabbing him, I listen to him. Eli has more common sense than Cady and me—put together and multiplied by ten.

CHAPTER 20

cadence

WHEN I COME INTO THE kitchen, I go straight to the coffee maker where Bradley's parked while he sips from the Grouchy Smurf mug I got him for Christmas last year when he *was* actually grouchy and not so freshly inspired by life.

I'm disconcerted, because I have no clue who brought me home last night. If I had to guess, I'd say that the car is still parked at The Burger and Dairy Bar. If it's not, I've managed to lose Mom's Volvo and I don't think I can put a positive spin on that. I hope caffeine will soothe my aching head and give me the energy to get into the shower, which will, in theory, provide motivation to figure out where I left the car. I pour myself a deep mug of black coffee.

"You're hung over." Bradley can either smell it or see it or sense it with his extrasensory addiction-intuition that he gained at his fancy rehab.

"Shut up," I say, suddenly a twelve-year-old. Or maybe *I'm* the Grouchy Smurf now.

"I'm not going to shut up, Cady. I give a shit about you." I'm pretty sure he's studying me, that his eyes are full to the brim with tears of heartfelt concern. But I can't say for sure, as I refuse to look directly at him.

I sigh, roll my eyes so hard it hurts, and leave the kitchen with my coffee mug in hand. I don't want breakfast anyway. I'd probably barf it up, because maybe I *am* slightly hung over.

❀ ❀ ❀

eli

I SEE HIM COMING FROM three telephone poles away. He waves before I can make out the fake smile on his face. Anyone could see it—Cooper's a hurting unit. Not that he's ever come right out and told me, "Dude, losing Cady broke my heart." But he doesn't need to. I know what it's like to lose folks. I know what it's like to long for them. I'm an expert on this, so I know.

He's been great to me, though. Every day Cooper drives me to the Baron Brothers headquarters in the morning and picks me up after work. Every night he helps me make lunch for the next day. He shares his bedroom and his mom with me. What Cooper's done for me isn't small potatoes; nobody's ever looked after me this well. I know this is a sorry thing to say, but it's also true. So, I want to help him find the same happy spirit he had when he was with Cady. This means we need to get back together with her.

I hop into the passenger seat of his car.

"How was work, dude?" Cooper asks.

"Hot as heck," I reply.

"I got you a Gatorade." He glances at the drink holder.

"Blue. My favorite." Cady's return to his life could mean that I'd be out. I swallow hard. "Thanks."

His sad smile grips me by my belly and squeezes. I don't want to lose Cooper. I don't think I could lose him and bounce back too good. I got more of a real life now than I ever had: a house without wheels and a couple of friendly faces in it. I want to keep these things.

"How about *I* take *you* out to dinner tonight?" Seems like the least I can do.

"You're saving your money, dude. Remember?" Cooper adds, "Plus Mom's making tacos. It's Dad's recipe so it's gonna be damned tasty."

I want to touch his arm.

I want to laugh. I want to cry.

But all I do is shrug and say, "Sounds real good."

❀ ❀ ❀

cadence

He's everywhere I am. I seriously have a stalker. I'd call the police, but I can't because he's my stupid brother.

"What are you doing here?" I ask when I step off the front doorstep of Mad Eats and notice Bradley balancing on his mountain bike on the walkway in front of the building.

"I'm looking out for my sister."

"Don't bother. I'm fine."

"Cady, you aren't fine. I see the signs. I lived the signs." He sighs and extends an arm to me. "We need to talk."

Without a thought, my hands go to my hips and I bend just enough to get the satisfying breath I'm going to need. "I lived

170

the signs right beside you, Bradley. I sat by and watched as you tore our family apart, so excuse me if I don't spill my guts to you upon request." I storm past him on my way to the car.

Bradley's determined. He swings his leg over the crossbar and pushes his bike as he follows behind me. "How come you never hang out with Cooper anymore?"

"That's none of your business." I unlock the car and open the driver's door.

"Tell me where you're off to tonight."

I don't reply, but I notice that his gray-blue eyes are exactly like mine, minus the bitterness.

"Come with *me* tonight, Cady. I need somebody to go running with, and you're one of the only people who runs fast enough." He laughs. "I need a challenge. Dad always lags way behind."

I don't laugh or smile or even acknowledge that he spoke. All I say is, "You're on your own tonight, Bradley."

I slide into the driver's seat and head to The Burger and Dairy Bar to meet up with my new BFF, Cece.

CHAPTER 21

cooper

WITH ELI IN MY LIFE, it's like having the brother I always dreamed of. We sleep in my full-size bed together, and it's not awkward. Once three nights passed and we hadn't grabbed each other and gotten busy, the pressure I felt for us to be "lovers" disappeared. Friendship offers freedom. It allows a safe distance between us so we can appreciate each other better. And Eli and I are on the same page—we want to be friends more than lovers. I can tell by the way he looks at me, *with* trust and *without* stress.

Maybe sometimes I still want to kiss him, but it's an urge I control.

The more I think about it, the more I'm convinced that this is the reason Cady and I aren't friends anymore. We were too gutless to accept that we had feelings for each other. And when she got the picture that I wanted her for a friend rather than a girlfriend, she decided it would hurt less if she left. But I don't know any of this for sure. I never asked her how she felt.

We should have talked about it, but instead we pretended that the only important thing was a meaningless bucket list. I could have told her I wanted something *else* with her, but not something less. Now it's too late.

I focus all of my friendship energy on Eli now. I managed to switch my shifts to days, so I get up at six with Eli and drive him to his landscaping job in Ellis by seven, grab coffee and get to my job at eight thirty, and I'm off in time to pick him up at five. Eli isn't afraid of hard work, which I also respect. He landscapes full time for Baron Brothers, and over the weekends he helps deliver furniture for The Sugar Street Home Store.

"Hey, dude. They kept you late tonight," I say when Eli comes out of the Baron Brothers office.

"Had to stick around until the bitter end if I wanted to get my paycheck." He waves a white envelope, hops into the car, and tosses his dusty cooler in the back seat. "Sorry I made you wait."

"Not a problem, dude. And tonight's a library night, right?" Eli has lived with me for almost two weeks, and we haven't yet studied for his GED. It's important, though, and I'm not going to let it slide, so tonight's the night.

Instead of eagerness, a strange expression crosses Eli's face. He seems a little worried, but more depressed. "I guess." He rubs his face with dirty hands. "I kinda thought Cady was gonna study with us, too."

"I can't do much about that—haven't heard from her in weeks." I refuse to dwell on this topic because it hurts. "Let's put our checks in the bank and go home for showers and dinner before we head out to the library. Mom's making shepherd's pie—Dad's recipe."

This news makes Eli smile.

cadence

CECE BLEW ME OFF AGAIN. When I got to her house and knocked at the front door, her mother answered wearing a guilty expression. "Oh, dear, I'm so sorry, but you just missed Cece. She has a date tonight with Darrell Walker. He was a starter on the Wellington High School football team last year, you know." *Nice, but Cece's date's elite athletic status doesn't make being blown off even an ounce more fun.*

"Thanks, ma'am." I'm tempted to ask Mrs. Tucker to give Cece a message for me and then flip the bird at her, but Mrs. Tucker doesn't deserve that treatment. And to be honest, I don't much care that I've been dumped again. I don't like Cece; she's so self-obsessed it's practically intolerable. What I *do* like is to drink until I can't think, and it's easy to do at Cece's house.

I consider asking if I can come in and help myself to their well-stocked liquor cabinet. When I drink I forget that Cooper's gone, and my new best friend couldn't care less about me if she tried, and I used Eli as if he were toilet paper, and my brother is one hundred percent right about me heading down the wrong path. But instead of begging for booze, I shrug like I don't care and trot down the steps as if being dumped again is no big deal. Then I drive straight to Macey's Liquor Store in Wellington, which is without doubt a stupid move.

"Will you buy me a bottle, sir? I've got a twenty, and you can keep the change." I stand outside and ask no less than ten customers—some of whom were probably on the PTA with my mother—until finally a young woman with a little boy either takes pity on me or needs some extra cash. I end up with a very cheap bottle of vodka.

Whatever. Whatever. Whatever. Whatever.

I say this one simple word to myself over and over as I drive home. And when I get there, I stuff the bottle into my backpack and head on foot to the only destination I can think of where I'll be able to drink as much of this bottle as I can get down, completely undisturbed. *Whatever.*

Nobody would ever suspect I'd booze it up there.

I laugh out loud because I came up with the perfect escape. As I slowly get bombed, I'll be able to do a little reading about pyramids. It will remind me of a better day.

cooper

THE LIBRARY IS PRACTICALLY EMPTY, because who on earth goes to the library on a Friday night in late July? Not a single soul our age, from what I can see. But I'm cool with it this way.

Before we start GED prep, Eli wants to show me some of his favorite books about pyramids. It's embarrassing, but I don't have a clue how to find a book at a library anymore. I vaguely remember something about the Dewey decimal system from grade school, but I haven't seen the inside of the Wellington Public Library since I was ten. If I want a book, I go onto Amazon. com and order it like the rest of the world does—well, the rest of the world except for the six or so old people scattered around on stiff wooden chairs and cozy corner loveseats in the stuffy library tonight. Eli and I increase the total number of quirky Friday night library-dwellers to eight.

"I'm gonna check and see if my favorite book is here." He seems to know exactly where it's shelved.

"You've been to this library before?" I ask.

"Yup. I been to about every library near every fairground in New England, and this one's not too far from where we set up in Ellis," Eli replies as he studies the shelf. "I love this certain book that takes you on a walk through the pyramids of the world. I don't see it, though." He sounds disappointed, but grabs a few other books. "These are okay, but the best one is missing."

I follow him as he leads me to the back corner of the library. He knows this place inside and out.

"A super soft leather couch is hidden back here, and almost nobody ever sits on it. It's real comfortable, Cooper."

When we arrive at the couch, however, somebody is already there.

"Cady…" I don't remember her ever coming to the library before. Neither of us did; we did research on our laptop computers in my bedroom or at her dining room table. When Cady turns around, her eyes roll back. She quickly refocuses.

Eli walks around the couch so he stands in front of her. "You're reading my favorite book," he says and smiles.

A book about pyramids is open on Cady's lap. "Issa great book." Her voice is too loud, and her grin is wider than I've ever seen it. Something is definitely wrong.

I jump over the back of the couch and plop beside her.

"Careful, Murphy, ya don't wanna s-s-spill my drinkie now, do ya?"

An open bottle of vodka pokes out of her backpack. Almost half of it is gone. I check around the couch for the cap and ask, "Where did you get this?" I find the cover on the floor and screw it onto the bottle.

"I gots friends in l-low p-places," she stutters.

I never knew I could be thrilled to see somebody and, at the same time, so pissed off, worried, and shocked. For a minute, all I can do is sit and stare at her.

But Eli seems to know just what to do. He kneels in front of Cady and closes the book gently. "Cooper, tonight may not be the right night to study for my GED."

"Good call." I stand, sling Cady's backpack over my shoulder, and help her to her feet. "You're coming with us." And suddenly I'm acting on autopilot. First, I push aside the intense relief at seeing Cady when we haven't had contact in weeks. If I want to help her, I need to put my emotions on hold.

Cady stands and staggers to the other side of the leather couch. "Gotta pee." She laughs too loud, grabs Eli's face between her fingers and thumb, and turns it toward her. "You get my meaning? I gotta *whiz*." She finds this unspeakably funny and breaks into a fit of giggles.

"I know where the closest bathroom is," Eli replies. He puts his arm under one of Cady's shoulders, I put mine around her waist on the other side, and we help her down an aisle that's way too narrow for three people.

Miraculously, we don't knock over a bookshelf and manage to get her to the bathroom. When Cady leaves us to go inside the ladies' room, I ask Eli, "How are we going to get her out of the library without the librarians noticing? Some of them are friends of her mother." I can't let her parents find out about this, although she really needs to be caught by someone.

"I also know a back way out of here."

"Of course, you do," I mumble, unsurprised.

A few minutes later we go into the bathroom to get Cady, as she doesn't come out on her own. We find her curled into a tight ball on the floor beside the wastebasket. She gazes at her fingernails, which are painted for the first time since I've known her. She flashes them in my face when I squat beside her. "Spent a little girly time with Cece and Trish and Mara. They always wanna do shit like paint their nails. You likey?"

I don't like dark purple nails on her because it isn't Cady, so I don't answer.

"You likey?" She asks again and louder, and then she asks Eli, "*You* like my Metallic Plum fingernails, don't you?"

"Be quiet, Cady!" I hiss before we take her to Eli's secret exit.

Once we're outside, I look around the parking lot for Cady's mother's Volvo wagon.

"I walked here," she says, reading my mind. "Got my booze and drove home and then snuck out and walked here." She giggles as if she just farted in church. "*Onward, Cady—to the library to get bombed!* That's what I said to myself."

"Good choice in not driving," I reply. I don't want to consider Cady behind the wheel in her current condition.

Eli and I help Cady to my car. He climbs into the back seat with her. "Maybe we should get her a cup of coffee," he suggests, sizing up her condition.

"First we need to figure out what to tell Mrs. LaBrie." After years of dealing with Cady's overprotective mother, I've grown adept in placating the woman. Still on autopilot, I pull my phone out of my pocket, lean against the driver's side door, and dial. "Hi, Mrs. LaBrie. Yeah, it's Cooper… Oh, I've been working way too many hours, so I haven't had any free time to drop by…

Bradley's home? Uh, yeah, Cady mentioned that… Well, sure, I'll stop by and see him next week. Anyway, I just wanted to let you know I'm gonna pick up Cady at the library tonight. She said she wants to talk."

In the backseat, Cady is either asleep or unconscious against Eli's shoulder.

"No… I don't think anything's wrong. Maybe she's bummed out about us going to different colleges soon. And I wanted to call you because Cady forgot her phone, and she's in the bathroom. And we're gonna rush off to a movie, so we don't miss the previews." I lie easily to Mrs. LaBrie because, over the past four years, every time Cady and I wanted to do something her mother wouldn't approve of, even if it was just something stupid and safe like going to a late night fondue festival at a local restaurant, we had to come up with stories so she'd let Cady go.

The Midnight Belgian Chocolate Fondue Festival—last December's holiday party for the staff of Mad Eats—was epic! Arrival time was ten p.m., which is Cady's usual curfew. All of the guests had to bring unusual food items that would have their flavor "enhanced by a swim in a Belgian chocolate fountain," which is what it said on Cady's fancy paper invitation. And Dad gave us his secret recipe for gingerbread shortbread, which was the chocolate-dipped hit of the party. Cady was proud of this, in addition to being happily infused with high quality chocolate. She looked so damn adorable with a messy chocolate moustache after she wrestled with a tall stalk of Savory Choc-Broc, chocolate-coated oven-roasted broccoli.

Cady has always been game for any kind of fun that's rated G. Too bad we had to tell her mother that she had to work the event, so attendance was mandatory. But we never got into trouble, and that's how we gradually earned Mrs. LaBrie's trust.

"I'll get her home early tomorrow, then. And say hi to Bradley for me."

I end the call, slip inside the car, and glance into the back seat to confirm that Cady has passed out. She's sprawled, semi-upright, on top of Eli.

"Now to smuggle her into my house," I say.

Eli nods and eases Cady's head to his lap. "We can make her coffee."

"Or let her sleep it off."

MOM IS CONVENIENTLY OUT OF the house when we get home, so Eli and I carry Cady down the hall to my room. We place her on her belly in the middle of my bed.

"Now what?" I ask.

Eli knows what to do in situations where I'm clueless. We tag-team well. "I'd say we let her sleep. And when she wakes up we get her to drink lots of water. The coffee can wait."

CADY DOESN'T WAKE UNTIL THE middle of the night.

"Oh, my God!" she shouts and bolts upright. Eli springs from the chair he fell asleep on, and I sit up beside her on the bed. "Mom's going to think I died! Oh, God!" Then she grabs her head and says it again, this time in a lower tone. "Oh, God..."

Eli takes a bottle of water from the desk and opens it. "Drink," he tells her firmly.

"Are you gonna hurl?" I ask. It's an indelicate, but important, question.

She sucks down half the bottle and shakes her head. "I don't think so… maybe…" She burps. "I don't know. What time is it? My mother's going to have kittens—"

"No worries, Cades. I called your mom earlier. Everything's cool. I told her I was gonna pick you up at the library and take you to a movie, and that you planned to stay here tonight."

Eli adds, "Because you wanted to *talk*." It's obvious what he wants to do.

Cady looks at Eli. "What are *you* doing here?"

"Right now, I'm opening a bottle of Advil so you can take a couple and not have a worse headache next time you wake up." He seems to think that Cady needs more sleep before we try to talk. I trust him on this.

"No, I mean, what are you doing *here*, with Cooper?"

I answer this one. "We bumped into each other at the home store one night when I was at work. Eli's been staying here ever since."

"You're boyfriends now?" Strangely, it's not an accusation. It's just a question.

Eli and I shake our heads. "It's not like that," we say in unison.

"What do you mean?" Cady rubs her temples and groans. Then she takes a better look at Eli. "Your earrings—"

"They're gone." He doesn't explain. "Now go back to sleep."

She nods once and flops back on the bed. "Thanks, you guys, for, you know."

Yeah, we know.

"When we wake up, I also want to…" She fades away.

When she wakes up, she's going to want to talk. I want to talk. And Eli has a stake in this, as well.

CHAPTER 22

"Ohhh…"

Although I'm still half asleep, I hear Eli say, "You're never gonna drink booze again, right, Cady?" At some point over the course of the night, Eli moved onto the bed with Cady and me. We ended up lying sideways across the bed, on top of the covers. I'm at the head of the bed, sprawled across the pillows, and Eli is stretched along the foot. Cady is curled into a ball, writhing and moaning, between us.

All she says is, "Water."

I grab the bottle of water that waits on my night table and hand it to her.

After she finishes it, she asks, "What time is it?"

I glance at my phone on the night table. "Six in the morning."

"Can I borrow a toothbrush?"

"You can have a new one. You know where we keep the spares."

It takes a lot of effort, but she drags her ass off the bed and goes out into the hallway in the direction of the bathroom.

"Think she wants to talk?" Eli asks.

"I think she needs to." I look out my bedroom window to see if my mother's car is in the driveway. "Mom's already gone to the gym so we can make coffee and talk at the kitchen table."

"I'll put on the coffee." Eli slips out of the room.

When Cady comes back, she heads right to my bureau, pulls off her plain white T-shirt, and replaces it with one of mine, which hangs to her thighs. "You've already seen this show," she mumbles and pulls off her joggers. "Number one on the stupid bucket list."

It seems as if The Weekend Bucket List happened a lifetime ago. I stand beside her in front of my bureau and pull my smallest pair of Nike shorts out of the bottom drawer. "Here. Put these on and come to the kitchen."

She nods, apparently obedient this morning.

The coffee is already brewing when I get to the kitchen. Eli leans against the counter with his arms folded over his bare chest, a mug in one hand, looking like a model for the Mr. Coffee company. Cady shows up less than a minute later.

"How's your head, Cady?" Eli asks.

"It's been better."

He grabs two mugs from the cabinet over the counter and fills them with coffee. "Sit down, and I'll get the milk and sugar." After he places the mugs on the kitchen table, Eli goes to the refrigerator and takes out the carton of milk. I'm glad to see him so at home in my kitchen. Maybe in some small way I've given him *something*. Not something huge and amazing—just a little bit of normal life and some comfort in a real home. A little break from being a "globe-trotter," as he often calls himself. Once he puts the milk, sugar bowl, and spoons on the table, he grabs his own cup of coffee, and we all sit.

cadence

183

"BRADLEY'S HOME FROM REHAB." I haven't seen Cooper in weeks and this is what I lead with. I'm either completely clueless or a genius in the art of distraction.

"I heard," he replies.

"I hope he's ready to live among the societal impure because Mom will lose it if he gets carted away in an ambulance again." Fear of the conversation we so badly need to have bubbles up in me. I'll talk about anything to avoid the subject at hand.

"What are his plans?" Cooper asks.

"Bradley's plan is to go to summer school at Wellington High so he can brush up on his classes. He wants to go for his GED at the end of the summer."

Cooper nods. "That's similar to Eli's plan."

Eli clears his throat. "Does your belly hurt?"

"A little. Plus, I'm sweating buckets." That pretty much covers my physical symptoms.

"The AC is on," Cooper points out. "You should be cool."

"Well, I'm hot as hell." We get nowhere fast, obsessing over my body temperature. "I… I don't know if I'm ready to talk about the serious stuff."

"You're never gonna be ready, Cades. Let's just get it over with right now. I'm sick of missing you and I'm done being pissed off at you."

"Tell me how you *really* feel, Coop." At times like this, sarcasm rules.

Eli suggests, "Maybe we should start with… I think we need to start with why you were in the library last night, drunk off your, well, you know. You were pretty wasted."

"I hang out a lot with this girl from high school, Cece Tucker. We like to go to parties and drink. It's not a criminal act." *Even if it actually is.*

"But you weren't at a party, Cady," Eli points out. "You were drinking alone in the library."

He's right. I'm not just a drunken loser; I'm a drunken *reject* loser. "Maybe I just felt like having a couple drinks last night." It's a weak excuse, but it's all I've got.

"If you don't want to talk about *why* you were drinking alone at the library last night, then maybe we should talk about what's going on between us." Cooper usually beats around the bush, but not today. "Or, *not* going on between us."

So I steal a line from Cooper's playbook. "You go first."

"I will, I will, Cady. I want to get things straight… Our relationship is too important to screw up any more than it already is." He gulps. *Not good.* "On that Saturday night, the night we kissed… well, you need to understand that I *was* attracted to you. And not just because of the kiss. It was because of how we are together, or how we've been since we were fourteen years old in PE class."

"You *were* attracted to me?" I ask, noting the past tense. I suspect a "but" is coming and brace myself.

"But…" Cooper starts, but pauses as Eli rises to his feet.

"Maybe I don't need to be here for this; it's private, and it's not about me."

"I want you to stay, Eli," Cooper insists. "You're part of this."

Eli looks at me to check if it's okay that he stays. "You don't have to go," I tell him. I'm not scared of him anymore because I somehow suspect that he's not my enemy. Whoever makes

185

Cooper happier is who he should be with, and I'll accept it if that person is Eli.

As soon as Eli is again settled in his seat, Cooper continues. "But even though we were attracted to each other, and maybe still are…" He lays his hand over his heart like he plans to take an oath. "…I knew after we kissed that I love how it *already is* with us. I want friendship with you, Cady."

At his rejection, my eyes fill with tears. Cooper can't stand it when I cry, but this morning I can't control it. "You want Eli instead of me, don't you?"

He shakes his head. "What I want of him is *his* friendship."

"You don't love *either* of us?" I'm nothing but a bundle of questions with a hangover.

"No, Cady. I love *both* of you… as my two closest friends."

Although the world is still blurry through my tears, it's obvious Eli is touched by Cooper's unexpected declaration of love. He doesn't seem to think that the platonic love Cooper feels is in any way less than if he were head over heels in love with us, as he sits across from me smiling sweetly. "I'm sorry, Coop, but I don't get it."

Cooper nods and says, "What we have is so much better than being lovers."

Even as I cry over Cooper's romantic rejection, I agree with everything he's said so far about friendship, which I realize is crazy. I've never been certain of what I wanted to happen between Cooper and me, but I still caused so much pain because I was afraid of a rejection so he could be with a boy. Maybe rejection was never on his mind. "I thought what we had together was fragile, Cooper, and maybe… maybe it wasn't fragile at all."

Cooper shakes his head. "It's strong, Cady. Our friendship is strong enough to let Eli in."

We glance at Eli, who stares into his cup of coffee. "The last thing I want is to break up your friendship," he says, almost too quietly to hear.

It's my turn to be brave. "I'm the one ruining everything. Not you, Eli."

He looks up at me. "How do *you* feel about *me*?"

"Well, I'm glad you were my first kiss," I admit.

Eli's cheeks redden. "I'm glad you were mine too."

Cooper and I catch eyes. Eli is as new at this type of declaration, *and* at kissing people, as we are.

"I want to spend more time with you, Eli. You're a very kind and open person and you make me laugh. Before, I thought three was too many people to be best friends with," I add. "And I figured that only two people could fall in love. Either way, one of us would be left out, and I didn't want it to be me."

"Know what I think?"

Cooper and I look at Eli. "We won't know unless you tell us," Cooper says with a smirk.

"I think you guys care more about the rules than you do about people." We must look offended, because he quickly adds, "Don't worry so much about what you're *supposed* to do and let's do what feels right."

This kid is a genius. Maybe he seems naïve, but he understands more about life than Cooper and I put together.

"I think you have the right idea, Eli," Cooper says.

"I really, badly, want another chance with you guys." Without a thought, I let the truth slip. To hear this plea come out of my mouth shocks me, and by Cooper's open-mouthed, wide-eyed expression, it has caught him off guard too.

But Eli just nods. "Of course, Cady. That's what friends do." He squeezes my hand, and then I squeeze Cooper's.

I have no idea how I got to be the lucky girl to share a bond of friendship with these two amazing guys, but I am and I plan to enjoy it.

cooper

I'M RELIEVED TO HAVE CADY back in my life and to have Eli here with us, although I'm still slightly overwhelmed. It's as if I have my cake and can eat it too, which is supposed to be a big no-can-do in life. But the three of us talked it over. We can make our own rules for our friendship, now that the pressure to be "more" to each other is gone. I don't really understand why being lovers is considered being "more" than being friends. Maybe I'll never get it. To me, friendship is huge. It's everything.

Mom's gonna be home from the gym at any minute and the three of us need to spend more time alone.

"Let's go for a ride," I suggest. "We can go to Tamarack Lake. It's still early and the summer camp won't have opened for the day. Nobody will be around."

"*Hello,* Cooper. I'm wearing *your* clothes, and the jury is still out as to whether I'm going to barf." Cady's still got her smart mouth. I wouldn't want her any other way.

"And if we go somewhere, I'm gonna need to put a shirt on."

Eli's right. I'm the only one dressed for public viewing, so I even the score. I rip off my bright yellow Pikachu T-shirt, drop it on the kitchen floor, and expose my freckled torso. "Let's go just as we are."

It's surprisingly easy to motivate our scruffy little gang to head out the door and pile into the Honda. Cady hops in the back seat, which allows Eli to climb in up front. It's a small gesture that shows Cady accepts that we're three friends on equal ground.

We roll down all the windows, open the sunroof, and, although it's closer to a rainy day than a sunny one, let the damp wind blow in. I drive as fast as I dare on the wet roads in the direction of the town beach.

It's a dreary day, and, aside from a single dog walker and his furry companion, we're alone on the soggy sand. The last time the three of us sank our feet in wet sand was the night when we checked number eight—"run naked on a beach"—off the bucket list. This time, we race along the shore, smiling and shouting to each other with the simple relief that we're together. When we reach the end of the beach, where No Trespassing signs warn us that we can go no farther or we'll be on some rich family's private lakefront property, Cady pulls us down so that we're a tangle of bodies on the sand. And we break into laughter—the pure, fearless kind.

I want to freeze time. This is so good.

CHAPTER 23

eli

I RAKE LEAVES FROM A planter that hasn't been cleaned out in years. This gives me plenty of time to think. What's going on with Cady, Cooper, and me is a whole lot to take in. I'm scared it's not real, but then I'm also scared it *is* real, because if it's real I *need* it to go on forever. The summer's almost at its end, and then my two best friends will move on to bigger and better things than a three-way friendship with a guy like me. Cady and Cooper have futures with colleges and smart people's jobs and mega-success. All I've got is the will to work my ass off in jobs nobody else wants.

"Time for lunch, Stanley. You're off the clock for twenty minutes." The site manager interrupts my thinking, and I come back to earth. I lean the rake against the house and head for the shade tree where I left my cooler at break time. I drop onto my butt in the grass and pull out the turkey and cheese sandwich Cooper made for me last night along with a Ziploc bag of chocolate chip cookies Cady brought me from Mad Eats.

My back against the tree, I take a bite of my sandwich. I let my brain have one last thought: This summer friendship isn't gonna end well for me. So I'm gonna enjoy it while it lasts.

❈ ❈ ❈

cooper

WHAT'S GOOD WITH CADY, ELI, and me gets better and better.

Although Cady couldn't manage to change all her work hours to daytime, we've still been able to find plenty of time to spend together. Earlier tonight, Eli and I came home from work and showered, and then we sped right over to Mad Eats so Cady could serve us old-fashioned macaroni and cheese, tonight's special. Mad Eats' Homestyle Mac and Cheese with Maple Bacon is better than Dad's macaroni and cheese, not that I plan on telling him. I wouldn't want to crush the man.

We sit in her section, and I notice that some of Cady's quasi-friends from high school are seated two tables to our right. I'm pretty sure that Cady hung out with them during the weeks we were apart because Cece Tucker has called her cell phone every time we've been together over the past few days. Cady always lets the calls go to voice mail.

"Ah, look here—it's the arrival of the loser contingent from Cady's past existence."

"Those are some mighty big words, coming from you, Cecelia," I reply. "I'm impressed." I don't normally look for trouble, but I try to stay ready in case it comes looking for me. Eli's jaw drops; he's never seen me act this way. But Eli's hot, so I'm sure he never got accused of being a card-carrying member of the loser brigade, as Cady and I did all through school. People like us learn to live ready.

Cece sits with this girl named Trish, who was the prettiest girl in the Wellington High School senior class if you go for blonde hair, blue eyes, perfect makeup, and expensive clothes that always match. She's not as nasty as Cece, but then she isn't the sharpest tool in the shed either.

"Hey, Cooper. Who's your gorgeous friend?" Trish *is* smart enough to recognize that I sit across from the best-looking guy in town—and the hottest guy in the whole state if you go for the sultry Savior-of-Humankind type.

I admit that Eli looks more stunning than usual tonight, but then he's always drool-worthy when he's wearing white. In his loose, white polo shirt and tan cargo shorts, he channels Ralph Lauren, which is right up these mean girls' alley. He sends me a "who, me?" glance, but doesn't wait for a nod. He's too busy flagging down Cady. The guy may be an eleven on a hotness scale of one to ten, but he doesn't seem to have the first clue about it.

Cady comes to our table balancing a tray with two glasses of ice water. "Hi, guys." She places the glasses on the table. "I'm only on the clock for another hour, and then the night is ours. Got big plans for us tonight?"

"Escaping from the in-crowd is first on my agenda," I mumble, and then elbow-point at Cece and Trish.

Cady glances at them. "Yeah, escaping them is a top priority."

"Who's your friend, Cady?" Cece calls, her eyes on Eli.

"This is Eli… Eli Stanley." Cady only a half-introduces him. She doesn't tell Eli the names of the girls who are looking at him like he's dessert.

"OMG, Cady. Are you're *dating* that hottie?" Trish exclaims. "You bitch!"

"He must be the reason you dumped us this week. I'd dump you, too, if I could get horizontal with Eli." Cece's smile is wicked. "Now we know *what*… I mean, *who* you've been doing instead of hanging out with us. Smart girl."

"It's not… exactly… like that, Cece." Cady is again evasive. Maybe she's worried that Eli may want to date Cece or Trish.

"Well, way to go, Cady, because he's adorbs. When he gets bored with you, send him my way." Cece looks directly at me. "But I'd suggest you guard Eli from your high school BFF. Cooper Murphy will try to steal him from you."

"Cece, cut it out. I'll be right over to your table." Cady doesn't defend my honor, but it isn't such a big deal. I guess.

I glance at Eli, who is biting his lower lip with confusion, as if he doesn't understand why Cady didn't tell Cece to take a hike. He doesn't understand; things don't work that way in a small town. You bow down to your superiors, or you live to regret it. Cady has clearly learned the ropes since graduation.

The only other option is that she's still worried about the possibility of losing our new friend to Cece and Trish's charms. I don't think she should worry, though. Eli is too genuine a person to fall for girls who care more about the shade of their fingernail polish than how to be a decent human being.

"What do you guys want for dinner?" Cady asks with a grin. I can feel Cece's eyes on us, but high school is over and she isn't my problem anymore. Cady pulls a notepad out of the back pocket of her jeans. "I'm ready when you are."

"I've got a craving for Mad Eats Mac and Cheese," I say.

"Cooper says it can't be beat, so I'm gonna go with the same thing."

"I'll bring you a couple of cokes, too." Cady jots it all on her notepad and then looks at us with a serious expression. "Don't pay attention to Trish and Cece. I can handle them."

To be honest, I've never seen Cady "handle" anybody except Bradley, Eli, and me, but still I nod. She walks over to her friends and speaks to them in a low voice. Then she takes their bill and rips it up. "Remember, you promised to head out of here without a single word to those guys."

Cady's actually bribing the mean girls to leave us alone. *My hero*—forgive me if I don't bat my eyelashes. Cadence LaBrie is a strange breed. But maybe this is how she looks out for us.

Eli's puzzled. "Who are those girls?"

"Do you remember the popular girls in your high school?" I answer him with another question. "Girls who think their shit don't stink?"

"Sure do."

"Well, that's who they are."

Eli tilts his head. "But you guys aren't in high school anymore. Why do they matter to Cady?"

"It's just how things are, dude." Time to change the subject. "Anyway, let's decide what to do with Cady tonight when she gets out of work."

He rests his chin in his hands.

"Should we study for the GED? The library's open until eleven," I suggest.

"Thought maybe we'd go to a drive-in movie tonight. I never been to one." Eli kicks my foot under the table. "We can study tomorrow."

"How about we compromise. We can study until nine and go to the drive-in afterward."

I love it when Eli laughs, especially when I'm the one who makes it happen. "I can live with that."

I join in the laughter and don't even notice when Cece and Trish leave.

cadence

WE PUT THE FRONT SEATS down as far as they'll go and then crawl into the back of Cooper's Honda Civic. It's a tight squeeze for three, but this makes it more fun. Cooper sits in the middle and holds the popcorn. To be honest, I have no idea what movie we'll be seeing and zero interest in popcorn. I'm just happy to be here. My relief at reuniting with Cooper, and getting this chance to build a friendship with Eli, hasn't diminished.

I learned something important from The Weekend Bucket List: Once you take a step forward in life, you can't un-take it. So maybe I started drinking on that weekend, but I've given it up since we've been back together. "To check off number six, I got drunk for the very first time. And it was much easier to go drinking the next time, and easier the next."

It's a random comment, but Cooper agrees. "That's how habits form."

Eli echoes, "Number six..." but neither of us explains.

"I stopped drinking because I don't need it... and I never want to end up where Bradley is," I add. He's an addict—alone at our house night and day. And he's not even a high school graduate when he should be.

"Maybe we should have invited him to the movies with us tonight," Eli says.

I shake my head. I'm scared of closeness with Bradley. I lost so much when I lost my brother to alcohol and drugs. I won't let that pain happen again. "Or maybe not."

When the movie starts, it draws Cooper and Eli's attention to the big screen, but I'm still submerged in deep thought.

I don't plan to lose this friendship the way I lost my relationship with Bradley. A memory of a different movie night pops into my head. Bradley and I hadn't even invited our school friends to the pizza party Mom had set up at the Nickelodeon Retro Pizza Cinema when we turned twelve. It had been, by our request, a private party—just the four LaBries and a double feature of *Grease* and *Flashdance*. But the best part of the night was afterward, when Bradley and I made an epic fort of blankets in our living room between the two couches. We sat inside, and by the dim glow of a flashlight, shared a half gallon of chocolate peanut butter ice cream with two spoons and zero bowls.

My eyes sting with the bittersweet memory and I promise myself never to take Cooper and Eli for granted again. But Bradley… when I think about him my heart sinks.

I ignore the movie and focus on Cooper and Eli. What I've got with these guys is so good. I know Cooper's sense of humor and the way his mind works inside and out, and likewise, he knows just about everything about me. But the addition of Eli's sweet openness to our friendship glosses over every rough edge and fills in the blank space that separated Cooper and me before.

Three is the right number for us.

CHAPTER 24

eli

I BOUGHT A CALENDAR, BUT I didn't hang it on Cooper's bedroom wall. I don't leave it sitting out on his desk either. It's a private calendar, just for me, so I keep it in my duffel bag under the bed.

The only months I care about on the calendar are July and August. The days in July are mostly all crossed off with big red Xs. We only have some of August left.

At the end of August everything will change. Cady and Cooper head off to college. And I'll turn into a traveling man again, I suppose. No more home, no more friends who are more like my family.

I try not to think about when Mom officially left home, but I right now can't help it. It took about a week for me to know for sure that she wasn't coming back, seeing as she hadn't been spending much time at the various places we'd called home for a couple years. After not seeing her before I went to bed for five nights in a row, I gathered up my courage and snuck into Mom and Dad's bedroom to find answers.

I didn't like the answers I found there one bit. Mom's half of the closet was empty. All that hung on the rack was a few bent wire hangers and her pink fuzzy robe that had seen plenty of better days. And her drawers were empty, too. Seeing her empty socks and underwear drawer hit me hardest—like a slap in the face. For some reason, the sight of this drawer—in a little white bureau that had come with us from one home to the next—empty of all her most personal belongings, made it real that Mom was gone and wasn't coming back. Even though I was in a state of shock, I managed to sneak out of their room before Dad caught me snooping. He never talked about why Mom left, except for making random comments every now and then about how the souls of Stanley men need to wander, and Mom got sick of it.

And that was that. I had no mother.

I got a strong feeling I'm going to get left high and dry again. No explanations, no goodbye—one day Cooper and Cady will just be gone. I hope I can get my GED by then. If not, I better pray another traveling fair comes by, scoops me up, and takes me with it, because I got no options.

I cross off another day in July with Cooper's red Sharpie marker, and then close the calendar, shove it in my empty duffel bag, and kick it under the bed until tomorrow.

❊ ❊ ❊

cadence

I HAVE TO BE AT work in an hour and a half: just enough time to feed Daisy, grab a quick yogurt, go for a run, shower, and drive to Mad Eats. No time to put on makeup or do much with my hair besides comb it, not that I care. Since I left Cece and her Bratz-doll crew in my dust, I have no need to impress anybody. And when I left, I gave them no explanation, which was rude, but they are the rudest people I've ever met, so they probably didn't even notice. I never call them and don't return their calls, and that's a good enough goodbye for me. In the end all they were interested in, after they caught a glimpse of Eli, was hooking up with him.

I take the steps to the kitchen two at a time. Bradley stands in front of the stove, scrambling eggs. "Hey, Cady. You're up early. Are you working this morning?"

I dump a can of cat food into Daisy's bowl thinking that Bradley's been so friendly since he got home from rehab. But he's totally rehab-obsessed. It's all he thinks about and the only thing he wants to talk about. At least that's my story and I'm sticking with it. I still can't let him in my life the way I did when we were young, as if he were part of me. He's just somebody I loved and lost and don't need back. "Yeah. I work ten to four."

"You keep yourself busy, and that's good. And you're hanging out with Cooper more now."

"Yeah, and this guy, Eli. I'm with both of them a lot."

"Cooper's a good guy." In other words, Cooper gets Bradley's blessing since he's not a drunk or a druggie.

"Glad you approve." I laugh, but my sarcasm makes the words ring hollow. "*We* managed to stay on the straight and narrow throughout high school." *For the most part.*

"When I first got home, you were drinking a lot." He looks into my eyes. I know he wants me to confirm or deny his accusation.

"Well, I'm not drinking now." I'm thankful that it wasn't hard for me to quit drinking after I worked things out with Cooper and Eli. But Bradley has no right to force me into a corner and make me confess. And I won't let him.

Bradley scrapes the eggs out of the pan onto a paper plate. "I should have focused more on my goals when I was in school, but at rehab I learned that it isn't too late. As long as I don't mix it up with my old gang, I'll be okay." He shakes some salt onto the eggs. "I've been focusing a lot on staying fit. It helps keep my head in the right place."

"I don't focus enough on exercising, but if I have a few extra minutes, I go for a run," I say as I slowly back out of the kitchen. "I'm going running right now."

"If you can wait for a few minutes, until I make some toast and eat, I'd love to go with you." He takes a step toward the toaster.

"It'd be cool to run with you, too, but I only have a couple of minutes before work. I really should have left ten minutes ago." Yogurt is a pre-run luxury I can do without. "Maybe we can go tomorrow or Friday... or something."

I'm out the door before he pulls a slice of bread out of the package.

CHAPTER 25

cooper

WE SPEND THE MORNING DOING practice questions for the GED at Wellington Public Library. By noon we're ready to break out and let loose. It's raining outside, and not just a sprinkle here and there. The wind gusts, and as I drive I have to avoid stray branches that have fallen all over the road.

"So maybe we should just go to the mall," Cady says without enthusiasm. She's one of the only girls I know who would rather rake leaves than try on clothes. This sounds like a stereotype about girls, but it has been my experience. I admit to a very short track record with girls, though.

"What are we gonna do *at the mall?*" I ask. I'd prefer to stay as far away from my workplace as possible on my day off. Plus, shopping sucks.

"When I was a little kid and my mother and aunt took me and my cousins to shop at the mall, we used to play hide-and-seek in the big department stores," Eli offers.

He rarely talks about his childhood. It must be one big sore spot.

"When I was young, my mother never let me out of her sight for five seconds in the mall," Cady says and rolls her eyes. "And mall security was on a first name basis with Mom in middle school, when she first let Bradley and me go to the mall un-chaperoned."

"My mother does all her shopping online," I add, "but I want to hear more about this hide-and-seek thing."

Eli sits beside me in the passenger seat. "For a couple years when I was around ten we lived near my aunt and four cousins in Maine. I got tons of good memories from those days." I glance at him and he seems wistful. "The five of us kids hung out every day, and when we played Mall Hide-and-Seek, we agreed on some rules for the game. Like, we promised to stay on a certain floor, or in a particular department, and not to leave our hiding spots until we got found."

"Sounds way better than shopping; we should try it," Cady declares. As always, she's game for anything.

At the mall, I park outside the biggest department store, Marx's, which happens to be the Rustic Valley Mall's major competitor with The Sugar Street Home Store.

We huddle together on the main floor between the perfume and pocketbooks, and Eli says in a hushed tone, "We'll play the game on level three."

Cady raises her hand as if she's in lit class, and asks, "What are the rules?"

"It's easy. Just hide some place tricky and wait until you get found without moving to a different spot. Last person found wins the game and gets to be the seeker next."

"Who hides first?" I ask.

"It's my game, so I'm gonna be the first seeker."

"Duh, Cooper!" Cady laughs. "But, Eli, what if you can't find us?"

"That won't happen. I'll find you." Eli is confident, which is as unusual as it is adorable. "I'm gonna go over by the ladies' shoes and count to fifty. You guys go hide on the third floor."

"May the best man or woman win." I head for the escalator. "And a big lunch is on our agenda after I kick your butts."

The third floor is where the home goods are kept—bedding and bathroom stuff and kitchen appliances and furniture—and I have to fight an urge to straighten everything out as if I was at work. Cady and I wander into the bath department and then over to the comforters. I find a good spot to hide in the bedding department. I drag a couple of packaged comforter sets out of the display rack and climb in behind them with my back flat against the wall, and then I pull the packages in on me. I'm sure they stick out from the others, but I can't do much about that. Once I'm settled in my hiding spot, I stay still and listen for Eli.

"Oh… Hi, Bradley." Instead I hear Cady's voice. "What are you doing here?"

"Just getting a new bedspread and maybe some curtains. I'm blinded by Mom's tropical décor every morning."

Cady laughs, but she sounds nervous. "I almost told her that neon went out of style in the eighties, but she was so excited about her decorating job."

Bradley laughs, too, and then says, "I'm starving. Want to grab a bite to eat when you're done shopping?"

I know that the five-second silence is a bad sign because I know Cady. "I don't think so, Bradley. I've got to meet… some people."

I can't come up with a reason that Cady doesn't ask Bradley to come to lunch with us. But she doesn't.

"Oh, that's not a problem, Cady. No problem at all." Bradley is quiet for a few seconds. "I hope we have a chance to hang out before you head off to school."

"Yeah, me too. I'm sure we will." This isn't regular Cady. This is the scared version of Cady who makes the wrong choices. "I'm late, so I'd better go."

"See you tonight at dinner."

I don't get why Cady blew Bradley off. She was so crazy about him during the first few years of high school, but she, along with her parents, spent the second half of sophomore year and most of junior year tracking him down. I'm sure that sucked. And it really messed her up when she found Bradley on the night he OD'd. Maybe she's still pissed off and so she's avoiding him.

I only have a few seconds to dwell on this because Eli pulls a comforter package away from my face. "Gotcha!" he shouts, and I slither out of the rack. The expression on his face is pure joy. It doesn't take much to get Eli excited, which is one of the best things about him.

"Did you find Cady yet?"

"Nope—you're my first victim." He giggles and I see the little kid in him.

I follow Eli around the third floor as he searches for Cady. I notice her before he does, but I don't say anything. I want him to experience the full thrill of the hunt. He finds her tucked into the twin bed that's on display. Cady's pretty skinny, so her body doesn't make too much of a lump under the plaid pastel bedspread. She arranged the throw pillows on top of her in such a way that her body is pretty well disguised. Just her face pokes out between two stuffed animals, and shit, it's cute.

"I found you, Cady! You hid real good!" Eli pulls her out of the bed, and then the two of them make the bed together. "That was the best hiding spot ever. It reminds me of my little cousin, Mandy. One time she hid inside a shower stall display and even wrapped a towel around her head!"

I make a note to myself to ask Eli about his cousins at lunch today. He hasn't mentioned his family much, and it's time we learned more about his background. I also make a mental note to ask Cady why she blew off her brother.

"Now it's Cady's turn to find us. Let's go hide on the second floor, in the toy department and ladies' underwear."

"I count to fifty, right? And you guys had better hide like pros. I'm awesome at stuff like this." She closes her eyes and starts to count. Cady isn't lying—she's great at finding other people's secret spots, but she's hard to find when she's the one in hiding.

AT LUNCH, ELI OPENS UP to us about his family.

"I have four cousins. Mandy, who I told you about, is the youngest, and Maddy is her big sister. And the boys, Kurt and Caleb. And then me. We did almost everything together when we lived near them, along with Mom and Aunt Gina."

Eli doesn't mention the details of why his mother left or the bad shit that went down between his father and him or anything about how they moved from place to place every few years, but I still get a sense that his rare memories of family moments mean a lot to him. He has lost more than I can imagine. Eli tells us so many stories about his cousins when they were little that I don't have a chance to ask Cady why she didn't invite Bradley to lunch. But when I think about Eli's loss, I'm reminded that Cady also experienced a loss during sophomore year of high school when she first lost Bradley to alcohol and drugs and the rough crowd that went with those things. And as our junior year went on, she lost more and more of her brother to drugs, until the night last summer when she found him unconscious on his bedroom floor.

I look at the tiny person with a bucket on her head that Cady had inked on her wrist. What she tried to accomplish with The Weekend Bucket List finally sinks into my brain. Not only was she hiding from the confusion about what she felt for me, but she was trying to escape her fear of losing me like she lost Bradley. Her obsession with The Weekend Bucket List makes complete sense to me now. It was the ultimate distraction.

The thing is, she's still hiding.

❀ ❀ ❀

As we head to the town beach, Eli says, "You guys have got great families." Eli has been obsessing over family ties since he told us about his cousins. "When am I gonna get to meet the rest of your family members?"

"Well, you know my mom. She hugs you every night before you go to bed," I remind him. "And Dad hasn't been home from the West Coast to meet you yet."

We turn expectantly toward Cady. Eli and I have been to her house a few times, but never to hang around. We just pick her up and drop her off. What Eli really wants to understand is how he fits into our lives. I can't blame him, so I'm anxious to hear what Cady has to say too.

"The time will come to meet my family," Cady mumbles. That's all she says on the subject, and it's fairly cryptic. I don't think the reason she hasn't introduced Eli to her family has anything to do with Eli, though. She's going through a rough patch with her brother being back from rehab. But Eli doesn't understand. How could he? Her silence has been pretty loud.

I park at the end of the lot, close to where we usually hang out. Cady hops out of the car and, when Eli jumps out, she grabs his hand and leads him into the woods. I follow along. But it's dark, so I shine my cell phone flashlight ahead of us.

"Eli, do you have your pocket knife?" Cady asks.

"Sure. I always do." He pulls it out of the front pocket of his jeans, and Cady snatches it from his hand.

"See this tree? I want each of us to carve our initials in it." She still hasn't told Eli when he'll meet her family, but we go with her newest plan. Cady presses the knife into the bark, and it takes her about five minutes to etch a very primitive CL. Under it she makes a plus sign. She passes the knife to Eli. "Your turn. Carve your initials and then a plus sign under it."

He does as she asks and then he hands the knife to me, and I carve in my initials. We look at the little equation: CL+ES+CM. Underneath she carves an equals sign and under that BFF. "Nobody will ever see this because it's hidden in the woods," Cady tells Eli as she traces the letters with one finger. "But it's still real, right?"

Eli nods.

"And even if you don't actually meet my parents and my brother, our friendship is real. See what I mean?"

"Sure, Cady," Eli says. In my opinion, it's a poor comparison, but Eli accepts it, so I go with it too.

What she says next surprises me. "The three of us—our relationship—is *so* real. It's the only real thing I've got." And she pulls us into a hug.

When she releases us, Eli heads toward the beach. He's quiet until we sit on the sand in a circle. This is when he asks the million-dollar question. "What happens to our friendship when you guys go off to college?"

If I could have it my way, the summer would never end. I've got no clue how to make the intense kind of friendship we've built work over a long distance. And we don't have a clue where Eli will go after his summer job ends.

I'm glad when Cady answers. "We'll work it out, don't worry." But again, her answer leaves me unsatisfied. I can only imagine how Eli feels. "And guys, none of us is going anywhere for two weeks yet, so let's make the most of it."

Although our time is limited and the sand is wet, the rain has stopped and the sky has cleared, so we lie down on the beach and stare at the sky. When I blow my troubles out between my lips, everything seems, for the most part, right. The stars are out, and my best friends are beside me. This beach is suddenly *our* place, and I like it here out in the open much better than in the woods by the tree in which we carved our initials.

CHAPTER 26

cadence

ELI AND COOPER DON'T COME to my house very much, but since Mom has gone to a quilting convention in Massachusetts for the day and Dad's at work, we meet here. Before she left, Mom hinted that maybe I should spend the day with Bradley. Since he hasn't hooked up with the guys he used to get in trouble with, he spends most of his time alone or with my parents. Part of me wants to hang with him, but another, bigger part of me gets in the way. I just can't say the words, "Bradley, do you want to do something with me today?"

All I have to do is get through the next two weeks and then I'll be gone to college and the Bradley problem will be gone with me. Anyway, he took off on his bike for a long, lonely ride to God-knows-where before Cooper showed up with Eli.

"Something's off with my windshield wipers, Cades. I'm gonna go take a look at them!" Cooper shouts up the stairs.

"But it's not raining. We don't need windshield wipers today!" I yell back.

Cooper doesn't respond, so I figure that his obsession with functioning windshield wipers is a car-owner thing.

"Hi, Cady." Eli steps into my room and checks it out carefully since he hasn't been here before. Mom is serious about protecting my virginity, so the rule is "no boys upstairs." Not that Eli has ever been here when Mom's around to enforce the rule. It's easier to keep my family in a separate compartment from the one where I keep my friends.

"Hey, Eli. What's the plan for today?" I bend over on the bed and tie my sneakers.

"I think we're going zip-lining."

"That'll be a blast." Bradley would have loved to hit the zip lines with us. He's into natural highs lately, as they're the only kind he's allowed to get. I shake my head in an effort to lose the guilt, and I concentrate on my sincere hope that Cooper won't experience an acrophobia relapse high up in the treetops.

"Cooper isn't sure of the hours and prices, though. He asked if me and you could figure it out."

"No problem. Get on my computer and find it in my bookmarks. The zip line place is called Weekend Joy Rides."

"You know I'm not so good with computers. Maybe you should look it up."

I go over to the bureau to grab an elastic band for my hair. "You can do it. I've shown you how to find things on my computer a bunch of times." Eli has never owned his own computer and seems pretty scared of mine. He worries he'll push the wrong button and break it. "Go ahead and try."

I bend so the top half of my body is upside down, and fasten the elastic to make a messy bun on top of my head.

"The Weekend Bucket List…" He reads aloud.

"Don't look at that, Eli!" I scramble to the desk and try to snatch my laptop, but he stands taller and holds it above my head.

"Get drunk… run naked on a beach… sneak into a movie…"

"Don't read that list! It's stupid—it's nothing!" And this is the truth. The Weekend Bucket List did nothing for Cooper and me but postpone an inevitable conversation with a clever distraction.

As my laptop is out of reach, all I can do is watch helplessly as Eli's eyes flicker over the list. "Number seven… have a first kiss."

He places my laptop in the middle of the desk, snaps it shut, and says, "I'm leaving." But he doesn't leave right away. He folds his arms across his chest and looks at me.

"Eli, it was just a dumb plan we made to have a little fun before graduation. You know, so we could prove some things to ourselves." And so we could change a subject we were too scared to deal with.

Eli's face has grown red. He's upset. In fact, I've never seen him this emotional.

"But we met you through it, so it worked out for the best for all of us."

He stares at the floor and then tugs his faded jeans that have drooped low enough to expose his tattoo. The short sentence fits perfectly on his hip. I want to fix my eyes on it and read over and over about how he found two life-changing friends, but Eli spins around and runs out of my bedroom.

I follow him down the stairs and out the door, and when he sprints past Cooper, who's bent over the open hood of his car, Cooper shouts, "Hey, what's going on?"

"He found out about The Weekend Bucket List!" I yell and chase Eli down the street.

Cooper races along behind us. Eli's faster, though, and soon he's out of sight.

When Cooper catches up to me, he shouts, "What the hell happened?" He grabs my arm, and I finally stop. "What happened?"

I'm out of breath, but manage to spit out, "He was using my laptop to look up Weekend Joy Rides and instead he found The Weekend Bucket List."

"Shit."

"Yeah. He probably thinks we were just using him, and that all the stuff we do together now is some big joke."

Cooper studies his sneakers. "We *were* just using him, Cady."

"Maybe at first, but it turned into more."

I worry that Cooper may have a stroke. His face is brighter red than Eli's was, and he's breathing way too fast. "Think he went to my house?"

"Probably. He doesn't have too many places to go."

"Let's give him an hour to calm down, and then go try to talk to him," Cooper suggests, and rubs his temples.

"Okay, sounds good." I need time to calm down too. My eyes fill with tears, and I do nothing to stop their flow. I've screwed up again—in a big way—maybe in an unfixable way this time. I don't know yet. "I keep on loving people and losing them." I murmur and don't care one bit if Cooper hears.

He *does* hear and he sighs and then pulls me into his arms and squeezes. I need this hug so much, and I figure Cooper needs one too, so I hug him back. "We'll find Eli and figure this whole thing out. No worries, Cady."

I'm less convinced.

WHEN WE ARRIVE AT COOPER'S house an hour later, Eli is gone. And when I say gone, I mean that all his stuff has been removed from Cooper's bedroom. It wouldn't have taken very long to fill a single duffel bag, though. All that's left is a note written on the back of a paper plate, propped on the toaster, that says, "Mrs. M—Thank you for putting me up. You are the greatest. Your friend, Eli."

Cooper and I stare at each other. I say, "He's either at the library or the Travelers' Haven Motel."

"You're probably right." Cooper drops into one of the chairs at his kitchen table. "But we need to give him some time to think things through. He'll realize that a lot has gone down with the three of us since the weekend of the bucket list and then he'll come back."

I'm not so sure Cooper's right. I'm not so sure of anything except I screw up a lot. "I'll wait at my house for him, and you wait here. Call me if he comes back."

"Let me drive you home," Cooper offers.

"No, thanks. I'll walk." Eli isn't the only one who has some thinking to do.

❊　❊　❊

I CALL CADY IN THE morning before work. "I kinda stalked him last night. Eli's definitely staying at the Travelers' Haven."

"Well, we'd better get there and fix this right now. We don't have much time left with him, Cooper. We leave for school a week from tomorrow."

I suspect this is part of why Eli took off, maybe even a bigger part than finding The Weekend Bucket List on Cady's computer. The fact of the matter is, Cady and I are about to leave for school, and we never talked about what will happen to him when we go. Will we stay in contact with each other and get together enough to keep a long-distance friendship going? Or will the bond we share fade away?

"We never even tried to talk to Eli about what happens to him when we leave. If I was Eli, I'd have taken off on us too." I speak softly into the phone. "Cady, I don't think we can fix it this time."

I'm pretty sure she drops the phone. When she responds, she's frantic. "What the heck are you talking about? We have to fix it!"

For the first time in as long as I can remember, hopelessness drags me all the way down. "Maybe this *was* just a summer thing with Eli—a meaningless offshoot of the pointless bucket list. Friendship with a virtual stranger who has no home base can't work; you and I both know this. Eli knows it too. Maybe he just knew it first."

Thanks to Eli and the bucket list, Cady and I are fully prepared to go off to college. We've gained some real-life experience. We've done the shit "normal" kids do—gotten drunk, stayed out all night, snuck into a movie, been pierced and tattooed, and sucked face with two different people. Maybe if I tell this shit to myself over and over again I can make myself believe it.

"No, Cooper. No!" Cady's upset, but it's too damned late. We screwed up again, and Eli was smart enough to run away before we left him on the sidelines.

"I have to get in the shower. I've gotta be at work in forty-five minutes." I love Cady and Eli. I love them as the best friends I'll ever have. But a three-way friendship between a sarcastic girl, a gutless boy, and a down-on-his-luck stranger just can't be done. It can't work in the real world, and that's that.

Cady hangs up without a goodbye. I hardly notice. Something has broken inside me. And I care even less.

❀ ❀ ❀

cadence

I STOP BY THE TRAVELERS' Haven Motel at about the time I expect Eli to come home from work. I wait in the parking lot no more than fifteen minutes before a pickup truck pulls into the circular motel driveway. Eli jumps out and waves at the driver.

I hop out of Mom's Volvo and race over to him before he can escape. "Eli! Eli, please listen to me for one minute." He stops and turns around.

It's as if a thick wall of glass stands between us. And maybe he hears my words through it, but he can't sense my need. Through it, I can't detect his sweetness or his kindness or that special thing that makes him Eli. He's cold and distant.

"What do you want, Cady?"

"I want to explain about the list—The Weekend Bucket List."

"You don't need to explain. I read the list. I was number seven, and I helped out with some of the other numbers, too." Eli is perfectly calm, as if he isn't torn apart. And who knows? Maybe he's not ripped into pieces; maybe I'm the only one who is. "You don't need to explain anything, Cady. Maybe you should just say thank you."

215

This is not the Eli I know. This is Eli-through-a-thick-wall-of-glass, and I need to shatter it so I can reach him. "Cooper and I were stupid when we wrote that list... and when we carried it out. We thought it would help us to grow up, or magically make us real players in college life. But since then, we've grown to love you."

He shudders when I say the word *love*. Wide, dark eyes meet my gaze. Briefly, their expression is warm and soft. But then Eli turns his head and blows some grass off of his shoulder, adjusts his workpants, and shakes his head, as if our love is no big deal to him. He lets his cooler drop to the ground and then bends to pick it up again. Eli would do anything to distract himself from what I just said. "I don't want to do this anymore. I don't want to be best friends with you and Cooper."

"Eli, what are you talking about?"

"Say goodbye to Cooper for me. And thanks to both of you for all the help studying. I got a good chance of passing my GED test now."

I nod because the only other thing I can think of to do is pull Eli into a hug and it seems to be the wrong moment for that.

"Bye, Cady."

Before I'm able to collect myself enough to beg, he's gone.

eli

I FEEL LIKE CRAP AS I walk away from Cady and head into the motel. But I did what I had to do, not that it was easy. Now Cady's off the hook and soon she'll tell Cooper I'm long gone, and he'll be off the hook too. And best of all, *I'm* off the hook—the sharp, dangerous hook that would've tore me apart in one short week.

Sometimes in life you got to get done with people before they get done with you. Even if they *say* they love you and that you're their best friend in the world. Words are just words—spoken out loud or written on a bucket list—and I been hurt by them too many times. I'm tired now.

I got some planning to do. Time to find another carnival to drift away from here with.

CHAPTER 27

cadence

MOM ALWAYS HOVERS AROUND BRADLEY. She asks him how he *feels* and what he *needs* and if he wants to *talk*. She hasn't seemed to notice that I've spent less than zero time with him this summer, aside from the occasions on which I'm home for a family dinner. Or maybe she *has* noticed and is in denial of my absence in his life. Our family is excellent at denying stuff we don't want to see. "Avoiding Bradley" has become a sport that I'm good at. I'm an Olympic caliber Bradley-avoider.

Until now, I've worked a minimum of forty hours weekly and spent all of my free time with Eli and Cooper and was never at home. With less than a week left before I leave for college, I'm now trapped inside the four walls of my family home when I'm not at work. My only prospect for freedom will be when Mom and Dad cart me off to college.

So maybe I'm officially moping. *Teenagers are hormonal; we're supposed to mope around our houses, aren't we?* It's not against the law. There aren't "moping police" standing ready to arrest me and drag me away to bad-attitude jail. And why shouldn't I enjoy this experience of intense self-pity? Maybe I *want* to revel in a show of grandiose brooding.

But a girl can't even mope properly around this house anymore. The new and improved version of my brother comes into the kitchen as I try to concentrate on indulging in self-pity at the kitchen table while I wait for the coffee to brew.

"Hey, Cady." Bradley doesn't give the coffee machine enough time to beep, letting us know its brewing job is done. He grabs the pot and pours coffee into the mug I left on the counter. "At rehab we drank hot cocoa instead of coffee. You'll never know much I appreciate coffee now." He takes a sip. "Despite the fact that it *is* too weak." He sticks out his tongue.

I don't apologize for my weak brew. In fact, I have nothing to say to him.

He plunks himself into the chair beside mine. "Why the long face?"

"My face isn't long. It's perfectly round." My sarcasm falls flat. Neither of us smiles.

Bradley presses on with, "It's just an expression, Cady." *As if I don't know this.* "What I mean is, why are you so miserable lately?" He places the mug beside my elbow. "You can tell me."

I can't prevent the subsequent eye roll, not that I try particularly hard. "I've just got a few things going on in my life, that's all." I drop my forehead onto the kitchen table.

"Then go ahead and vent."

I lift my head from the table to look at him. "No, thank you."

"Why not?"

"Don't worry, bro. I'm not going to go off and drink away my problems."

"Well, I'm glad to hear *that*." He slurps noisily from the mug that was meant for me, and says, "But I still want to know what's up with you."

"Maybe I don't want *my* stupid problems to drive *you* to drink." My nasty remark sizzles in the air, forcing us to bask in its tense afterglow.

"You had nothing to do with my drinking or drug use, Cady. And I'm sorry for what my bad behavior did to your life for the past few years. I apologize and intend to be a better brother to you now." Bradley's a brave guy; he actually places his hand on my arm. He's got to be terrified that I'll bite it off. "So, talk to me. Okay? Tell me what's up. Maybe I can help."

I can't bring myself to utter a word because I'm scared to death to tell Bradley my secrets. Not that I'm worried he'll blurt them out to Mom and Dad, because in that sense, we've always had each other's back. I'm more afraid to make an emotional investment in my brother, because a bottle of beer or painkillers could end it all in a moment of weakness. And where would that leave me? "It's nothing, Bradley."

"Yeah, and I'm the Marlboro man."

His reply makes so little sense that I say, "My God, Bradley. The only vice you *don't* have is smoking cigarettes." We laugh, and it lifts my spirits.

When we stop, Bradley gets up and pours a cup of coffee for me. He comes back to the table, places it in front of me, and asks, "So what's up with you?"

I make a sudden decision that I hope I won't regret: I'm going to tell him. "I have two best friends I can't live without, but I have to."

"Yeah? I knew about Cooper, but not the other one."

"We met the other guy earlier this summer. Cooper and I did this dare; we called it The Weekend Bucket List. One of the things on it was to have a first kiss. And so, the other boy—his name is Eli—kissed Cooper and me."

"I want to know what happened with the three of you, but prepare me—is this gonna be TMI for your twin brother's innocent ears?"

"Not a chance. We didn't all kiss each other at *the same time*. It happened one kiss at a time."

"We? You mean you *and* Cooper kissed Eli?"

I nod. "Yeah, but, like I said, at different times. I got jealous because I thought Cooper was more into Eli than me. And I messed everything up between us. Cooper and I even stopped hanging out for a few weeks, but the three of us figured out how to work things out."

"Just tell me, is my twin sister is part of a sexy love triangle?" He sounds mostly floored, but a little bit impressed.

"No, so get your mind out of the gutter. We're best friends… the three of us. Or we were until I screwed it all up again."

Bradley's eyes are as huge as Frisbees. I think I've blown his mind.

"It's all upside down again. Eli found out that we were using him for number seven—the first kiss. You know, to check an item off the bucket list."

Bradley shakes his head. "Well, that sucks."

It feels almost like a dose of harmless revenge to shock my brother, who was always the one to shock me with his reckless behavior.

"And you want to be this guy, Eli's, friend?"

"Cooper and I want to be his *best* friends."

"Then I think you have to make amends to Eli, the one you screwed up with," he says.

"That sounds suspiciously like you want me to work one of the twelve steps."

"Maybe so. But you need to show him something different than you showed him before—something better."

I have an answer for that. "Eli told me he doesn't want to be friends with us anymore."

"Have you made an effort to change his mind?"

"No—*I told you*—he doesn't want to see us again." I roll my eyes because it always makes me feel cooler than the person I roll my eyes at… except this time.

"You should go visit him, but only when you have something better to offer him."

"Like what? Cooper and I are leaving for college in a week. The only thing we can offer him is a goodbye."

"Where does Cooper stand in this mess?"

"He's frustrated with the whole situation. I'm pretty sure he wants nothing more to do with either of us. He's been through a lot this summer too."

Bradley walks across the room to look out the kitchen window. He studies the bird feeder and then proclaims, "You need to make a better bucket list."

"What are you talking about? The stupid bucket list is what got me into this situation in the first place."

"Then make the bucket list you should have made, or at least make a bucket list that will prove to Eli and Cooper that you've got your priorities in order."

I stop to consider what Bradley just said. "I could try, I guess." Cooper actually created a lifetime self-improvement bucket list for his graduation speech. I can make a better bucket list for a single weekend.

"Of course you can. I have faith in you. But first, let me make us a couple of omelets and maybe we can go for a run," he offers. "Or a bike ride."

It's still a little scary, but I want to hang out with my brother. Maybe I even need to. "Sounds like a plan, bro."

"I'm glad you'll be hanging around here a little more. Daisy was starting to miss you."

CHAPTER 28

cooper

I DON'T HEAR FROM CADY all week and I'm okay with it because things have gotten way too complicated and painful. I can always email her once I'm settled into my dorm. We can be email pen pals. *Oh, joy.*

It's actually way more complicated than that. In fact, I can hardly believe I lost Cady; we've been best friends forever. But I just can't reach out to her right now. Everything is way too broken this time.

And then there's Eli. How many times can you screw a person before they say, "Take a permanent hike"?

Friendship is supposed to be something pure. It's supposed to help you to be all you can be and make everything about your life more alive. The friendship I shared with Cady and Eli started out that way, but has since forced us into the worst versions of ourselves. It hasn't made our lives more vivid, but more dismal.

And the most important aspect of friendship is that each of us *chooses* to be in it. Eli has chosen to leave our friendship—in fact, he literally ran from us without saying goodbye just like we once did to him. I'm no longer committed to our relationship; the thought of repairing it seems futile and depressing. Cady is off the radar, too, and it isn't the first time she has taken a breather from Eli and me. If none of us want it, our friendship doesn't exist.

I don't think our friendship exists.

❉ ❉ ❉

THIS MOTEL ROOM IS BETTER than the one in the basement, seeing as it costs more. It's above ground, so it's got no long-legged bugs running past me, and all of the furniture doesn't have that greasy feeling, like it's wet, when it's dry. I plan to watch the heck out of the TV while I'm here too, because I got a suspicion that I'm never going to have this many channels again.

They filled my spot in the Ellis Crossing Over Project for Men, so I'll have to spend most of what I saved over the summer on this motel room, unless I can find a job with a place to live attached. I might have to join the army, but I can't do that without a GED. I hope I don't have to put off going for my GED, but survival has to come first. Food to eat and water to drink and a bed to sleep in—these things are most important.

I got too much on my mind to fall asleep. I have to figure out where to go and what to do. And I have to do it alone. Before I met Cady and Cooper, alone was just the way I was. Now alone means *without Cady and Cooper,* and it's worse.

I don't sing it; I just say it. "Alone again, naturally."

❉ ❉ ❉

As I WALK THROUGH THE party store searching for just the right balloons, I admit that the challenge involved in setting this whole thing up has been trickier than I thought. It makes SAT preparation seem like a cakewalk. I'm calling myself out for all the ways I screwed up with the original bucket list, because I think that somewhere along the line I lost all of my compassion.

I've grown insensitive in my effort to protect myself.

And maybe I'd rather study for the AP US History exam than examine my soul in order to make a better bucket list. But I'm doing it anyway.

"Heart-shaped balloons. Perfect!" I call to Bradley, who is still in the candle aisle.

❀ ❀ ❀

cooper

I FIND A NOTE ON my windshield after work on Thursday.

"Be at Our Place at the end of the town beach Friday night at 9:00 PM."

The note isn't signed, but it doesn't have to be. I recognize the handwriting and the demanding tone.

cadence

I'VE BEEN SITTING IN THE lobby for two hours now as I wait for Eli to come home from work. The three ladies at the front desk very kindly have not ordered me to leave, although I'm certain that I'm loitering, and I saw a red and white sticker on the glass door in the front of the building that clearly states it isn't allowed. The ladies send me periodic patronizing smiles, since I explained to them how I needed to wait for an important person so I could make a necessary apology. I know pity when I see it, and repetitive, regretful smiles indicate pity.

They think my effort here is sweet and they think I'm sweet. Those ladies have no idea how un-sweet I've been lately.

It's nearly eight o'clock by the time Eli comes through the lobby doors. When he sees me, he stops short, and his horrified expression tells me he's considering escaping onto the street as a viable option. But Eli is a quality person and, although he doesn't *want* to talk to me, he decides not to cut and run, as I'd have done in his shoes.

I walk over to him, actually shaking with a bad case of frayed nerves, as the ladies at the front desk stare, enthralled by this moment. I force myself to smile, to be glad I can provide them with some quality entertainment. They work hard; they deserve to be amused.

See universe, I'm more compassionate already.

"Awww," the ladies murmur in unison.

I resist the urge to ask, politely of course, that they mind their own damn business, as I look directly into Eli's eyes. "I admit that you owe me nothing, Eli. But before we never see each other again, I have one small request."

Eli sighs, and, in the sound, I hear impatience. He wants to get this over with. "What do you want, Cady?"

"I want you to meet me on Friday night at our special place on the town beach. At nine o'clock. I want to do something; I *need* to do it before I go to school."

Eli studies my face. He wears the same expression of hurt disbelief that he wore when he caught sight of The Weekend Bucket List on my laptop. He still thinks that *I* think it's all about me—what I want and what I need. And he can think that, for now. "Is Cooper going too?"

It's a fair question. "I invited him."

Again, Eli sighs as I sweat bullets. Finally, he answers. "I guess I'll go."

I swallow as noisily as Cooper usually does. "Thank you."

This time, I'm the one who walks away. I *want* to run—to get the heck out of the motel lobby before he changes his mind, or the ladies behind the desk shout, "You go, girl!" and spoil the mood—but I find the inner strength to walk.

CHAPTER 29

cadence

"IS THIS COMPLETELY OVER THE top?" I ask.

Not only did Bradley help me create the list, but he also helped me set everything up. He put the pink tablecloth on the picnic table where I very much hope Cooper, Eli, and I will sit to talk, while I tied helium-filled, heart-shaped balloons to the table's four legs.

"It's not over the top for the Queen of Cheesiness, but for you, Cady, it's… let's say, *excessive*."

"Good," I reply. "Eli and Cooper deserve *excessive*, and more."

"It's 8:45 p.m. We should light the candles now." Before I have a chance to argue, Bradley snatches his lighter from the table and strides onto the beach to light the candles we have scattered in the sand. I pushed for arranging the candles in a heart shape, but Bradley said I need to prove to the guys that I have squelched my need to control every last detail, so I let Bradley place them in a random formation on the beach.

Bradley and I spent the entire afternoon dipping strawberries in chocolate, and, as I pull back the foil that covers them, I call, "And that makes you the official right-hand man to the Queen of Hearts. You are the Jack of Hearts—*not cheesiness*."

When he finishes lighting the candles, and I've scattered rose petals on the tablecloth and the sand, we meet beside the picnic table. Bradley glances around at the dreamy scene and says, "Well, Cady, you sure came out of your comfort zone to impress these guys."

"I've screwed up a lot with them. I had to do something big to show how much I care."

Bradley surveys the beach a final time, and states, "You can rest assured that this is big." He grabs my hand. I feel as close to him as I did in middle school, which scares me a little, but not enough to pull my hand away. "You have your cell phone, so call to let me know what goes down with the three of you. In the event that you need a ride home, I'll be ready to come get you. And if necessary, you can cry on my shoulder all night."

It isn't a choice when I pull him into my arms and squeeze—I have to do it. "Thanks for everything, Bradley."

"I'm Jack now, remember?" My brother, the Jack of Hearts, squeezes me hard. "Good luck. And don't forget to call—either way it goes." He walks through the woods to the parking lot. And when I think he's gone, his voice, from the other side of the woods, surprises me. "I've got your back, Cades!"

I'm left alone with all of my hopes and regrets and my incredible fear of risking it all on two people who may very well walk away. But the night is clear and warm and breezy and it somehow assures me that, even if I fail, the right thing to do is to try.

A car's engine rumbles, and I'm not sure if it's Bradley pulling away or Cooper driving into the parking lot. Or maybe it's a friend dropping Eli off. In any case, the night is unfolding, and the last thing I do in preparation is pull a sheet of pale pink stationary, covered in my handwriting like it's a cheat note for a vocabulary quiz, out of my backpack and place it on the table and tuck the edge under the plate of strawberries.

To my surprise, Cooper and Eli emerge from the woods together.

Cooper answers my unasked question as he gazes around at the romantic scene. "We didn't *plan* to come here together. I saw him walking on the side of the town beach access road, so I picked him up."

It's dark, but Eli is close enough to the candles that I can see his eyes fairly well. "What's this supposed to be?" he asks, and gestures to the scene before him.

"This is…" I'm nervous. I stop talking and take a necessary calming breath. And I gulp the way Cooper used to do. Then I start over. "I hope this is the beginning of The Better Weekend Bucket List."

Cooper and Eli first exchange glances and then look around the beach at my decorations, but they don't ask any questions. They just look.

Since neither of them has run away screaming, I press on. "This time we have to do the list in order." If they go along with the plan…

I walk over to the picnic table and sit, fully aware that I will likely be sitting alone. The guys stare at me, and then Cooper follows me to the table.

"Sit down, please," I say. "Have a chocolate-dipped strawberry."

Cooper sits across from me, obediently picks up a strawberry, and bites into it. Juice drips down his chin, but I decide not to offer, sarcastically, of course, to clean it up with my tongue. It could send mixed messages, and it's definitely not the right time for humor.

Eli squats where he's been standing since he got here. He takes a rose petal from the sand and sniffs it. "I… I don't…"

"Just sit down and have *one* strawberry, Eli. I made them myself. Well, with the help of my brother."

"They're pretty good." Cooper is already on his second one. "Almost as good as Dad's."

Lucky for me, Eli is too much of a nice guy for his own good. He slowly approaches the picnic table and sits on the edge of the bench, but stays as far from me as possible. He picks up a strawberry and holds it by the stem, but doesn't take a bite. "What's going on here?" he asks.

I slide the paper out from under the plate. "I told you before. I made a better bucket list and I want to carry it out with both of you."

"Don't you think *one* bucket list was enough, Cady?" Cooper is openly cynical, and normally I would use this moment to put him in his place.

But I don't. "No. We created the last one for all the wrong reasons. And Cooper, I take full responsibility for that. Yeah, I wanted to stop being such a model citizen and perfect daughter for one weekend and find out what it was like to be a regular kid."

Eli places his strawberry on the pink plastic tablecloth. I have already managed to kill his appetite.

"But what I wanted even more, Cooper, was to figure out…" This is going to be extremely difficult to say.

"Figure out what?" Cooper snaps.

"I wanted to figure out how we felt about each other."

Silence, except for the waves that slosh on the shore and the breeze that wafts through the trees.

"I thought if I had a chance to kiss you, I'd know for sure whether you were the right person for me. But I also needed you to kiss a boy, so you could find out if you'd rather be with a boy than with me. And Eli was perfect, so handsome and sweet."

Eli stands. His expression says, *I don't need to sit here and listen to this crap.*

I have to say the rest before he leaves, so I blurt it out. "But instead of clearing everything up, we found ourselves liking you."

He stares at the water. "I fell into friendship," he murmurs, but not specifically to Cooper or me. "Like an idiot."

I refuse to be distracted. "So, I guess I'll start with number one on The Better Weekend Bucket List." I point to the paper. "Number one is to apologize to somebody."

I'm nervous because neither boy has said much or even yelled at me like I deserve. I get up and walk over to Eli. I study his face, but he refuses to meet my gaze. So, I take his stiff, cold hand in my warm one and squeeze. "I'm sorry for pulling you into our first bucket list and not considering how it would affect you. We were selfish, but honestly, the reason you got hurt was because I was jealous. I was jealous I'd get left out of whatever it was that was growing between you and Cooper."

"Shit," Cooper mutters.

But this is my apology to Eli, so my attention remains on him.

"Cady... I'm not sure I can forgive you. You hurt me." That's all Eli says, so I try not to cry or beg. It's best to let him think it over before I resort to those tactics.

I move on to Cooper. I sit beside him on the picnic table and say what needs to be said. "I'm sorry I never leveled with you about how I felt. I was afraid that if you knew how much I cared, it would scare you away, especially if you decided you wanted Eli to be your boyfriend."

I don't think Cooper is going to reply, but he surprises me. "You should have told me, or maybe *I* should have told *you*, because I felt a lot for you too. Sorry, Cady. We screwed up."

Eli sits on the edge of the bench, and I choose to take this as a sign he plans to stick around for a while.

In the spirit of number one on the new bucket list, Cooper stares across the table at Eli. "Eli, I have to say sorry to *you*, too. I knew I wanted to get to know you better as a friend, but I let you go when I wanted to hang on. And I promised you shit I didn't follow through with. That was a big mistake."

Eli stares across the table at Cooper and then addresses me. "Can I have a minute to think about number one on The Better Bucket List?"

"Of course, you can," I reply.

And for the next five minutes the three of us sit in dark silence. The breeze is nice, and I'm confident with what I've done so far, so the wait that should kill me, doesn't.

"Cady and Cooper... I got a sorry to say too."

Now *this* I didn't expect. Cooper doesn't expect it either; he gulps and coughs a few times.

"When I read about the bucket list on the computer, I was surprised. But I walked out, even though I already knew you guys were sorry and when I knew you guys were the best friends I could ever have." His eyes grow wet, and I feel guilty, but I don't interrupt. "I left before you guys could leave me. That's what I did."

Cooper nods. He seems to understand. "You had good reason to worry about that; we never talked about what came next with us, once we were off to college."

"If you stick around this weekend, I think we can fix that," I say to Eli. "We can talk about everything important in the future, and you can meet my brother, because he's the only person in my family who gets me."

When Cooper says, "Count me in for The Better Weekend Bucket List, Cady," I can't stop my smile. We look expectantly at Eli.

"What about you, Eli?" I don't mean to press him, but I do. I guess I'm bossy by nature.

He shrugs before he answers. "I'll try, I suppose." He finally picks up his strawberry, eats it in one swallow, and then gulps down three more. "These are good." He smiles, and I'm pretty sure he mostly forgives me. It's awesome to see a glimmer of the Eli I know.

"What else is on the better bucket list, Cady?" Cooper asks.

I snatch the paper so only I can read it. "Important things… but as I said, this time we have to do them in order."

"That's cool," Eli says, and licks his fingers and then his thumb.

"Will you guys let me lead you through them?"

"What have we got to lose?"

I laugh and say, "I guess you'll have to wait and see, Coop."

"But first, I want to sit in the sand, like we always do when we come here." Eli gets up, grabs us each by a hand, and drags us toward Tamarack Lake. Before he sits, he scurries around, grabs a few candles, and places them close by so we are visible to each other.

"Okay," I say. "Number two is a promise."

Eli and Cooper stare at me, caught up in my words, and I suspect that this matters as much to them as it does to me. "We need to promise that this weekend we'll speak only the truth to each other."

"No lies?" Eli checks.

"That's right," I say.

"It might be harder than we think." Cooper is the voice of reason.

"That's true, but I think it'll be worth it."

"Okay… and what comes next?" Eli is eager.

"Number three is to start a tradition. We don't necessarily have to do it right this minute, but I want to put it out there so we can keep it in mind until we come up with a good idea."

"I already got an idea for number three." Eli gets up and goes over to the tree closest to the beach—a tree everybody who walks along the beach can stop and look at, not hidden away in the woods. He pulls out his knife and carves his first name into the bark. "Now you guys do it."

Cooper and I take turns carving our names beside his.

"This is our summer tradition," Eli declares. "Every summer we'll find a tree in a special place—a spot that everyone will see—and carve our names into it to mark another year of friendship."

He wants our friendship to be visible to everyone and expects it to last for a long time. "That's so perfect, Eli."

"Let's clean up the beach. We have a lot to do tonight!" Now that Eli seems to be all in, I'm excited. However, the items on the new list aren't just fun or novel or daring; they are essential.

cooper

As I DRIVE TO THE Burger and Dairy Bar, Cady calls her brother from the back seat.

"Hey, Bradley, you don't need to pick me up at the beach. Things went better than I hoped. Thanks for all of your help setting up. I owe you big time. So how about if I take you to breakfast tomorrow morning with my two best friends?"

I study her smile in the rearview mirror and then I check out Eli. He smiles too, as Cady has just proposed an introduction to her brother that suggests to Eli he's permanent in her life.

"Great. Can you tell Mom I'm sleeping at Cooper's house? And not to flip out, but I won't be home until Sunday. You can let her know I'm all packed for school."

I catch eyes with Cady in the rearview mirror. She looks smug, which is so very Cady.

"I love you, too, bro, and I'll let you know where to meet us for breakfast. I have some ideas about you and Eli, but I'll tell you in the morning." She ends the call.

"*That* was honest," I tease.

"Total honesty *is* number two," she replies. "Duh!"

Eli laughs along with me. Last time we talked about numbers on a bucket list, he was left out of the secret. I like it better with him in on it.

CADY AND I KNOW AT least half of the customers at The Burger and Dairy Bar since it's a late-night hangout in Wellington for the high school and college crowd. Not that we ever hung out here. Social outcasts usually steer clear of post-keg party "drunken munchies" food stops. As we cross the parking lot, Cady scrambles between us and grabs Eli's hand and then mine.

"Here goes nothing," she says, and we march to the window. "And by the way, 'no more hiding' is number four."

"Three cheeseburger dinners with cokes, please. The name is LaBrie." Cady orders for us. She lets go of our hands when it's time to pull money out of her pocket. Once she's paid for the food, she again links arms with us and, like a paper-people chain, we move toward the only open table in the courtyard.

"Cady LaBrie! You must be drunk, clinging onto *two* dudes like that—well, that is, if you consider Cooper Murphy a *dude*!" Cece's verbal harassment stings, but I try not to let it get in the way of our goals for the weekend. "And why are you three sitting *all the way* over there? Our table has plenty of space."

Cady is smart, though, and she must have taken us here so we would deliberately run into these girls. The only reason she would do this tonight is to prove a point. She replies, "We are celebrating, Cece, so we're going to sit here. Alone." Cady dismisses her easily. "But good luck at college!"

Cece is shocked, as she's never before been brushed off by the likes of Cady LaBrie. She stands abruptly and stalks to our table, naturally followed by her two human security blankets. "So, Cady, you're cozying up to your high school nerd counterpart. But, whoa girl, you're hanging onto this cutie, too." She points at Eli. "Eli's your name, right?"

Eli nods.

"Which one of them is your boyfriend, Cady? Because there comes a time when every girl has to choose."

That was certainly direct. And what it comes down to is that this is Cady's big chance to put number four—no more hiding—into action.

"I did choose," Cady replies simply.

"And?" Cece asks with interest, but Eli and I are even more curious about her answer.

Tonight's awesomeness continues when Cady tells them, "I chose *both* of them."

Three perfect chins drop in unison and they're not attached to the faces of Cady, Eli, or me.

"Burgers are up for LaBrie!"

Eli and I jump to our feet so we can grab the food, and I have no idea what Cady says to Cece and crew, but they're gone before we get back to the table.

"Stories are going to spread all over town about the three of us," I tell Cady after she steals a french fry from my plate.

"Let people think whatever they want. All that matters is what we know, and that is we're three best friends." Cady steals a french fry from Eli's plate.

Eli takes it all in, but says nothing.

It seems as if it's been forever since the three of us have been alone together in a place where we won't be interrupted. Tonight, Eli lies between Cady and me on my big bed as we listen to the eighties pop songs on the local family radio station. Not cool, but so cool.

We lie here for such a long time that I wonder if Eli and Cady have fallen asleep, but suddenly, "Time for number five!" bursts out of Cady's mouth sharply enough to make me jump.

"Number five is to say how we feel about each other—of course, with complete honesty, which is number two."

"You go first," I say to her, and hear Cady's laughter. "At least I'm predictable."

She pushes us apart just a little, and looks from me to Eli. "I love you guys, and I'm not going to lie about something. To me, you're both really attractive." She's breathless, which is very un-Cady-like. "But what we have—our amazing friendship—is what I want."

Cady took a chance. She let us know that some of her feelings for us are more than platonic. And she's not alone, so I offer a bit of truth. "I've had the same feelings for you, Cady, since the end of sophomore year. And they tortured me, because I knew that if I acted on attraction, I'd run the risk of losing you as my friend."

"They say friends can turn into lovers, but lovers never turn into friends," Cady offers. I figure that the "they" she refers to is society, and I'm not sure how wise society is, but this time, I agree.

I continue with my big reveal. "And Eli, you mean more to us than number seven on a freaking bucket list. My confession: When I kissed you, I knew I liked kissing boys, too. And, sure, I see you as desirable. But you aren't an experiment, and friendship is a choice. And I choose you—both of you—to be my friends."

"Um, this isn't Pokemon." Cady's humor alleviates the sappy effect of my declaration. "Hate to tell you this, Eli, but we can't check number five off The Better Weekend Bucket List until you spill your guts."

Eli has been relatively quiet tonight. Maybe he hoped to skip this part. The truth is, Eli hasn't been very lucky in love. Not with his mother, who left him, or his father, who didn't care about him, and then there's the way we treated him. But Eli's brave. He draws in a breath and says, "When I took off from home senior year of high school, I never thought I'd *not* be alone again. I wanted to be in a relationship with somebody so bad, and, believe me, at the carnival I got hit on by girls right and left, so I didn't have to be alone if I didn't want to. But I stayed away from having girlfriends. It wasn't right for me."

This makes sense. Eli has never expressed an interest in romance with Cady or me.

"But I gave it a shot with you guys because in the tent that night, I told you, I felt like I was home."

"We were your first, right?" She asks the right question. "Your first kisses?"

"Uh-huh."

"I figured you *had* to be experienced because, just because of how you look," she admits. "You know what I mean… you're gorgeous."

"Maybe I'm a natural-born kisser, so I did it pretty good on my first two tries," Eli suggests. "But I want *friends*—the kind that last. And about how I feel, how I feel is scared that I'm going to lose you guys again."

I don't know what to say, but thankfully Cady does. "Number six will help with that. But you'll have to wait until tomorrow."

She yawns, and, since yawns are contagious, Eli and I yawn too.

Honesty provides plenty of peace.

That's all I remember.

241

CHAPTER 30

cadence

BEFORE WE MEET BRADLEY FOR breakfast, the three of us sit around the Murphys' kitchen table and drink coffee.

"It's time for number six," I inform them.

The guys ask at the same time, "What's number six?"

"Number six is to make a future plan for our friendship—a plan for how we'll keep in touch when we're in three separate places."

Eli is scared that we'll leave him behind, so it doesn't take long to notice his relief. As he closes his eyes and exhales, his shoulders slump slightly.

Cooper recognizes Eli's relief too. "How about if we spend one weekend a month together at my school and one weekend at Cady's?"

Luckily, we have single rooms in our dormitories. "We'll have to pull the blankets off the bed and sleep on the floor, though, because all three of us will definitely not fit in a twin bed," I add. As usual, I focus on practical stuff. Practical is a comfortable place for me.

"One weekend each month, we can visit the place where you have a job or are going to school, Eli." I'm glad that Cooper takes the reins. "And one weekend each month we'll probably have to spend missing each other like crazy. But we'll get together three out of four weekends, which isn't as good as every day, but is still pretty decent."

Eli seems unable to spit out a single word. He opens his mouth a few times, but nothing comes out.

"And tonight, Eli, you're moving back into my house. You can stay with my family and study for your GED and live here as long as you need to after that. Mom will love the company. She's dreading an empty nest," Cooper insists. "And come to think of it, Dad will love to cook for you. Your appetite isn't as big as Cady's, but you've got time to work on that."

"We'll help you figure out what you want to do after you get your GED." I stand and ruffle Eli's dark curls. "Oh, look at the time. We'd better get going so we're not late to breakfast."

THE NEXT TWO ITEMS ON the new bucket list are relatively easy to check off.

At breakfast, I complete number seven, which is to hook up Bradley and Eli, or, as I so eloquently phrased it in The Better Weekend Bucket List, "to join our new lives with our old." I introduce my brother to my new best friend. The most brilliant part is that nobody except me has a clue that this is a bucket-list item.

After a hearty meal of scrambled eggs, bacon, *and* pancakes—a girl has got to eat to have enough energy to complete a bucket list challenge—I say, "Bradley, you and Eli are studying to get your GEDs. When Cooper and I go off to school, you guys should study together." I act as if the idea just hit me, although it has been very well thought out. And like I hoped, it gets the ball rolling.

"I been studying my butt off," Eli tells Bradley.

"Me too, but it would sure help to have somebody to go over everything with."

I hope these guys will end up as friends. They're both people who need support in life, and who have hearts big enough to offer support to someone else. They shake hands and promise to have many future study dates.

Number seven… an artfully done deal, if I don't say so myself.

NUMBER EIGHT TAKES LESS THAN five painful minutes to accomplish.

We go to the mall, to the very same Piercing Pavilion where we got our ears pierced last time. Eli picks out the same "diamond" earrings and sits on the same stool. Judging by the way he grits his teeth, it hurts a little more to get pierced than it did the first time around, but within a minute we get to watch him admire his sparkling ears in a handheld mirror. *Déjà vu.*

I buy "diamond" earrings for Cooper and me too. We replace our original earrings with them, although technically we haven't had our ears pierced long enough to change earrings yet. Sometimes you have to break the rules.

And despite the fact that it isn't on the list, we swing by the Verizon Store and pick out an iPhone for Eli. He's a little nervous about how he'll pay for it, but Cooper and I promise him that friends lend each other a hand and a few bucks when necessary. It's mandatory that Eli has a phone so we can stay in touch, and the cost of him not having a phone is much higher than the cost of him having one.

eli

JUST LIKE LAST TIME I went to the mall and got pierced, I make a pit stop in the men's bathroom by the big fountain. And just like last time, I tell Cady and Cooper that I need to whiz, but what I really need is to get my head together.

I go into the bathroom, but this time I go straight to the sink. Before I look in the mirror I bend over and throw some water on my face because this whole better-bucket-list thing has made me sweat. When I straighten up and look at myself, I see a guy with wild eyes and tight lips and his usual messy hair, who's caught between the most happiness he's ever felt and being as scared as a rat in a corner.

But I *do* believe it's true friendship with Cady, Cooper, and me. We got a plan of how we can stick together when we're far apart. Still, I'm afraid, because when I can't *see* people anymore, it usually means that they're gone from my life.

I got a decision to make—to either trust in this promise of friendship, or not to. As I stare into the mirror, the reflection of my new diamond earrings catches my attention. Cady insisted I get my ears pierced today so the three of us could match again. Maybe she wants me to feel connected to them when we're not together. And I will. Every time I look in the mirror and see my earrings sparkling, I'll remember my best friends' earrings are sparkling too, even if they're far away.

mia kerick

cooper

"I CAN'T BELIEVE I'M GOING to a carnival." Eli sits in the passenger seat and shakes his head.

I pull my car into the grass parking lot at the annual end-of-summer Up-North County Fair. Eli doesn't get out of the car when Cady and I do.

"Come on, Eli. This is gonna be fun," I urge.

"I haven't been at a fair for the fun of it since I was a kid. I only ever *worked* at fairs."

"But we need to do number nine on The Better Weekend Bucket List. And we can only do it here." Cady's in all-business mode. I want to know what she has planned. But maybe it's better I don't.

After a few minutes, Eli drags his ass out of the car. As soon as he emerges, Cady and I grab his hands and drag him toward the entrance.

AT FIRST ELI IS QUIET as we walk around the fairgrounds, and I figure he's thinking of the years he spent working at the carnival. But the Up-North County Fair has all kinds of animals that his little traveling carnival didn't have, and they fascinate him. We spend an hour watching oxen pull heavy shit from one end of a field to the other, and the fastest kids ever catch greasy pigs. We have a hard time getting Eli to leave the petting zoo.

And Cady and I find out that Eli's *amazing* at the games on the midway. He knows all of the tricks and wins Cady and me too many cheap, rainbow-colored stuffed animals to count. We give most of them away to little kids who are walking near us and drooling, wanting the toys with every fiber of their beings. We can't carry them all, anyway. But Cady and I each keep one to put on our dormitory room beds.

Cady keeps a bright pink pig and I hang onto the last stuffed animal that was rejected by all of the kids, probably because it's not actually an animal at all. It's a giant, stuffed-purple-crayon backpack, and it reminds me of the day we waited for Eli to meet us so we could take him on the road trip. Luckily it has straps, so I sling it over my shoulders like a total dork and I walk around the fair.

"Food!" Eli shouts when he smells the aroma of food coming from the row of booths where country-fried chicken, apple pie, and ice cream are for sale.

"Nobody likes to eat more than I do, but we should wait to eat until *after* we do number nine on the list," Cady suggests with a meaningful glance in my direction.

Her warning look makes me nervous. "Oh, God, what's number nine?" I ask.

"Um… I'll tell you when we're on the Ferris wheel." She says this quickly, but I hear every syllable.

I can't miss the enormous Ferris wheel that looms in the distance. It's twice as tall as the one we rode in Ellis. "I don't know…" The way my belly churns tells me this may not be the best idea Cady's ever had.

"You already faced this fear, Coop. It'll be a cakewalk." If I could only have Cady's confidence. I fight nausea as I push the thought of cake from my mind, just as I did last time I went on a carnival ride.

Eli's worried about something entirely different. "You guys aren't gonna try to stand again, are you? Because that's real dangerous, and I don't wanna get kicked out of this fair until I had a piece of apple pie or two. And a spicy sausage."

As we approach the ticket booth, Cady promises, "We're not going to stand up."

I breathe a sigh of relief. Maybe I can handle the ride if we keep our asses on the bench. Eli and I stand in the line by the Ferris wheel while Cady buys the tickets. We wait our turn, but it takes a while, as the line is long. Everybody and their mothers come to the annual county fair.

Eli climbs into the chair first, and Cady, then me. My heart pounds: a reminder that I haven't entirely overcome my fear of heights. Slowly but surely, all of the carts are filled, and by the time we're at the top, I concentrate on steady breathing—in through the nose, out through the mouth—that I hope will prevent a rainstorm of barf from falling on the folks below. But when the ride starts, our hands all come together on the safety bar, and I feel unexpectedly safe. I cling onto Cady and Eli's hands and manage to keep my eyes open as we go around.

I've just started to enjoy the ride, when Cady asks, "Are you guys ready for number nine?"

Eli nods, and I shrug because I'm not at all sure I'm ready.

"The plan is that next time we reach the top, we kiss."

"We kiss?" I'm not sure what she means. Kissing seems to fall more in the romance realm than the friendship one we chose.

"On the cheek… We're friends, remember?" She winks at me.

"I'm in…" Eli is enthusiastic. "It'll be as if we're blessing our friendship, right?"

I nod. "I think I can do it." Cheek-kisses shouldn't rock the cart too much.

The next time we summit, the three of us exchange quick kisses. When we're finished, we lean back in the cart and enjoy the ride and the late summer breeze.

On our last full day together.

THE REST OF SATURDAY AT the fair is awesome in that bittersweet way, when you're having the time of your life, but you can't forget it's soon coming to an end. We sample way too much food. Cady eats more maple walnut fudge than Eli and I combined. We go on a few more low-to-the-ground rides and play a few more games. But the drive back to my house is stone silent because we're all in shock. Tomorrow we have to go our separate ways, and today seemed to pass way too fast. We only just found the best friends in each other.

Again, we sleep in a row in my big bed, but we don't touch and we don't say a word. I'm the lucky one to be in the middle tonight and I try to memorize the feeling of safety and acceptance lying between two people I chose to be in my life as best friends. We stay awake as long as we possibly can and fall asleep without "goodnight" because "goodnight" seems too much like "goodbye" and we don't need to face that until tomorrow.

CHAPTER 31

cadence

COOPER, ELI, AND I SPEND a lazy morning together. We make pancakes and drink coffee in Cooper's kitchen. His mom stays in her room, and this gives us the time and space to be alone and say goodbye. But too soon it's time for number ten.

The biggest part of me is aware that I'm lucky to have the opportunity to do number ten with Eli and Cooper because I almost lost them. But I didn't lose them, and so we have no choice but to say goodbye. To say goodbye artfully isn't a typical bucket-list type of item. But this is *our* list and it's meant to serve *our* needs.

We drive to the Traveler's Haven Motel, where Eli will stay until Cooper's parents have returned from following him to Bennigan College. And then the three of us squeeze together on the pleather couch in the front lobby, and I force myself to say, "We have one more thing to do before we go."

Cooper and Eli frown. They're gloomy, like the world is coming to an end, and my job is to change this. To do it, we need to look at the bright side. Although we have to spend time apart, we still managed to come together.

"The rule for number ten is," I begin, "that we don't say goodbye."

Eli sighs dutifully, but Cooper's response is less submissive. "What the heck…?"

"Number ten on The Better Weekend Bucket List says that we leave each other in a *different* way. And we start by admitting that we are going to be apart."

Eli and Cooper just stare at me, because, of course, they already know this. And Cooper mumbles, "No shit, Sherlock."

I continue. "Next, we tell each other to be safe."

Eli decides to play ball. "Cady, please don't walk alone across your college campus in the dark unless you got a can of pepper spray in your pocket. And Cooper, wear your seatbelt whenever you drive your car."

I offer my best advice for safety. "Eli, don't lift anything too heavy at work. And Cooper, don't so much as *touch* your cell phone when you're behind the wheel."

Cooper's still reluctant to join in, but he says, "Don't do anything I wouldn't do, you guys."

"Now, we need to let each other know how important our friendship is. I'll start." I grab their hands. "I love you guys. You're my best friends and always will be."

Eli goes next. "I'm so glad I met you two. Thanks to you, I've got an awesome future plan."

Out of the three of us, Cooper has the hardest time with this not-a-goodbye. He looks over our heads, but still opens up. "I learned from you guys… that friendship is everything. In good times, bad times, and ugly ones, friendship is all you need."

That about sums it up.

"The last part of number ten is that we need to promise to see each other again."

Eli is the first to say, "I'm gonna miss you both so bad, but we have plans to meet up at Cady's college in two weeks, when you're all settled in."

With a smirk, Cooper tells us, "I plan to hold my breath until I'm with you guys again." He may not be entirely serious, but he makes us laugh. And we need it.

And then it's my turn. "I'm just going to say 'hello' in advance of the next time we're together." It's sappy, but I don't care.

We stand and face each other. Cooper puts his hands in the middle of our little circle, and Eli and I pile our hands on top, as if we're a three-person sports team. I gaze into Eli's eyes and I'm glad that I don't encounter as much fear as I expect. When Cooper pushes his glasses onto the top of his head, I can easily see the wetness in his eyes, but he copes with this by sniffing hard. I'm not sure what they see when they look at me, but it holds their attention. We stand here, frozen in place, for a little too long.

Before one of us breaks into actual tears, I say very softly, "We can check number ten off the list."

Then we let go of each other's hands and go our own ways.

But we're not alone.

With a friendship like ours, we'll never be alone.

THE BETTER
WEEKEND
BUCKET LIST

1. apologize to someone
2. speak only the truth
3. start a tradition
4. stop hiding
5. say how you feel about each other
6. make a future plan
7. join your new life with your old
8. become a matched set
9. kiss cheeks on top of a ferris wheel
10. never say goodbye

ACKNOWLEDGMENTS

THANK YOU TO MY EDITOR, Annie Harper, for opening my mind to new possibilities. Thank you to my cover designer, CB Messer, for doing the same, in visual terms. In fact, I'd like to acknowledge the entire team at Interlude/Duet Press for helping to shape my raw story into a relevant and refreshing Young Adult book.

And, as always, I'm indebted to my husband, Randy. His patience, support, and truly exceptional talent with a crockpot allow me ample time to fixate on plots.

ABOUT THE AUTHOR

MIA KERICK IS THE MOTHER of four exceptional children—one in law school, another in dance school, a third at school at Mia's alma mater, Boston College, and her lone son still in high school. She writes YA LGBTQ fiction when not editing National Honor Society essays, offering opinions on college and law school applications, helping to create dance bios, and reviewing English papers. Her husband of twenty-five years has been told by many that he has the patience of Job, but don't ask Mia about this, as it is a sensitive subject.

Mia focuses her stories on the emotional growth of troubled young people. As a teen, Mia filled spiral-bound notebooks with tales of youthful conflict and stuffed them under her mattress for safekeeping. She is thankful to Interlude Press for providing her with an alternate place to stash her stories.

A social liberal, Mia cheers for each and every victory made in the name of human rights. Her only major regret: never having taken typing or computer class in school, destining her to a life consumed with two-fingered pecking and constant prayer to the Gods of Technology.

Her books have been featured in Kirkus Reviews magazine, have won a 2015 Best YA Lesbian Rainbow Award, a 2017 Best Transgender Contemporary Romance Rainbow Award, a Reader Views' Book by Book Publicity Literary Award, the Jack Eadon Award for Best Book in Contemporary Drama, a YA Indie Fab Award, and a Royal Dragonfly Award for Cultural.

Contact Mia at miakerick@gmail.com or visit at www.MiaKerickYA.com to see what is going on in Mia's world.

an imprint of interlude **press**

@duet**books**

Twitter | Tumblr

For a reader's guide to **The Weekend Bucket List** *and book club prompts, please visit duetbooks.com.*

also from  duet.

Snowsisters by Tom Wilinsky & Jen Sternick

High school students—Soph, who attends private school in Manhattan, and Tess, a public school student who lives on a farm in New Hampshire—are thrown together as roommates at a writing conference and discover unexpected truths about friendship, their craft, and how to open their hearts to love.

ISBN (print) 978-1-945053-52-8 | (eBook) 978-1-945053-53-5

The Rules and Regulations for Mediating Myths & Magic by F.T. Lukens

When Bridger Whitt learns his eccentric employer is actually an intermediary between the human world and its myths, he finds himself in the center of chaos: The myth realm is growing unstable, and now he's responsible for helping his boss keep the real world from ever finding out.

ISBN (print) 978-1-945053-24-5 | (eBook) 978-1-945053-38-2

Summer Love edited by Annie Harper

Summer Love is a collection of stories about young love—about finding the courage to be who you really are, follow your heart and live an authentic life. With stories about romantic, platonic and family love, Summer Love features gay, lesbian, bisexual, transgender, pansexual and queer/questioning characters, written by authors who represent a spectrum of experience, identity and backgrounds.

ISBN (print) 978-1-941530-36-8 | (eBook) 978-1-941530-44-3

CPSIA information can be obtained
at www.ICGtesting.com
Printed in the USA
BVHW04s0824180418
513728BV00001B/20/P

9 781945 053580